POWER STRUGGLE

A.D. ELLIS

ONE

PAUL POWERS

"PAUL, you know I trust and respect you." Betty Short, the superintendent of Valley Hill School Corporation, leaned on her elbows behind her desk. "I'd prefer to wait until our other guest joins us, but I'm going to give it to you straight."

"Betty, we've known each other our entire careers. You know I'm thinking the worst." I rested my elbows on my knees and leaned forward.

"It's not good, I'll admit that." Betty scowled. "But I don't think I'd call it the worst. I've got five years before retirement and I'm not going down without a fight."

I glanced at my watch. Where the hell was the other person we were waiting on? Being late to a meeting with the superintendent was beyond unprofessional. "Who are we waiting on? And what kind of fight?"

"Oh, I asked him to pick up a Diet Coke for me on his way." She waved me off. "Did you know there's a large majority in this town who want to shut down the whole Valley Hill School Corporation and bus all the kids to Sugar Creek?"

I huffed. "Yeah, that's been talked about for more than a couple years." My eyes went wide. "Oh, hell no, is that what's happening?" We'd been out of school for the summer break a single day and I had a sinking feeling that the already-too-short-and-jammed-packed-with-work-summer and upcoming school year were going to be the roughest of my career. At fifty, I still had a lot of energy to pour into my school and my students. As principal of Valley Hill West Elementary, I was highly concerned about the lack of money, talk of closing, and loss of teachers. Betty beating around the bush wasn't doing anything for my anxiety.

I'd been a proud principal of the West Wasps for seven years and the school was everything to me. My gut was screaming that I wasn't going to like what Betty had to say, but I was determined to make it work. I wouldn't let my school fail without a fight.

The door opened and I barely contained my groan.

Jamison Powers.

Of all the damn people in the whole school corporation, why did it have to be Jamison? The guy was friendly—bordering on flirty—and I didn't dislike him, but I avoided him as much as possible. For…well, reasons.

"Sorry I'm late," Jamison announced and handed Betty a large Diet Coke before turning his broad, beautiful smile my way. "The drive-thru was crazy. Hi, Paul." He took the seat next to me and I suddenly felt like we were two kids in the principal's office.

Betty took a long sip and sighed. "Ah, that's just what I needed. Thank you, Jami." She clasped her hands together and smiled. "Well, here we go. My Power Team. You're kinda my last hope here."

My stomach plummeted. "Last hope? What the hell is going on, Betty?"

"We have to consolidate. There's no other choice. And even this may not save the corporation. I've hand-picked the two of you because of your reputations and histories. I know you will give your best and make every effort to save Valley Hill schools." Betty took another drink as if fortifying herself.

"Consolidating?" Jamison squeaked. "Can you

give more specifics? One school? We're both principals. How's that going to work?"

"Hell no," I grumbled. "I have fifteen years more experience than him. No way I'm losing my position to him."

Jamison scowled—and I felt as if I'd been punched in the gut as I recalled our nineteen-year-history—and crossed his arms over his chest. "You may be fifteen years older than me, but we've both been principals for seven years. We have the same administration experience. Plus, I have age on my side."

"Gentlemen, let me give some details before you rip each other's heads off." She shook her head. "I picked the two of you because of that passion right there, but I'll need you to temper yourselves. You're going to have a very long summer and school year working together."

Jamison huffed.

I pinched the bridge of my nose. "Explain, please."

"Valley Hill has two elementary schools, a middle school, and a high school." Betty took a sip of her Diet Coke and shook a few chocolate candies onto her desk—if Betty was chomping on chocolate, it was proof she was stressed. "The elementary schools are both at about half capacity. Our enrollment has gone down every year for the past five. The middle school was built to contain a much larger number of classrooms and students than what it's currently housing."

"What about the principal at the middle school?" I knew the Valley Hill Middle School Yellow Jackets leader was a brand-new hire. Surely the board wouldn't let her be the principal when I had so much more experience.

"We'll get there. First, we're going to put both elementary buildings into the middle school. We'll save thousands; upkeep on one building is much cheaper than upkeep on three buildings."

"So, the elementary buildings will just sit and rot away?" Jamison asked.

"We're hoping to rent them out, but that's a different problem." Betty popped more chocolate into her mouth and waved away Jamison's question.

"So, who is principal of the new consolidated school?" I asked.

"I don't suppose the two of you could come to an easy conclusion on that?" Betty asked wearily.

"No," Jamison and I both bit out.

"Well, you're both amazing and I'm not going to make that decision either. So, let me tell you my idea. I was thinking you divide the school into squads. One of you take Squad A and one take Squad

B. At the end of the year, whichever squad has the best attendance and test scores, that man will be the principal the next year. The other will be the assistant principal." Betty winced and watched us for our reactions.

The idea was ludicrous, but I wasn't going to argue it at that moment—I needed, hell, I wanted my job—if dividing the building was what Betty thought was best, I'd deal with it. And I'd win. I sighed. The idea was beyond stupid; I'd need some time to think it over and find a better solution. But first, there were other concerns. "How many teachers are going to lose their jobs?"

Betty shook her head. "Between resignations and retirements, I don't think we'll have to displace anyone. We may have to shuffle some positions, but I don't think anyone will lose a job." She rubbed her chest. "Believe me, that's one of the only good things I've been able to find in this mess."

"What about Danika Smith at the middle school?" Jamison asked.

"Well, she's brand new. She will be offered an assistant principal spot or she may opt to go to Sugar Creek. Heavens knows how, but they are hiring." Betty leaned back in her chair looking every bit as irritated, worn out, and concerned as I felt.

"So, that's it? Two squads and the best man

wins?" I clenched my jaw. What was she not telling us?

"Well, yes. Unless my Power Duo can come up with a better idea. Believe me, I'm open to better solutions." Betty's eyes shifted to the side. "And, um, along with needing to work together a lot this summer, I'm sending you to a week-long conference in Indianapolis."

What?!

"We can't afford to keep our schools running, but there's money to send us to Indy?" I muttered. Indy was about an eight-hour drive from Valley Hill which meant no airfare—as most places in the Midwest were driving distance, but I assumed hotel and at least some meals would be covered.

"The conference organizers offered scholarships. I applied for one and was chosen—you know I'm always on the lookout for scholarships and grants. It's just too bad I can't find a grant to save all of our schools." Her lips twisted into a wry smile. "Thanks to the scholarship, I can send two people and you're my choice. You'll be given gas cards, a meal allowance, hotel, and entrance to the conference with all of the breakout sessions covered." Betty rubbed her temples. "I know this is less than ideal, gentlemen. But I also know that you two have worked together very well over your careers. There are no other people I'd trust to help me make this work. Can I ask for commitment?"

I glanced at Jamison. Fucking Jamison Powers. Bad enough we had the same last name. Even worse the memories I'd tried unsuccessfully to push to the far corners of my mind. He was an amazing teacher and administrator; I didn't want to compete with him. I most definitely didn't want to spend my summer with him. But what choice did I have?

He narrowed his eyes at me, but smirked.

The little shit.

"I'm in," Jamison answered without taking his eyes off me.

"Yeah, I'm in." I took a deep breath and looked away.

"Excellent. I'll trust that you two can make your own plans for meeting. I'll email you all of the conference details." Betty glanced at her phone. "Now, I hate to kick you out, but I have another meeting with Transportation to start discussing the new bus routes."

I followed Jamison out of the office. We didn't speak until we reached the central office parking lot.

"So, I guess we're going to be seeing a lot of each other, huh?" Jamison asked with a smile and a wink.

I grunted. "Where do you want to meet?"

"I can check, but I'd assume there's going to be a

lot of cleaning and moving going on at our new building. Along with the usual extermination, painting, and waxing, I'd guess we'd be better off meeting outside of the building." Jamison opened his car door and tossed his bag into the passenger seat.

"I've got a decent deck in the shade," I offered begrudgingly.

"I've got a pool," Jamison answered with a saucy grin.

"We'll play it by ear depending on the weather," I suggested.

"Okay, let's talk on Sunday and figure out what Monday's going to look like." He eyed me up and down with a salacious smile, gave a little wave, and drove off.

What the hell?

I got into my hot car, blasted the air, and did everything I could to stop thinking about Jamison on my way home. But it was no use. Those bright blue eyes, that smile, the dark hair. And good Lord, that body. I growled.

My mind traveled back to the year I'd first met Jamison Powers. He was a smart mouth, cocky-as-hell, too-smart-for-his-own-good sixteen-year-old. I was filling in as a long-term sub in a literature class at the high school. I was dating a very serious boyfriend, totally in love, adored teaching, and welcomed the challenge of the snarky Jamison. The entire year, he'd pushed back on every assignment, every grade, and every word we read as a class. But he'd also done amazing work, seemed to love the content, and had an easy smile for me every time he thought he was getting to me.

On the last day of school, I'd unexpectedly stumbled upon Jamison giving an upper classman a blow job behind the gym bleachers. I remembered the day clearly. I'd heard noises after the final send-off of the buses behind the gym and went to investigate; all of the students should have already left the building. As my eyes adjusted to the darkness behind the bleachers, I realized Jamison was on his knees sucking Tim Olson as if his life depended on it. I'd watched for one second too long before clearing my throat and telling them to break it up. Tim had shoved Jamison off his dick, tucked himself in, and ran off.

Jamison on the other hand had wiped the back of his hand across his mouth, licked his lips, let his eyes wander up and down my body, and then grabbed his backpack. "See ya later, Dick Power." He'd given a seductive little moan as he walked past.

"It's Mr. Powers," I'd muttered, but Jamison was already out the gymnasium door.

My parents had named me Richard Paul Powers—

Richard after a grandfather—but the thought of their son being Dick Powers was worse than P.P. So, Paul Powers was what they'd chosen for me.

Jamison's cheeky smile had done something strange to me that day and I'd gladly accepted a position at the middle school the next year. I definitely didn't need whatever trouble Jamison Powers could bring me.

And he definitely brought me trouble a few years later. Fate seemed to think it was funny to continually put Jamison in my path and he was my kryptonite in a variety of ways that I didn't even want to analyze.

As the memory faded, I realized I'd been sitting in my driveway for several minutes—I loved that my home was outside of the subdivisions in Valley Hill and I had relative privacy. I mean, I had neighbors, but the houses were farther apart in my area of town. And I had the perfect little bungalow style house on a corner lot with a wooded area behind and to one side. My home was definitely my sanctuary.

I pulled the car into the garage, went into the house, and immediately poured myself a glass of wine. It was two o'clock in the afternoon, but it was also summer break. I needed to get into school, gather my belongings—fuck, I'd need to let the teachers know they needed to pack up and prepare for a move—and leave Valley Hill West Elementary. I sighed. At least I wasn't losing my teachers or my students; we were just relocating. I had to try to see the positives of the situation. My head ached with the thought of all the change and upheaval—and frustrated teachers and parents.

I took a deep breath. I had two days to rest and collect my thoughts before I had to deal with all of that. Before I had to spend my entire summer with Jamison Powers.

"Heaven help me," I muttered as I sipped the sweet red and flopped onto the couch.

TWO

JAMISON POWERS

I TOOK the rest of the day to simply lounge by my pool. The summer was clearly going to be even more packed with work than a usual summer—and even my usual summers were often brutal; definitely not a lot of down time no matter what people thought of educators getting a summer break—I needed at least a little bit of a breather before facing it all.

Forcing myself to leave my laptop and anything work-related in my cute little ranch-style house—I'd lucked out finding an amazing house with a pool in an older Valley Hill neighborhood—I poured a chilled sweet red wine, put the bottle in a bucket of ice, and changed into my tiniest swim trunks.

My pool and backyard were private thanks to a fence, a corner-lot, and a wooded area at the back. I probably could have sunbathed naked, but I didn't think Valley Hill East Principal, Jamison Powers, Sunbathes in the Nude; What Type of Role Model is This For Our Children was the headline I wanted to see in the Valley Hill Daily Times. So, I kept to my slinky black Speedo, dove into the cool water, and swam a few laps. With the tension at least somewhat eased from my muscles, I left the refreshing water, plopped down on my towel-covered lounge chair, and took a long swallow of the wine. It was early afternoon, probably too early for wine, but the news I'd learned earlier and the major changes coming warranted a drink. It was summer break, after all.

As the sun warmed my skin and the wine warmed my blood, I closed my eyes and couldn't help but smile a bit. I was likely facing one of the toughest years of my life—at least as far as my professional life was concerned—but I had to admit, even if only to a tiny part of myself, that I wasn't dreading spending the summer with Paul Powers.

Oh, I was one hundred percent sure Paul was dreading it. I chuckled to myself. Somehow, I got the feeling that Paul saw our history very differently than I saw it.

I'd met Mr. Powers when I was sixteen. A very snarky, cocky, smart-ass-is-my-middle-name sixteen I might add. He was thirty something, filling in for the year in my literature class, and I spent the entire year picturing him every single time I jacked off. The look on his face when he'd caught me blowing Tim Olson behind the bleachers was priceless—a very interesting mixture of shock, curiosity, embarrassment, and lust. Sadly, he'd never been my teacher after that year.

However, and this is where I started to believe fate had a sense of humor, I ended up being Paul's student teacher during my final year of college. True, there weren't all that many schools in Valley Hill where I could have been placed, but the fact I ended up assigned to spend an entire semester with him was just too good to be true.

By that time, I was twenty-one and ready to take on the world. Paul had changed though. He'd seemed so full of life and excitement about teaching only five short years before, but at thirty-six he just seemed down, burned out, and joyless.

Despite his change in demeanor that year, I valued him as a mentor teacher. He was still great with his students, still had an amazing presence in the classroom, got his class to really think, and made sure the kids were having fun. I learned a ton from him that semester.

But I also didn't have it in me to curb my push-back. Paul was a great teacher—even if he seemed to be struggling in his personal life—but I often found myself challenging plans, methods, ideas, choices. And he'd push back—sometimes with vigor, sometimes wearily—and we often ended up in long, passionate discussions into the early evening hours as we graded papers and prepared for the next day.

While I definitely valued him as a mentor teacher, I also found myself drawn to him personally. Something was going on with him, but he wasn't one to spill about his personal issues. I wanted to chat with him about more than just school, wanted to know what was bringing him down, wanted to wrap him in a hug and tell him it was going to be okay. Yeah, and I wanted to do more than that. I was definitely hot for teacher. But even I knew any kind of relationship with my mentor teacher—despite us both being of-age and consenting—would be a very, very bad decision.

So, on the last day of my student teaching program—pretty much the moment Paul had signed off on all my papers and requirements—I blurted out an invitation for celebratory drinks.

Paul's eyes had narrowed and I saw the exact moment he started to say no, but then something had changed. He'd nodded with a slow smile. "Sure, first round's on me. Congrats on finishing this semester."

We'd finished up our usual afterschool tasks and

said goodbye with the promise to meet up at a bar outside of Valley Hill. We were both adults and no longer in a power imbalance, but it felt safer—more neutral maybe—to go outside of our town.

I remembered that night as if it were yesterday. I'd dressed in tight jeans and a black t-shirt along with my red Chucks and nearly swallowed my tongue to see Paul dressed casually in perfect-fit jeans and a maroon button-down with black dress boots. We'd found a corner booth, ordered drinks and an appetizer, and spent hours laughing and talking about the semester and our students.

Paul—after a few drinks—had slipped and mentioned a break-up. After the cork was pulled, and likely thanks to the alcohol loosening his lips, he spilled all about how he and the boyfriend of several years had broken up and how he wasn't dealing well with it all. It had sounded like Paul was thinking marriage and then the boyfriend up and dumped him. So, it made sense that Paul had been having a difficult time that semester.

We'd spent some time discussing exes, bad breakups, and the see-saw of emotions that came with being a gay male teacher in a small town. When the bartender announced final rounds, we'd stared at each other with glassy eyes, shrugged with tipsy smiles, and each ordered one last drink.

When we'd stumbled our way to the parking lot, the cool evening air bringing us to our senses just a bit, we'd both come to the conclusion that we'd had too much to drink. We weren't drunk, but tipsy was too much to drive.

I remembered the hesitation in Paul's eyes as he glanced toward the all-night diner down the road. "Want some coffee?" he'd offered.

A couple hours later, full-to-the-brim with coffee, water, and waffles, we'd made our way back to our cars at the bar. I'd realized I'd just been on the most enjoyable date of my life and I didn't want it to end —deep down, I knew it couldn't continue. Wouldn't continue; Paul would see our age and positions as a definite no even after I was no longer working under him.

But, the pull between us had been too strong. With only the soft glow of a neon sign from the back window and a half-moon shining above, I'd stepped into Paul's personal space and took his hand.

"Jamison," he'd tried to protest.

"Thanks for a great semester. I'm hoping to land a job soon and I know I'll be better for it because of you."

"You're going to make an amazing teacher," he'd said softly. "I'll get that letter of recommendation sent to you by Monday."

"I'm really sorry about your breakup," I'd whispered, a fluttery feeling filling my chest and making me wonder if the alcohol was making a comeback in my bloodstream.

"Shit happens. It's not anything for you to worry about. I'll deal," Paul had answered.

I'd smiled softly and bit my lip. "I never did get a chance to thank you for not turning me in when you caught me behind the bleachers."

Paul's eyes had gone wide and he choked out a laugh. "Yeah, well. I probably should have, but I think I was so shocked and ready to bust out of there on the last day, I just conveniently let it go."

Stepping close enough that our hips touched, still holding his hand, I'd swallowed thickly. "Do you think, if we ever find ourselves in a different set of circumstances, you'd ever find yourself willing to play school with me?" I'd kept it light, teasing, but God how I'd wanted to lean in just a bit and kiss him.

"Jamison," Paul had whispered. "We…"

"I know. Age difference and all that," I interrupted.

Paul had frowned then and chuckled without humor. "Yeah, I guess that should be a reason, too. Something must be wrong with my head that I didn't even let that cross my mind. It's more—at least to me—the fact that you were a student of mine, you just today finished being a subordinate, we definitely aren't equals," he'd said and continued when I'd started to protest, "I don't mean you aren't as good as me. I just mean that I have years of experience, I've been in a position that would be looked at as your boss. It would look bad for both of us, especially me."

I'd licked my lips and met his silvery blue eyes. "But if that wasn't standing between us, you'd be interested?"

Paul had swallowed thickly and closed his eyes. "Heaven help me, but yeah. So damn interested."

Not caring that it was a bad, bad idea, I'd leaned in and feathered a kiss against his lips before trailing my mouth along his cheek and whispering, "Then I guess I'll just have to hold on to hope that someday we'll be equals."

Paul had tensed, his breathing paused, and he'd pressed his cheek into mine. "Best wishes in your career. I expect to hear great things. Take care," he'd whispered and placed a light kiss on my cheek before turning away, climbing into his car, and driving off.

As the memory of that night cleared, I smiled, took another drink of wine before refilling my glass, and stood. Diving into the pool—which now felt much colder thanks to the sun warming my skin—I swam a few more laps as I thought about Paul.

He'd been the hottest teacher in school when I was sixteen. Okay, a lot of the guys thought Ms. Casen was the hottest, but I only had eyes for Mr. Powers—and yes, I'd thought it was beyond cool that we shared a last name.

Paul had been even more attractive when he was my mentor—I likely had a case of wanting what I couldn't have, but there was no doubt he was hot.

Over the years, Paul had never seemed to get old. He just got more and more distinguished. He had a great sense of fashion, and even dressed in jeans and a Valley Hill sweatshirt at football games somehow managed to look like he'd walked off a runway. His silvery blue eyes, salt-n-pepper hair, and trimly muscled body never ceased to make my head turn. Even the glasses he now wore were totally him—hip, fashionable, a splash of color—as if he was saying, "If I've got to wear them, I might as well look fabulous in them."

And Paul knew he looked good, but it wasn't a stuck-up type thing. He took pride in his appearance and always presented himself as professional and put together. But even though he exuded confidence, precision, and control, he never came across like the type of guy who thought too highly of himself. He wasn't conceited, didn't act as if men should be begging at his feet. No, Paul seemed to have given up on a love life after that jerk dumped him. He was completely devoted to his students, staff, and school.

It was funny how fate played out sometimes. Paul and I ended up back in each other's orbit about seven years later, but we still weren't equals and Paul had made it clear back then that he preferred to forget about our little conversation in the parking lot.

Even now, he seemed to think that ignoring the attraction would make it go away. As if pretending he hadn't said he'd be interested would make it so. But I definitely hadn't forgotten.

I smiled as I climbed from the pool and wiped a towel over my face before plopping back down on the lounge-chair.

The thought of straight-laced, always-in-control Paul unraveling and letting loose before me was something dreams were made of. We might have had an unequal professional relationship in the past, but we no longer had that unequal footing. We were colleagues and had the exact same position—at least for now, although I hated the Squad A, Squad B idea —and I was completely in favor of making our required summer work a little more enjoyable.

We could enjoy ourselves and work hard to save

our schools and our jobs. Or we could pretend we didn't have a history and mutual attraction while still working hard to save our schools and our jobs. Either way—despite how much I admired him as a fellow educator and administrator—I wasn't going down without a fight.

I closed my eyes and sighed. It would just be a lot more fun saving my job if a naked and quivering Paul was in my bed while I did it.

THREE

PAUL

I HAD a tension headache that wouldn't let up.

A car packed full of my office supplies that couldn't yet be taken to my new building.

Texts, calls, and visits from staff members concerned about the changes and the move.

Questions beginning to pour in from parents— Valley Hill's rumor mill was one of the strongest in the Midwest.

And the only thing my mind seemed to want to focus on was Jamison Powers.

Glancing around my Valley Hill West office, grabbing the stuffed wasp a student had given me my first year as principal, I wandered the halls until I found myself at the custodian office.

"Got quite a change happening, huh?" Roy Carmichael squinted his rheumy eyes and smiled around the ever-present toothpick between his teeth.

Roy had been a life-saver over my time at West. He knew the ins and outs, could get things done, and kept his small-but-efficient-and-dedicated-crew in tip top shape so our building always looked fantastic and functioned smoothly.

I often found myself taking a fifteen-minute break in Roy's space. Partly because he was good to chat with. Partly because he was great at bouncing around ideas and solutions. And partly because he somehow had the best damn coffee in the building.

"Don't suppose you'd reconsider that retirement? Come to the new building with me?" I gave Roy a rough time as I poured a cup of coffee; I knew the man was beyond ready to hang it up after the summer closing procedures were officially done.

"No way, no how. I've got grandbabies to spoil." Roy laughed. "You're looking a bit frazzled. I've got to go supervise a load of furniture being packed and taken to the middle school. But relax a bit and drink your coffee." He glanced out to the hallway. "Can't believe the ruckus some of the teachers are making —and on a Sunday even. Seems to me it's not your fault and they should be glad to still have a job. I'll close the door; take all the time you need."

I flopped onto the cozy couch Roy had kept in his

office forever. What I needed to do was check in with my staff to see if I could alleviate any concerns and get any questions answered before going home and spending the evening plotting out how the next week was going to work.

What my mind actually allowed me to do was sip the delicious coffee, lean my head back, and think of Jamison.

The kid had been in my life for nineteen years.

Nineteen years.

First as that mouthy sixteen-year-old.

Then as a twenty-one-year-old as my student teacher. He'd been ready to take on the world. I'd been broken. He'd been ready to offer me something I wanted but definitely couldn't have. I'd at least been smart enough to say it wasn't appropriate, even if I was stupid enough to admit I'd be interested in a different circumstance.

You're definitely in a different circumstance now.

I swallowed my coffee like I swallowed that thought.

I'd lost track of Jamison after hearing that he got a job out west. Occasionally, I'd heard from his parents or folks in town that he was doing well. Dating, teaching, living the good life it seemed.

And I was happy for him.

I was.

It was for the best that he'd found someone his own age. Found someone who wasn't considered his superior. He'd moved on and so had I.

Not that there'd been anything to really move on from. He'd had a crush on an older man. I'd had a moment where I'd wished our circumstances were different. That was all.

And then fate threw me yet another curve ball when Betty Short hired Jamison to work at Valley Hill West.

As one of my teachers.

I usually had a lot of say in the teachers hired for my building.

But not with Jamison.

If I'd had my way, he would have gone to East or the middle school. I definitely didn't need to see him day in and day out in my building.

But there he'd been on the first day of teacher work days. Twenty-eight, only slightly taller than my 5'10" frame, purposely messy dark brown hair, eyes that shone like copper, and a smile that threatened to bring me to my knees.

And we'd been right back to our unequal footing.

Jamison had greeted me that day with a happy smile and a friendly hug. I'd had a moment where I thought perhaps whatever thing had seemed to flicker between us in the past had been extinguished.

But then we'd found ourselves as the last two people in the building early one evening and I'd offered to help him get the rest of his shit carried in so we could both go home.

"So, what brings you back to Valley Hill? California not all it's cracked up to be?" I'd asked as we carried in the last few boxes from his car.

"Something like that," Jamison had scoffed. "More like an epic break-up and being in the same state as that asshole was the last thing I wanted to do. Coming home seemed like the right thing. For my heart and my head. When I talked to Ms. Short and she said she had a couple openings, I knew there was no question. I was coming back." He'd plopped a box down on his desk. "Don't get me wrong. I loved California, loved my school, loved my students. But I couldn't stay there after Matt screwed me over—by screwing several other men in our bed while I was at school..." Jamison had winced. "Sorry, TMI. I'm still bitter. Midwest living is a lot more affordable, especially on a teaching salary."

"Hate to hear about the breakup, but glad to have you back in Valley Hill." I meant the words.

Jamison had cocked his head. "Isn't it weird how we keep ending up in the same places? It's like our paths are destined to cross."

I'd chuckled. "Yeah, fate seems to have a strange sense of humor."

"Still unequal footing," Jamison had hedged. "Guess you're my boss now." He'd winked. "Just so you know, I've got my administration license now. Betty knows I'm interested in a principal position. You may luck out and not have to deal with me for longer than a year."

"We're glad to have you on staff. I always knew you'd be a great teacher." I pretended to not know where he was leading the conversation.

"Once I move to administration, maybe we can revisit the whole if our circumstances were different convo from seven years ago," Jamison had said in a teasing tone, but I recognized fiery desire in his eyes.

It had been so long since someone had looked at me that way. So long since I'd allowed myself to feel something toward someone else. My ex, Douglas, had done a number on me and it seemed the safest to just keep all of that locked up and hidden away. I had my students and school to keep me busy and happy.

"Looking forward to a great year," I'd answered, ignoring Jamison's hint.

And the year had been a good one. Our school had shown amazing growth. We had great test scores, a growing social emotional learning platform that was showing fantastic results with our students, a garden and chickens that gained us media attention, and a real sense of family among staff, students, and parents.

Jamison had been voted teacher of the year for his work with his sixth graders, running the robotics club, and chairing the student council—with a focus on inclusionary practices for all students.

He'd also started casually dating in the spring of that year.

Which was for the best.

It most definitely didn't mess with my head and make me question if the squirmy feelings in my stomach were jealousy.

Not at all.

And then he'd closed out his one year at West by taking the open admin position at East. We'd become rivals of a sort. My West Wasps against his East Bumblebees—but in the long run, they'd all become Yellow Jackets at the middle school and Valley Hill Hornets at the high school, so it wasn't as if we were mortal enemies. But a little competition was good to keep staff and students striving for their best.

In the past few years, Jamison and I had fallen into a habit of friendly chit-chat at district meetings. We'd finally found that equal footing.

And for nearly seven years, even as equals, we'd ignored the past. Jamison dated. I convinced myself I wasn't jealous and buried myself in work. I'd accepted that my chance at love and intimacy—hell, even just sex—was something I'd given up long ago. I was happy with my work, even if my personal life was unfulfilling, sad, and lonely. That information was something I kept closely-guarded.

It was easy to co-exist with Jamison in our connected-yet-separate bubble.

Until we were thrown together in a way that was definitely going to make ignoring each other very hard.

It seemed like fate was back at it.

And I didn't know if I had it in me to fight against it this time.

Didn't know if I wanted to.

I'd fight for my school and my job.

But I suddenly wasn't sure I wanted to fight against whatever fate had in store for Jamison and me.

I swallowed the rest of my coffee, rinsed the mug, and left Roy's office.

After making a round to check in on teachers, I climbed into my car and drove home in a daze of confusion.

I really had no idea what to expect from these new circumstances.

BY THE TIME I arrived home, I'd convinced myself of two things.

First, I was committed to helping save the Valley Hill School Corporation. The school system had been part of me for my entire life. Back when I'd been in school, there was only one elementary and the middle and high school were in one building, but Valley Hill schools were where I learned and dreamed and decided I wanted to be a teacher. After my parents died, I'd considered leaving the place and starting over somewhere new. But I'd lived in Valley Hill my whole life and it didn't feel right to leave. Even after Douglas broke off our long-term relationship—right on the cusp of me thinking we were heading toward marriage and a long life together—I wanted the comfort and familiarity of my hometown. Now that the schools were in trouble—even more trouble than they'd been in over the last few years—I knew in my heart I needed to stay and fight. I was still at least a decade from retirement and I planned to retire from Valley Hill, not some neighboring school district.

Two, no matter the past between Jamison and me, getting involved with him would make a messy situation even messier. No matter the flicker that had started even before that night at the bar and now threatened to flash into a full-blown flame, Jamison and I needed to keep our relationship strictly professional.

But you're equals now. Valley Hill schools have more than a few dating and married teacher couples. For a small town, the folks here are about as open and accepting about differences as they can be. Betty likes both of you, she wouldn't balk at you dating.

"No," I muttered as I settled in with a cup of tea, my laptop, and a notebook. "What if it turned ugly between us. Who would step down? Who would be looked at as the bad guy?" My words fell flat in the empty house.

I knew Valley Hill liked and respected me, but they also considered Jamison their golden boy and were thrilled he'd come back home.

I didn't think our dating would be a problem except for two things.

One, we'd kinda been thrown into a competitive situation and, even though we were equals in title, one of us was going to have to either take a lower position or go to another district to keep our principal title. How would an intimate relationship affect that? How would a relationship—especially a new one—even survive that?

Two, if things went south between us, I feared the town would choose Jamison over me. The older folks would likely team with me out of respect for my parents. But the whole town loved Jamison—I had a feeling they'd side with him and I'd be made to be the bad guy.

Who says things between you and Jamison have to get ugly?

I shook my head and took a sip of my tea while staring at my laptop.

I hadn't even thought about being gay until my late teen years. Then, I'd pretended it wasn't true throughout college—despite a couple awkward sexual encounters that always left me feeling like I had even more to hide—and even in my first few years of teaching.

By my late twenties, I'd finally come to accept who I was. I came out to my parents—they took it wonderfully as I'd known they would; truly my biggest issue was with myself—and eventually met Douglas. I didn't announce my sexuality at school, but some of the people on my teaching team likely had their suspicions.

When I slowly started bringing Douglas to staff get togethers, no one really batted an eye. He and I fell into a simple, loving, easy relationship and I imagined it lasting a lifetime.

When he met me at the door to our house outside of town—his idea, he didn't like the older homes within the city limits—and told me he wanted me to move out, I was floored. Truly, I nearly fell over.

Douglas's words came back to me.

"You're so stuck in your ways."

"You're so controlling; you never let loose."

"You're happy to settle here and teach for the rest of your life; I want more than that."

"We're comfortable and boring after just a handful of years, how stagnant and resentful will we be in a handful more?"

Douglas, I later found out, had found an older man who'd promised him riches and world-travel and constant excitement. Last I'd heard, the older man had kept him around for about five years, found a younger, newer guy, and tossed Douglas out on his ass. I did feel a bit of vindication when I'd learned of that outcome.

So, thanks to Douglas, I had only one experience with actual relationships and it had gone down very badly. Sure, logic told me that not every relationship would turn out that way, but my past was all I had to go by. Which made picturing something with

Jamison being anything less than bad news extremely difficult.

Being around Jamison wasn't something I could avoid. I could accept that.

Getting involved with Jamison in any way that wasn't one hundred percent strictly professional was very much avoidable.

With my mind made up—even though my body and my heart wanted to offer counter arguments in the decision—I finished my tea, opened my computer, and began to make notes about what needed to be done during the week Jamison and I would be meeting.

As if he knew he was on my mind, Jamison texted.

JAMISON: Did you see the email from Betty regarding the conference?

Me: Not yet. Since tomorrow is supposed to be cloudy and cool, want to use my place to meet?

I WASN'T ALL that keen on the idea of working by a pool. Not that I had anything against swimming, but we needed to get actual work done, not sun ourselves and swim.

.   .   .

JAMISON: Sure. I'll need your address.

WE SET up a time for him to come over the next day and I sent him my address—I hadn't thought about it, but Jamison probably only knew of the place I'd shared with Douglas—if he'd even known of my location at all. Lucky for me all those years ago, I'd moved out of there, left Douglas with the lease he'd insisted be in his name only, and easily found my current home. No way I wanted to stay where all of those memories came crashing down around me.

Late that night, after hours of planning and a lonely dinner, I headed to bed with two books. A non-fiction title I was reading for school and a sci-fi title I was reading for pleasure. The fact that the sci-fi story featured gay characters and lots of steamy sex made me glad it was on my personal electronic device—easily kept secret when reading out in public.

When a particularly sexy scene had me hard in my pajama pants and my mind turning way-too-easily to Jamison, I tossed my e-reader to the side and quickly turned off the light.

No. No way was I thinking of Jamison when reading a sex scene.

As badly as I wanted to touch myself—and on normal occasions I would have just jacked off and been done with it—I had to keep control and stick to the decisions I'd made earlier that day. Which meant absolutely no thinking of Jamison in any situation that involved my throbbing dick.

I huffed and rolled to my side. A little delayed gratification—at least until my mind wasn't insisting I imagine Jamison sucking me off or spreading himself open for me—wouldn't hurt. I fell into a fitful sleep that turned out to be anything but restful.

The next morning, I ignored the fact that I'd dreamt of Jamison all night long and hopped into the shower. Steeling myself for the inevitable, I shampooed, washed, and rinsed before taking my aching shaft in hand.

I will not think about Jamison ran on a loop as I stroked myself.

I tried to picture some of my few and far between hookups—encounters that usually left me somewhat physically satisfied but never emotionally fulfilled. And the effort that went into setting up those awkward, less-than-amazing meetups was just too much; it had gotten to the point where it was easier just to watch some free porn or read a sex scene and get myself off.

Letting myself believe I was about to come while successfully not thinking about a certain someone was a huge mistake. As my soapy hand gave a final few strokes and my balls drew up tight, I allowed my mind to drift. Jamison's gorgeous pink lips, his copper eyes, and killer body filled my head just as an orgasm ripped through me.

With shaky knees, I pressed my forehead against the cool tile wall. I wasn't going to pretend I hadn't thought about Jamison as I'd jacked off over the years. But this time felt wrong—okay, not so much wrong as dangerous. I needed to keep space between us, keep everything completely professional, and avoid any potential messes outside of the school mess we'd been thrown into.

But a little bit later, when Jamison showed up at my door with hot drinks and a smile, my body thrummed and my heart sang.

Danger! Danger!

Keeping control of this situation was quite possibly going to be the biggest challenge I'd ever faced.

FOUR

JAMISON

"DID you know we live in the same neighborhood?" I asked as I walked past an obviously annoyed Paul. "How did we not know we lived so close to each other?"

Paul stared at me in disbelief so long, I started to wonder if I'd gotten the day and time wrong. But then he shook his head as if to clear whatever was bouncing around in there. "We do?" Then he shrugged. "I guess we had no real reason to know where the other lived until now. What street are you on?"

"Same street, just opposite end. Seriously, our houses are like the bookends of our street." I glanced around his cozy home. "Corner lots for the win," I joked and handed him a warm cup of chai latte. "I see you drink these at district meetings, thought I'd bring one as a peace offering." I knew Paul was not looking forward to this week, our trip, or the next school year with me.

"Uh, thanks," Paul mumbled as he took the chai latte. "Wanna set up on the deck? Weather is supposed to be cool. If it rains, part of the area is covered. Or we can come inside."

I gave a nod. "You have outlets on the deck? I may need to charge my laptop."

"Yeah, it's a good spot to work. Outlets, shade, comfortable chairs, nice view." Paul picked up a notebook, pens, and his laptop and headed through the sliding glass door. His usual tension and tight control seemed to be ten-fold.

I followed. Glancing at the two chairs separated by a small table, I wrinkled my nose. "Maybe best to push the chairs closer so we don't have to constantly turn our screens to show each other something?"

Paul looked like he wanted to argue, but instead he just shrugged and we quickly pushed the chairs together.

"Can you show me to the restroom before we get started?" I asked.

"Yeah, sure." Paul led the way and pointed to a door toward the front. "Right in there. The flusher sticks a bit, just give it a wiggle." His face pinked and I smiled.

"Give it a wiggle, gotcha." I winked and decided teasing Paul was once-again quickly becoming my favorite thing—and it was all appropriate and acceptable this time around.

When I got back to the deck, Paul was seated with his head in his hands.

"Man, you really dreading working with me that much?" I asked as I took the seat beside him.

He turned guilty eyes my way. "It's nothing against you. This whole thing is a disaster. I didn't want to lose my building. I don't want to compete with you—or anyone else for that matter. I don't want to watch the district shrivel up and die. And I don't want to lose a job I'm good at; being an educator—and most recently, a principal—is something I've always dreamed of. I'm good at it." He shook his head. "Don't get me wrong. I'm not saying you're not good at it, too. It's just that I've basically put my whole life into this career and it's scary to think about losing it."

I nodded slowly. "I think I get it. I know you're good at what you do. And I'm certain I'm good at what I do. This is your hometown just as much as it's my hometown—despite growing up here at different times. I don't like the idea of competing either." I frowned. "Well, that's not accurate. I love a good competition. But I know how good you are. I've been inspired by you since I was sixteen. I'm good partially because of what you taught me. I don't want to see either of us have to step down."

Paul scowled as if waiting for the punchline. "Thanks, those were kind words." He sighed. "Is there a way around this? Betty didn't seem married to the Squad A and Squad B option. Maybe we can come up with something new?"

I bit my lip. "Can we put that on hold for just a moment?"

Paul's eyes narrowed. "Why?"

I shifted in my seat to face him fully. "Just wondering if we should maybe discuss the elephant in the room?"

His cheeks flushed and I suddenly wanted to learn every inch of his body and find out all the ways to make him so deliciously pink.

"Um, it's probably best if we just agree that we're colleagues only. Agree to keep all of this professional and appropriate." Paul's eyes looked toward the wooded area off the back of the deck as he took a sip of his drink.

"We're colleagues, yes. But for the first time ever, we're equals. I think we discussed what we'd both want if we ever found ourselves in this situation." I took a drink of my spicy, creamy tea.

"That was a long time ago. We're not those

people anymore." Paul's eyes flitted to mine before he glanced at the deck floor.

"I may not be that young guy any longer, but whatever this spark is that's been here forever, it's not gone away." I tucked a leg under me. "I kept waiting for the years to diminish what I've always felt for you —yeah, it was just a crush at sixteen, but it was definitely something more at twenty-one. Nothing has diminished. If I'm being honest, I feel more for you now than I did as that horny college kid."

Paul's eyes went wide as he tossed another look my way. "It's just not appropriate. We have more to concern ourselves with. And you don't even know me."

"I've known you since I was a teenager. We worked daily together for half a school year. You may try—whether you mean to or not—to keep people at arm's length, but I've seen you in front of a classroom. I've seen you inspire a whole staff. I've seen you deal fairly and open-mindedly with students. I may not know you on an intimate, personal level, but I know enough about you to know that I like you. Even when you're being prickly and bossy and scared to lose control." I gave Paul a wink as I took a drink. His blush had me smiling behind my to-go cup. "Plus, what's not appropriate about two adults exploring something they've pushed away for over a decade?"

He huffed. "We're vying for the same position. You're fifteen years younger than me. We both have roots in this town; not easy to pull up and move on if things go badly." His frustration indicated he was grasping at whatever roots and rocks he could grab onto as he slid down a steep hillside.

"Who says things would go badly?" I asked quietly.

"You heard all about my sob story when Douglas threw me out. You've moved back home after a bad breakup. Do we really have pasts that seem likely to yield a good relationship?" Paul scratched at his scruffy chin, the mixture of hair there a perfect blend of brown and silver.

"Really? Just because a person has a breakup in their past it means they can't find happiness?" I scoffed.

Paul took off his glasses and rubbed at his eyes. "There's too much uncertainty. Our jobs for one. Hell, how would a couple work around one person having to basically be demoted while the other gets the top position?"

"Oh, I think we could share that top position," I teased.

The blush that painted Paul's face went straight to my cock.

"I, um," he sputtered, "only have experience with being principal. I never worked under anyone else."

I narrowed my eyes. Interesting. Was Paul speaking only about his job experience or was he insinuating something about his sexual history? "Look, in the bedroom department, I'm very happy being vers—just throwing that little tidbit out there. If we're talking about our jobs, I won't step down without a fight—or if Betty opts to move me—but I'm not going to consider my career over if I have to take the assistant spot for a year or so."

Paul's wide eyes studied me for several moments before he shook his head. "I'm going to choose to ignore that first part." He drew in a deep breath. "No, we'd eventually begin to resent the other if one of us has to step down."

"One of us is going to have to step down no matter what," I hedged.

"Which is why it's for the best if we're colleagues in a professional relationship only," Paul said.

I rolled my eyes. "I'll accept that answer for now. But I'm not giving up on this. There's nothing in our contracts that says we can't date colleagues as long as there isn't a power imbalance. We'd be doing nothing wrong."

Paul ran a hand over his face before putting on his glasses. "You don't think the folks of Valley Hill would have a heyday with the thought that one of us used the other to secure our position?"

I chuckled. "The folks of Valley Hill have a heyday with any and every rumor the mill generates. You and I'd know the truth and that's all that matters to me."

"Rumors like that can end a career," Paul said.

"Rumors like that mean nothing when there's no proof to back them up. Plus, we'd have Betty on our side."

Paul pursed his lips, but he didn't argue.

"So, my proposal—and we can revisit this later—is that we give ourselves a chance. Hell, maybe we've built it up in our heads so much that we'll laugh at how much of a flop we are. See if this thing between us is even worth taking to the next step. If it is, we talk to Betty and make sure everything is on the up and up. If it's not, we shake hands, stay friends, and do our jobs to the best of our abilities."

Paul stared at me and I could almost see the wheels turning in his brain.

For one small moment, I thought he was going to agree. My heart soared and my zipper area grew tight.

But then he sighed and shook his head. "There's

too much against us." He swallowed almost audibly. "And I've gotta be honest. It's hard enough living with the imagined idea of what things could be like between us. I don't know that I could get that small taste and then find out you don't feel the same or have Betty say we can't continue. It's best if we just agree to be professional colleagues and nothing more." He waved a hand my way as he pulled his laptop onto his lap. "You're young and hot; you'll find someone closer to your age, someone much more appropriate, and everything will work out for the best." He opened his laptop. "Now, let's look at the Squad A and Squad B options and see what we can figure out."

I narrowed my eyes. "You are one stubborn man, but that's fine, I like a challenge." I shifted to balance my laptop on my legs. "And don't think I missed the fact that you called me hot. There's something between us and we owe it to ourselves to explore it."

We settled in to work mode with moments of silence interspersed with chatter about scholars and teachers and schedules as we attempted to make the squad thing work out.

Two hours later, Paul slammed his laptop shut and I nearly threw mine off the deck. We'd been working to separate the students from Kindergarten to eighth grade into the A and B squads. The idea was ridiculous to begin with, but then we were faced with questions like:

Do we keep siblings in the same squad?

Should we evenly split the bus riders, car riders, and walkers among the squads or does that matter?

Do our special education students get split among the two squads? How will that affect the special education teachers as they try to service students in two separate squads?

What about our English Language Learners? It didn't seem fair to just split them by number since most were at varying levels of English proficiency.

And that fact brought us back to our special education students. We couldn't just split them right down the middle when we had students with a variety of different special education classifications which determined their level of needs and services.

How did we split up our free and reduced lunch and book rental students from our students who paid?

And how were we going to be sure that each squad got the exact same level of instruction? Every teacher was different—all of our teachers were good, but basing our jobs on the squad plan when there was no way to control every variable was bringing on a massive headache.

Even just trying to equally split into two squads

based on race and socioeconomic level was difficult, but then throw in transportation, siblings, ELL and special education classifications, and there was no way to make sure both squads were equally split.

"This is the stupidest thing I've ever been told to do," I complained and rubbed my temples. "Don't get me wrong, I respect Betty, but this wasn't her best idea."

"It's impossible," Paul grumbled. "Betty is my friend so I won't throw her under the bus completely; I know she's just trying to save jobs. But it's asinine to think any educator worth his salt would think it's a good idea for one leader to provide great things to one squad while a different leader offers different great things to another squad. Every single kid under our leadership deserves the best of both of us, the best of every teacher, the best programs and incentives."

Our eyes met and an electric current sizzled in my blood as we both smiled.

"So, we give them our best," I answered with a twist of my lips.

"What are you thinking?" Paul asked.

"I say we co-principal, with each of us taking lead on either Kindergarten through fifth or sixth through eighth. We each shoulder the responsibilities, but we focus on either primary or intermediate as far as checking lesson plans, doing observations, running grade level meetings, that type of thing. We tag team staff meetings and any kind of whole-school events." I was getting excited just thinking about the option. Honestly, anything was better than the original plan we were given.

Paul worried his lip. "It will mean a lot more work for us. What about Danika Smith?"

"She already agreed to the assistant principal spot for the year. She's young and eager. I don't think she's married, doesn't have any kids. I'm guessing she's ready to dig in and get her hands dirty." I smiled. "If we're able to be part of saving the district, it will look great on her resume if she opts to not continue with Valley Hill after this year."

"You're willing to give up a social life? Taking on the entire school—even split by grade levels—means early mornings and late nights, working weekends, spending evenings at school events. Even just the fifth and sixth grade and middle school sports schedule will be a full-time commitment if we try to go to as many events as possible."

I knew Paul wasn't trying to talk me out of the idea, just warning me of the hard work it would entail.

"Look, I don't exactly have a hoppin' social life as it is. The only person I actually want to spend time with—outside of visiting with my parents from time-to-time—is you. Looks like committing to what will likely be the hardest year of our careers has the potential to bring me fulfillment and satisfaction both professionally and personally. It's a win-win." I winked at Paul's flustered face.

"Us committing to work together to save the district and our jobs doesn't leave room for any type of fulfillment or satisfaction in our personal lives. We're colleagues working toward a common goal. Nothing else." Paul's eyes bore into me. "Right?"

"You keep telling yourself whatever lets you sleep at night, Powers," I teased. "I'm more on the side of combining our personal and professional lives gives us the best of both worlds and allows for career and relationship gratification. We'll have time to learn and grow and give our best as educators along with time to play as men who are highly attracted to each other." I pressed my lips together trying to hide a smile because I knew I'd ruffled feathers.

"You live in a fantasy world," Paul sputtered.

"Maybe you'll help me make some of them come true," I murmured as I leaned closer to Paul's cheek. "You already star in my fantasies…can't wait to get you in me, under me, on me…my fantasies are wide open." I smiled against his ear when he shivered.

"You've been trouble since you were sixteen,"

Paul stated gruffly before clearing his throat and standing up.

"Oh, I've been trouble since before that. Our problem is you've never been in a position to take on that trouble." I stood and stretched, knowing that my shirt riding up on my abs would catch Paul's eye. "But now? The Powers team is ready to tackle whatever trouble comes our way."

"School-related trouble only," Paul warned over his shoulder as he walked toward the house. "Come on, I've got food so we can work through lunch."

As he set out lunch, Paul peered at me. "How are you so damn good at what you do, so professional at school and district stuff? No one else sees this wicked side of you," he said under his breath, almost as if muttering to himself.

I chuckled. "Would you rather I show others my wicked ways?"

He shook his head. "No. And I'd rather you just stick to professional around me, too."

"Nah, where's the fun in that?" I reached for a croissant. "Seriously though. If I'm too much or you're uncomfortable, tell me. I'm playing around—and I'm very serious about wanting something with you—but I don't ever want to put you in a position that makes you feel uncomfortable."

Paul's eyes narrowed, but then his face relaxed

into a rueful smile. "I'm kinda damned if I do, damned if I don't in this situation."

I cocked my head. "How's that?"

Paul shook his head. "Never mind. I appreciate you looking out for my comfort, thank you." He slid a bowl of chicken salad my way. "Let's eat."

I was able to persuade Paul to just talk about school over our meal instead of mindlessly eating while staring at his laptop. Which is something I had a feeling he did a lot—I actually got the feeling that Paul spent most of his time alone, buried in work, and not taking very good care of himself emotionally. A weird feeling tugged in my chest as I realized I wanted to be there to make sure he took care of himself—to be the one taking care of him.

"This is really good," I said as I took another bite of savory chicken salad on a croissant. "I like that you put the grapes but not the nuts and celery. Honestly, I love chicken salad except for those two things."

Paul smiled softly. "Yeah, the crunch mixed with the creamy texture of the rest of it really throws me off. Most people would say my recipe is severely lacking, and I'll add the celery and nuts if I'm taking it to a pitch-in or something, but when I fix it for just myself, I leave them out."

"Well, if we ever have a pitch-in, please make a

bowl of the good kind for just us." I savored another bite. "This is seriously the best lunch I've had in forever." I gave Paul a wink. "Don't tell my mom that. Her funeral sandwiches would be a close second."

Paul chuckled. "Gotta love a good funeral sandwich."

"Did you know that people outside of the Midwest think we're crazy for calling them that? I mean, I don't even know what else to call them. Ham and cheese doesn't do them justice." I scooped more chicken salad onto a croissant. Healthy eating be damned when there was food this delicious. "I mentioned them out in California and people thought I was making them up."

"Did you tell them about funeral potatoes?" Paul teased.

"I did! I ended up making the sandwiches and potatoes for a small party and showing them the recipes online. Of course, they loved the food, but still thought the names were strange." I shrugged. "They kept saying cheese potatoes and ham and cheese sandwiches were better names."

We finished our sandwiches and Paul brought out a tray of tiny, iced, shortbread cookies.

"Are you trying to make me fat? Plump me up so much you can just roll me out of the building and take over?" I teased as I took two cookies and moaned at the sweet, buttery flavor that exploded on my tongue.

Paul laughed. "You're onto me. Damn, my plan was going so well." He rolled his eyes as he glanced up and down my figure. "Pretty sure plumping you up would take more than chicken salad and cookies."

Oh, something is plumping, alright I thought as his eyes traveled up and down my body once more before he cleared his throat and gestured toward the bathroom.

"Bathroom break and then back at it?" he asked.

I gave a nod, popped another cookie, and headed toward the hallway.

By the time we'd finished working for the day, I felt like we'd gotten an amazing start on our plans.

"Okay, so we meet with Betty in the morning," Paul said as he scanned down his perfectly bulleted list, "and Danika is coming to your place to work tomorrow. We'll hit the class lists and schedules tomorrow."

"We've also got the School Improvement Plan and the other reports we need to finish for the Department of Education," I reminded.

"Yep, those can wait toward the end of the summer I think. But we should be sure we're on top of the items we have to provide information for."

Paul tapped a pen on his notebook. "I think putting Danika in charge of testing coordination is a good plan, but she's going to need help. I think the instructional coaches can assist with that."

"Good idea. She seems highly motivated and extremely intelligent, but coordinating testing for the entire building is a job in and of itself. I think the middle school social worker and counselor should help with testing for sixth through eighth." I scribbled a note on my paper.

"Yeah, that's perfect. Luckily we have the technology for all the testing; getting that grant for the one-to-one devices a couple years back came at just the right time." Paul glanced up. "The grant pays for upkeep of the devices each year, but I think it's written to replace them next year? Maybe the year after that?"

"We really are lucky that Betty is so good at grant writing and finding money for the district. Can't imagine how up a creek we'd be if she'd not gotten us free money from so many different outlets." I couldn't help the yawn that escaped.

"Okay, we need to call it a day. We'll meet at your house tomorrow? Send me your address so I know I've got the right place, but just straight down my road to the corner lot?" Paul closed his notebook and stowed his laptop in his brown leather carrying case.

"Yep, it's the last house on the road, corner lot. My car will be in the driveway." I packed away my things. "I'll have lunch, although probably not as good as your chicken salad. I have water, pop, beer, cider, wine, and tea."

Paul cleared his throat. "Pretty sure a work-related lunch shouldn't involve alcohol."

I pretended to think about it for a moment. "You're right. We can save the drinking for when it's just us and we're on a date."

"That's not what I meant," Paul sputtered.

"Bring your swimsuit tomorrow. It's supposed to be really warm. My deck has sun and shade. We should be perfectly comfortable in the shade with the fans, and the water will help cool us down, but we can always go inside if needed." I hoisted my bag onto my shoulder and followed Paul into the house. "Any chance we want to turn off the professional and spend an evening working on the personal?" I waggled my brows.

Paul's eyes searched my face and for a moment I saw a flash of how badly he wanted to say yes, but he huffed and rolled his eyes. "Do you want to take some of this chicken salad home?"

Well, if I couldn't get a night of cuddling on the couch with him, I'd at least take his chicken salad.

"I'd prefer something else, but I won't turn down a couple sandwiches."

He smirked. "I guess I know the way to control you." Paul spread chicken salad on two croissants and put them each in a plastic baggy.

I stepped close to him, trapping him between the counter and my body. "Learning other ways to control me would be oh so much fun," I whispered against his ear. "But the real question is just how do I get you to lose that control you've got fisted so tightly."

Paul tensed for just a moment. I felt the shudder that traveled through him right before I stepped away.

"Thanks for lunch," I said. "And dinner." I held up the two baggies. "We need to plan our trip to Indy soon."

He gave a nod and walked me to the door.

I spent the rest of the evening simultaneously smiling over the potential I saw between Paul and me and grumbling over how damn stubborn and controlling he was. Don't get me wrong, there was definitely a certain level of desire that flamed to life when I thought of Paul taking control in the bedroom—although, I wouldn't mind at all getting my turn to take the reins. But the issue was finding a way to get him to finally give in and give us a shot.

We'd spent an entire day together, gotten a lot of work done, and not once had I wanted to be elsewhere. Paul and I got along great. We were very different, but we had enough in common—mostly thanks to our jobs—that we never really ran out of things to talk about.

Maybe there wasn't a magic button that would get him to give us a chance. Maybe my best bet was to just keep at him. Let him see how well we worked together, spend as much time as possible with him, and eventually wear down his walls until he had no choice but to let me in.

I had a feeling, once that happened, we'd be in for a wild ride.

FIVE

PAUL

I GLANCED at the two options I had as far as swimming attire went. A skimpy black speedo that I'd worn on a vacation back when Douglas and I were together, and a modest pair of board shorts.

I held up the black cloth. "Hard pass," I muttered and tossed the scant material aside. As if a man my age should ever be wearing that item of clothing, especially to a colleague's swimming pool for a day of work.

Bet Jamison would be happy to have you wear your skimpies over to his house for a late night, private swim.

The fleeting thought brought on a frustrated growl. Why hadn't I just taken the opening when Jamison offered to back off if he was making me uncomfortable?

You know why.

I scrubbed a hand over my face. Times like this—who was I kidding, I'd never had times like this, all of this with Jamison was completely foreign to me—were when I wished I had a best friend to talk things out with.

And I didn't have that.

I had staff members I respected and got along with.

I had Betty who I could chat with about school.

I had a couple cousins I was semi-close with. As in, we commented on Facebook posts and sent cards at Christmas.

But in all honesty, Jamison was the person I was closest too.

And holy fuck, that hit me like a ton of bricks right to the gut.

How? When? My mind sputtered questions as it attempted to short-circuit. We were colleagues, nothing more. Could I even call him a friend? And yet, lonely-ass old man that I was, I didn't have anyone I wanted to talk to more than a guy I had to keep things platonic with. Friends could be good. Yeah? Could Jamison and I do the colleagues and friends thing and ignore the rest?

I sighed.

I should have just told Jamison he was making me uncomfortable.

But that would have been a lie.

Kinda.

On one hand, I was uncomfortable. I wasn't used to the attention. I wasn't used to the feelings he stirred inside. After Douglas and a few failed attempts at random hookups, I tucked away all romantic notions and convinced myself that love wasn't in the cards for me any longer. And now, at my age, that still seemed like the best plan.

But Jamison had this way of chipping away at my carefully built walls. The banter and innuendo, the laughter and easy chatter, all of that was foreign to me these days.

So, yes, he made me uncomfortable. But not in a negative way. It was one of those push-me-out-of-my-comfort-zone feelings. Like before you go bungee jumping and you're kinda so nervous you could puke, but also super excited, and you know that you're on the precipice of disaster or extreme exhilaration.

I knew I faced both with Jamison.

And I didn't think I was strong enough to make the leap.

But what if you miss out on that exhilaration?

Pushing the thought away, I considered the other option to Jamison's offer of backing off.

If I told him he didn't make me uncomfortable, if I admitted to how much I liked spending time with him and all the flippy-floppy feelings he was stirring inside of me, Jamison would be encouraged. He'd think his plan could work. And I couldn't let that happen.

He was much too young for me—hell, I was fifteen when he was born—and we had to work together. Neither of us had plans to move to other districts unless forced to. Despite the fact there was no actual rule against colleagues dating, it seemed to be tempting fate to get involved with Jamison during a year when both our jobs—hell, the whole district—was on the line.

So, as I'd told Jamison earlier, I was damned if I do, damned if I don't.

I didn't want to lose the little slice of happiness and excitement being with him brought me. But I also didn't want to encourage him—or my heart and dick—that something real could ever happen between us. Hell, I didn't even know what level of relationship Jamison was angling for.

What about a fling?

I choked out a laugh. No, I wasn't the type for a fling. Okay, that wasn't true. I didn't know if I was the type for a fling because I'd never had one. Could I do just casual sex and then walk away? Knowing I'd see him day in and day out for at least an entire school year?

No, I didn't think I could.

But could I continue to stave off the crazy hot feelings I had for him? The way I imagined things could be between us? I remembered that kiss from so long ago and shivered. No kiss had ever moved me so much—and it was just a tiny thing as far as kisses went. I recalled the heat of his body in my kitchen the day before, the warmth of his breath against my ear, and sighed.

I didn't want to lead him on.

I didn't want to cut him off.

I didn't want to face the inevitable disaster that we could be facing—both professionally and personally.

But I was like Wile E. Coyote hanging from a cliff and Jamison was Roadrunner pecking at my fingers as if they were worms. I had a sinking feeling that he'd keep at me until I had no choice but to let go and fall.

The scariest part was having absolutely no idea what was waiting for me when I finally went kersplat.

How had being forced to interact with Jamison

for a few days—with weeks and months of working together ahead of us—gotten me so deep in over my head? If a few days could do this to me, what was an eight-hour drive and a week-long conference going to do to me?

I ran a hand through my hair. "Good God, man. Just put on your shorts and get going," I muttered, pretty sure I was facing a midlife crisis if picking out a pair of trunks had me in such a dramatic tailspin of emotional and mental overload.

I yanked on the board shorts, threw a t-shirt on, and put on flip-flops. I checked myself in the mirror. How did others seem to always look so effortless when they tried to look casual and I looked as if I'd spent three hours attempting to look casual? It seemed my casual was still tightly in the grips of my inability to let go.

Douglas had been right. I had no idea how to let loose.

But keeping a tight control on things—my heart, my job, my personal life—was the safest way to avoid heartache and loss.

I grabbed my laptop bag and headed down the road. The morning was already heating up and driving would have been quicker, but I figure the walk would help clear my garbled head.

As I neared the corner lot about ten minutes later

—I guess I hadn't realized how long our street was since I always took the opposite direction when I left —I saw Jamison out front of a cute little ranch-style home.

Looking as if he'd just stepped from the pages of the Boys Next Door magazine, Jamison wore swim trunks, a tank, and flip-flops as he directed a hose to rain onto his plants.

Plants—potted plants, shrubbery, decorative grasses, flower gardens—that looked like they took substantial time and care. Plants that looked as if they'd win awards from the town for adding to the beauty of our little neighborhood.

Because, of course, Jamison would be an amazing gardener on top of all the other remarkable stuff he did. I couldn't even keep a cactus alive.

I added this new knowledge to the already long list of things that were simultaneously impressive and intimidating about the man.

The next moment played out exactly how one might expect if one were to give it much thought.

But, of course, dumbass that I was, I didn't give it much thought.

Sidling up to stand on the well-kept little brick path next to where Jamison was watering what looked to be spider plants and ferns hanging on the porch, I did what any polite, professional person would do.

"Good morning," I said.

For an impressive and intimidating man, Jamison sure was jumpy.

He yelped, jumped, and turned to face me.

Without letting go of the hose.

Cold water blasted me right in the chest.

"Oh my God!" Jamison cried.

Luckily, the hose was dropped as he quickly moved toward me.

I removed my glasses and ran a hand over my face with a chuckle. "Good morning. I think I prefer coffee, but that was a nice little wakeup call."

"Paul, I am so sorry. I'm easily spooked. I was in my own little world and didn't notice you there." He grimaced and his cheeks flushed as he glanced toward the driveway. "Did you walk?"

I shrugged and replaced my glasses. "Yeah, wasn't too hot just yet and figured the exercise would clear my head. Didn't realize I'd get a cool-down spray at the end."

Jamison winced. "I really am sorry. Did your laptop get wet? I can get you a new shirt."

I patted the bag hanging from my shoulder. "Nah, it's safe and sound. We're just sitting on the deck, right? Shirt'll dry."

Gesturing to all of the plants, I smiled. "So, in addition to being an award-winning educator, master of the robotics club—and soon to be more groups, I'm guessing—and a principal our superintendent feels is worth keeping around, you're also a gardener? I'm impressed."

Jamison preened. "First, thank you. Second, there's a lot you don't know about me, Mr. Powers. And third, yes, I love to garden. I think I got it from my mom. She always talked about loving to get her hands in the dirt and watch her efforts grow —plus the sunshine and fresh air is a perk—and I used to think she was weird. But the older I've gotten…"

I scoffed and rolled my eyes.

Jamison smirked and ignored me. "…the more I've come to realize just how right she was. I had the shrubs and such planted by a crew. I don't have to do much with them. But the flower gardens," he pointed toward the colorful plots around his mailbox, around the shade tree, and lining the porch, "are a lot of fun. I love planning out the styles and textures and colors." Jamison rolled up the hose. "The potted plants on the porch spend the winter inside with me and the summer outside as long as I can keep them from the direct sun."

"So, just flowers and plants or do you grow

vegetables too?" I asked as I followed Jamison around the back of the house.

"I haven't ventured into vegetable gardening yet. I think I'd like to have tomatoes and green beans maybe. But honestly, I get so much joy from my flowers and plants, and I enjoy hitting up the farmers market for produce so much, that I don't know that I'll ever feel the need to have a veggie garden." He pointed to the shaded area on the deck. "Put your stuff down, I'll give you a tour inside."

I glanced at my watch. "Danika's coming, right?"

"Yeah," he said as he headed toward his sliding glass door. "She said she'd be here in about an hour. Okay, so kitchen. I loved the bright, airy feel when I was looking at this place."

"The vaulted ceiling and open concept into the living room makes it seem huge," I commented as I took in Jamison's lovely home.

"I know, right?" he smiled broadly. "So, the only thing I don't love about it is the fact that there's no half bath like what you have. If you need the bathroom, there's the one here in the hall," he moved to point toward the restroom, "and there's one in my room. There are two other rooms; one is a guest room that never actually gets used and one is my office."

"This is a great house," I said with a nod.

"I love it. The pool was what sealed the deal. I didn't even know I wanted a pool, but the day I came to see this place and saw all that crystal-blue water shimmering in the sun, I was done for." Jamison opened the fridge and tossed me a bottle of water.

"Is the pool a lot of work?" I asked before taking a sip.

"Eh, kinda. I do my part by sweeping it and keeping the cover on it. I put in whatever the pool guy tells me to put in every week or two. He comes every other week to check the levels, clean it, and basically do the upkeep on it that I don't want to do." Jamison took a long swallow.

"You have a pool boy?" I teased. "Isn't that like the start of a really bad porn?" The words were out of my mouth before I could think of how unprofessional they were. "Sorry, that was inappropriate." I cleared my throat and willed the fire on my cheeks to simmer down.

Jamison's eyes flashed and he grinned. "We'll need to dig deeper on that one someday, but I'll let it go for now."

Grateful, I followed him to the deck and helped in setting up our work space.

"So, class lists and schedules are our main goal today," I said.

"Yep, and we should take a look at the state site

for testing dates and get a schedule mapped out." Jamison tossed the decorative pillows to the side before flopping down on the couch. "Damn, it's hotter than I thought it was going to be. I'm already feeling sticky. Swim before we get started?"

After nearly swallowing my tongue, I gave a quick shake of my head. "Ah, um, no. I'm good here for now." I gestured to the shaded area and the ceiling fans—which really were providing a nice breeze.

Jamison shrugged and stood. "Okay, but all work and no play makes Paul a dull boy," he teased.

"Dull is my middle name," I quipped with a wink. Why in the hell was I winking at him? Winking could be seen as flirtatious and that was the farthest thing from what I needed to be doing. "Have fun. I'll get in later."

The sparkling blue water really did look inviting. Not one to enjoy the loud chaos of crowded public pools, I didn't swim a lot. Really, nothing about fighting for a place to lay my towel and wading through screaming, crying kids only to be splashed by the local teens who were roughhousing in the deeper water sounded appealing at all. But I definitely saw the appeal of a private pool with its cool crystal water.

Jamison sauntered toward the pool's edge and stretched a few times before stripping his tank over his head to reveal wide shoulders and a trim waist. His lean muscles were not the type one would get from hours and hours at the gym, but the type from swimming, yoga, possibly cycling, or running.

When he turned around to kick off his sandals, I looked away quickly, but I knew I'd been caught checking him out.

As if to give me ample time for viewing, Jamison walked toward me with a teasing grin. Stopping by the little table, he picked up his bottle of water and chugged the rest of it.

Which of course caused his neck to stretch and his Adam's apple to bob. My eyes traveled from his neck, to his chest—lightly covered in crinkly blondish-brown hair, down to his abdomen where my eyes couldn't help but follow the tantalizing trail of hair that disappeared below his trunks.

Forcing my eyes to leave his body, I yanked my laptop onto my lap and pretended to ignore Jamison's knowing smile as he tossed the bottle in the trash and walked toward the pool.

Glad to have something over my traitorous dick, I opened my computer and attempted to start some sort of work, but my mind wandered back to Jamison. Douglas had been a strict bottom and I'd mostly topped even before him. So, it made sense that, despite trying my best to not think about

Jamison in a sexual way, I'd automatically imagined topping him. And I wanted to. God, how I wanted to. I may not have been able to act on the desire, but I could at least secretly admit it to myself.

But I also let my mind drift a bit further to a scene where I bottomed for Jamison. The few times I'd ever attempted to bottom had ranged from disastrous to boring and every experience had definitely been unfulfilling. I'd never been able to get out of my own head enough to enjoy the sex—even the times when it hadn't been painful and over before I blinked. My experiences had left me wondering why I'd want to give up the control of topping to be at someone else's mercy.

Maybe giving up control is exactly what you need; maybe your inability to do that is why you're lonely.

My eyes traveled the length of the pool as I watched Jamison swim laps.

And maybe there's nothing wrong with being at someone's mercy if that someone is just as into making it good for you as it is for them.

An image of me on a bed, legs spread, Jamison sliding slowly into my body played through my mind.

I shivered. Could I ever actually let go and just enjoy?

Ever heard of topping from the bottom? Maybe

bottoming doesn't have to mean giving up control, but simply allowing your body to have what it wants with a person you trust.

I huffed and drained the rest of my water as I tried to push the damn thoughts from my head. None of my ponderings had anything to do with work—and would most definitely cause a messy problem if I allowed them to take over and guide my actions—so I pulled up our student information system and forced myself to begin scanning enrollment dates and building the class lists.

A bit later, Jamison emerged from the pool, water sluicing from his body and glistening in the sun. "Danika will be here soon. We can work for an hour or so and then grab lunch."

I gave a nod, but continued to look at the computer screen. "Wish I had printed these out, it's a pain going back and forth."

Jamison plopped down beside me, his cool, damp skin touching mine and making me shiver. "Here, let me connect you to my printer. Probably easiest if the three of us work together anyway. Having paper copies will help."

I sent the documents to the printer and followed Jamison inside.

After a stop by the restroom and grabbing the

papers, I returned to the deck to find Danika and Jamison laughing.

"Hi, I'm Paul Powers," I said and reached out to shake. I'd met Ms. Smith during a few district staff meetings, but hadn't had the chance to really get to know her.

"Danika Smith, nice to meet you." She returned my handshake with a smile. "I was just telling Jamison that the Powers team's reputation definitely speaks for itself."

We settled into our seats while continuing our small talk.

"I'm sorry about the shuffling and the way things have gone down with the consolidation," I offered.

Danika waved away my concern. "No worries. I just got my admin license in January. Landing the principal position at the middle school was exciting but quickly turned into a case of biting off more than I could chew. I'm energetic, ready and willing to get my hands dirty and assist the district in any way, but I can't say I'm upset to be working as just part of the team rather than being the sole person in charge of that building." She opened her laptop. "I learned a lot from Jenkins before he officially retired, but four months isn't enough. I'm looking at this summer and this year as a learning experience; I'm happy to be teamed with both Powers."

Jamison and I glanced at each other and smiled.

"Well, thanks for the kind words," I said. "We're looking forward to working with you. Neither of us wants to see this district fail."

We launched into the undertaking of building class lists.

I read from the paper copies of the teachers' suggested lists.

Danika made notes and marked off on the school master roster.

Jamison entered names onto the lists on the computer.

For the most part, since we knew all the elementary kids in our former buildings so well, Jamison and I were able to quickly make changes to suggested lists if somehow students had gotten misplaced or paired with another student they shouldn't be with.

Two hours flew by and we had the Kindergarten through fifth grade lists done by lunch.

We stood, stretching out the kinks, and headed into the kitchen.

"So, sixth, seventh, and eighth are going to be a bit more challenging for us since we don't know a lot of the kids," Jamison started as he pulled items from the fridge. "Although, we do know some of them if they were in Valley Hill as elementary students." He glanced down at the tray he was holding. "Shit, I totally spaced it and didn't even think to ask. Anyone have any allergies?" He grimaced. "Also, sorry about my language."

Danika and I both shook our heads.

"Oh, so no language concerns when it's just me, but when someone else is around, you're all concerned about being professional?" I rolled my eyes as I messed with Jamison. His cursing wasn't a problem for me, but his inappropriate insinuations could be curbed and I'd be just fine.

Would you?

"The counselor and social worker and I sat down at the end of the year and got most of the students into homerooms and class schedules. I'd say that part is eighty percent finished." Danika picked up a bottle of water from the little cooler Jamison had provided on the counter.

"Perfect. That's a huge help." Jamison set to work displaying several food items on the counter. "Okay, so I wasn't sure what to fix. Definitely not as delicious as Paul's magical chicken salad." He elbowed me.

"Magical chicken salad?" Danika asked.

"It's just plain old chicken salad without the celery and nuts," I said.

She wrinkled her nose. "But where's the crunch? I gotta have that crunch."

"Man, people really don't appreciate the good stuff," Jamison teased. "Anyway, I went with a meat and cheese tray with assorted bread options, veggies and fruits, and a spur-of-the-moment purchase of sushi simply because it looked yummy." He spread his arm to indicate the food. "And mini cupcakes for dessert. I got the mini ones because you can eat more of them. Like, I don't feel bad for eating five minis. Don't get me wrong, I could probably put away five full-size, but I'd be miserable and full of self-loathing."

We all laughed and kept up the good-natured chatter as we filled our plates and headed back to the deck.

"So," Danika began, "do you think Valley Hill has more of a problem with principals in a gay relationship or a black woman being assistant principal?"

I nearly choked on the mouthful of sushi I'd been enjoying.

"Oh, um," I sputtered.

Jamison stepped in to save me. "We're gay, but we're not together."

I almost expected him to tease with some comment about how he was working on it, just needed to get me on board, or similar. I was grateful when he didn't.

So why are you just slightly bent out of shape that he didn't?

"Oh, sorry. I just assumed." She glanced between us with a slight frown. "My bad." Popping a piece of sushi in her mouth, Danika continued. "I think we're kinda tied though—as far as bringing shock and awe to some of the folks in town. I'm new here and it definitely seems as if I'm the minority. I'd assume you are too?"

"Yeah, but Valley Hill isn't as backward as one might think," Jamison offered. "There are certain people, but the town as a whole is pretty friendly and open."

"So, if you two were dating," she hedged.

"A few people might cause a stink, but most would be fine with it. Jamison and I both have solid reputations and histories with the town." I cleared my throat before dipping a carrot in ranch.

"I'm hoping that holds true for me," Danika said. "I'm more accustomed to an urban setting, so the small town is a definite adjustment."

"Why the move?" Jamison asked.

Danika shrugged. "Bad break up, wanted a new start. I've got family in the Midwest. It's good to see that the schools do have some diversity. I'm looking forward to getting to know the students."

"We'll introduce you around. I know you'll be super popular with our students. Usually once the students like you, the parents are quick to follow," I said.

After lunch and finishing the middle school class lists and schedules, Danika stood and stretched. "As much as I'd love to enjoy that gorgeous water, I've got a training session this afternoon. Something for new employees that didn't get done in the spring."

"You'll definitely have to come back and swim before summer ends." Jamison stood as Danika gathered her belongings.

I walked with them to the front of the house.

"We're going to Indy next week for an education conference that Betty wants us to attend," Jamison started.

"Paid for by a scholarship provided by the organizers," I added. "Hate people thinking we're using district money to spend a week at a conference when the schools are barely hanging on."

Danika nodded with understanding. "That conference sounds really good. You guys will have to bring back all the knowledge you gather."

"Oh shoot," Jamison said. "We meant to talk to you about our change of plans."

Danika turned curious eyes our way.

I ran a hand sheepishly through my hair. "I'm not usually one to forget something like that. I'll blame it on the sunny location and good food."

"So, did Betty tell you about the squad idea she had?" Jamison asked.

A flash of something crossed Danika's face, but she gathered herself and nodded. "Yes, she explained the A and B plan."

"Well, she wasn't completely married to the idea and was using it just as a way to determine which one of us," Jamison gestured between himself and me, "would do the best."

"And we struggled with it for a bit and finally decided it was the worst idea ever," I cut in.

"Oh, thank God," Danika declared. "I thought it was a terrible idea."

We all laughed.

"So, we're doing a call with Betty today to let her know our new plan. Paul and I are basically going to co-principal. One of us take on more of the Kindergarten through fifth responsibilities and one of us take on more sixth through eighth. We're in charge of grade level stuff, but we'll share the building-wide stuff. You're our right hand for the entire building, focusing heavily on all things testing

—with the help of the counselor, social worker, and instructional coaches."

"That sounds like a better idea. Probably a lot more work," Danika hedged. "But how will the board decide which of you stays as principal and which bumps me out?"

I winced.

Danika waved off my reaction. "No hard feelings, I'm not completely committed to spending my career here. When the consolidation was announced, I assumed one of you would take the assistant spot—and I didn't envy the person who had to make that decision. I chose to stay because I want to work with you. Like I said, this is a learning year for me." She opened the car door and tossed her bag to the passenger seat. "Let me know if Betty doesn't go for it or makes big changes. I can meet a couple other times this week if needed. If not, I'll be tackling testing plans and attending trainings for testing coordinators with the state."

"Well, our hope is that the proposed referendum passes and we get a mayor who will work with the district to increase enrollment in the district," I said.

"And if that doesn't happen?" Danika asked.

I shrugged. "We'll face that when we get there. Even if Betty doesn't want to make the decision, I'm sure the board would have no problem deciding our fates."

After Danika drove off, Jamison and I made our way back to the deck.

"Call Betty, two more hours of work, and then we end the day with swimming?" he offered.

"Sounds good."

We went into the house and made the call from Jamison's office.

We explained our concerns about the squad plan, shared our plan, and waited with baited breath for Betty to speak.

"Well, I'm in complete agreement that the squad idea was likely my worst plan ever, but I was under pressure and didn't want to decide between the two of you." Betty steepled her fingers under her chin. "If my Powers team wants to take on the extra work, rely on the referendum and a new mayor, and you understand if those things don't work out the board will have to assign one of you to assistant, then I'm all for your plan. You've discussed this with Danika Smith?"

"Yes, she was just here. We had a working lunch," I said.

"Good, good. I'm glad you're all on the same page. Now, I'm sure you've got as much work to do as I do, so I'll say goodbye. Enjoy the trip to Indy.

Bring back some great ideas." Betty gave a little wave and ended the video call.

Jamison and I both sighed.

"Wow, I didn't realize how worried I was that she'd say no," he said.

"I wasn't so concerned she'd say no, but I was definitely nervous to tell her the original plan sucked." I chuckled. "Betty is a friend and colleague from way back and she comes across very mild-mannered, but she can be a bulldog."

Jamison shivered. "I remember when she was a dean at the high school. Even though you didn't turn me in for sucking cock behind the bleachers, I quickly learned that Betty Short was not an adult I wanted to mess with that following year. I pretty much toed the line just to avoid being in her office."

I tried to ignore the comment about sucking cock —but my dick perked up at the mention—and focused only on the memory of Betty as the dean of students at the high school. "She started as dean the year after I did the long-term sub position, that's right. I'd forgotten that. She's definitely done pretty much every job an educator in this district can do. She'll retire from the superintendent position in a couple years I'm guessing. I know she doesn't want a failed district on her plate as she plans her last couple years."

Jamison studied my face—I swore he was staring at my mouth—and teased his bottom lip with the tip of his pink tongue. "Well, we've got some of the smartest kids around so test scores won't be an issue. We'll work to get that referendum passed and get a new mayor voted in—one who will actually understand that the town needs to appeal to families in order for our schools to increase enrollment. We won't let Betty down."

We spent the next two hours finishing random tasks before Jamison declared it was quitting time.

"It's hot. We're done. Time to swim." He stood and yanked his shirt over his head and dove into the water with barely a splash. When his smiling face broke through the water, he wiped his eyes and gestured toward the water. "Come on! It's amazing. We need a break."

I knew that I did need to take breaks and relax or I'd work myself into a headache—a plain old headache if I was lucky, a migraine if I wasn't—so I moved my laptop to the side and stood up. I gathered all of my belongings and packed them away before walking toward the edge of the pool.

"I didn't bring a towel," I muttered right as I realized my fail.

"No worries, I've got some over in that cabinet. Grab me one too."

Was I stalling? Why did I feel the need to stall?

Maybe because I knew how I'd ogled Jamison when he stripped down to just trunks and I was nervous he'd do the same.

I was in good shape—especially for my age—but I wasn't one to do a strip tease.

I yanked two towels from the cabinet and tossed them next to the pool edge.

"Here goes nothing," I muttered and tried to push away the nervousness of Jamison seeing me in just swim trunks.

SIX

JAMISON

HOLY HELL.

Paul Powers was gorgeous no matter what.

In his fitted suit jackets and slim-cut slacks? Definitely.

Casual jeans—even if I knew they were designer —and a Valley Hill hoodie? Yep.

Trunks, t-shirt, and flip-flops? For sure.

But when the man pulled his shirt over his head and I caught a glimpse of his torso, I knew I'd have the image in my head forever.

Paul removed his glasses and placed them on his laptop bag before heading toward the pool.

The ashy-brown mixed with silver hair on his head for that perfect salt-n-pepper, silver fox look also made an appearance on his chest, his belly, and sneaking under his waistband. He wasn't bodybuilder built, but he hadn't gone flabby—and how strange was it that I wouldn't even have cared? Somewhere along the line, I'd lost my former immaturity and shallowness and now all I wanted was Paul, no matter his build. Of course, the fact that he looked damn hot didn't hurt. I wanted to climb from the water, trail my hands over his chest, and lick his dark pink, pebbled nipples.

Fuck.

I needed to stop gawking and get rid of the boner trying to escape my trunks. Opting to give us both a little privacy, I dove under the water and swam a few laps in hopes that Paul would take the opportunity to enter the water.

By the time I gave up on my laps, Paul had joined me and was shaking water from his hair.

"This water is amazing. Not too cold, but just cool enough to be refreshing," he said as he squinted across the water toward me.

"How badly do you need your glasses?" I asked with a grin.

Paul smirked and shook his head. "Badly enough that you're pretty much a blur of flesh tones against the blue water." He dunked his head and came up again wiping his eyes. "Like I can tell you're a person, but I can't make out facial features. If you had words on a shirt, I'd be screwed."

"Have you always worn glasses?"

"Yeah, since I was little. Both of my parents had shit eyesight so I guess I come by it honestly." Paul stretched his arms against the side of the pool and let his legs float out in front of him. "I wore contacts a lot during high school and college. I still have some that I can wear if needed. But my eyes get so dry and glasses—even though they can be such a pain in the ass—are just easier most of the time. What about you?"

I swam over toward Paul. "Can you see me better from here?"

Paul nodded. "Not perfect, but much better."

"I have always had twenty-twenty vision. My parents have perfect vision, so it must be somewhat hereditary."

"Of course you do," Paul deadpanned. "Jamison Powers, practically perfect in every way."

"Did you just Mary Poppins me?" I exclaimed in mock shock.

"If the shoe fits," Paul said with a smile.

"I'm so far from perfect, I promise you that." I lounged against the edge of the pool and closed my eyes to soak up the warm sun. "Just ask Matt."

Paul scoffed. "Nah, I have a feeling Matt just couldn't handle sharing the spotlight with someone as amazing as you. For real though, everything you do seems to turn out successful. Fabulous teacher, terrific principal, successful with the robotics club and the student council. You make being good at things seem like a cinch. I'd venture to guess that Matt was someone who wasn't super confident in himself and he felt threatened by that."

I pondered that for a moment. "So, I guess I need to find someone who is just as amazing at making success look like a piece of cake." I kept my eyes closed, but a smile teased the corner of my mouth. "Someone who is confident and mature enough to combine our successes rather than resent me for mine."

Paul was quiet for so long that I wondered if I'd said too much. I cracked an eye and found him staring at me with a serious look.

"Yeah, I guess that's who you need to find." He cleared his throat and pushed off the side of the pool, diving under the water.

We swam in silence for the next fifteen minutes before climbing from the pool and stretching out to dry on the lounge chairs.

"I was thinking that we'd drive together to Indianapolis if you're okay with that," I said as the sun warmed my skin.

"Yeah, that makes the most sense. From the details Betty sent, I'm pretty sure we'll only get reimbursed for gas on one vehicle anyway." Paul shifted on his lounger and propped his arms behind his head.

"The conference starts Monday, but Betty's email said we could check-in as early as Friday evening because we have early-bird access. What if we leave Friday late afternoon and then we can explore Indy all weekend before the conference on Monday." I glanced at Paul. When he gave a little nod, I went on. "Have you ever been to a conference that lasts Monday through Sunday? I mean, I guess the last actual workshops and such will be that Saturday, but we're not checking out until Sunday. Definitely the longest conference I've ever been to."

"Yeah, I think that's why this event is only every three years. It's long, but I've heard it's really good. We can leave late afternoon on Friday, that's fine. Once we check in, we should take a look at the finalized event schedule so we can figure out what we're attending." Paul's voice was low and bordering on sleepy.

"Sounds like a plan." I rolled to my stomach in hopes of drying the back of my trunks. "Is it weird that I'm kinda looking forward to the week away? I mean, I know we'll be doing school stuff, but I haven't been to Indianapolis for a while. I remember it being a fun city. It will be kinda nice to get away and I'm sure we'll be learning some great things. Plus, having gas, meals, and hotel covered is huge. I'm not hurting for money, but I definitely wouldn't be able to cover gas, meals, and hotel for seven days —the hotel we'll be in looks swank."

Paul chuckled. "Yeah, I think that's why a lot of people just go for three to four days. We really did luck out getting that scholarship—we'll have to thank Betty. I'm pretty sure the organizers give out like twenty of them—mostly need-based. Kinda sucks that our school district qualified, but maybe we'll be able to bring back some great ideas and breathe some new life into the schools." He sat up. "I'm going to need to head home; if I stay here any longer, I'll fall asleep. I'm not as fair as you, but I'd rather not burn."

I chuckled, trying not to think about how much I'd love to cuddle on the couch with Paul, take a nap, and wake up to eat dinner and hang out while watching a movie. "Yeah, I definitely have to get out of the sun since I didn't put on sunscreen. So, we work the rest of the week and plan on leaving on Friday?"

"That works." Paul slid his glasses back on his face. "My house tomorrow? It's supposed to storm."

"Sounds good. Want me to bring anything?" I asked as I stood and stretched.

"Nah, I'll come up with something or we can order in. See you tomorrow." Paul gathered his bag and headed toward the front of the house with a little wave.

I cleaned up the deck and covered the pool before going inside to clean up the kitchen. Since we'd worked all day, I didn't even feel the least bit guilty about cracking open a bottle of wine and chilling out in front of the television with a movie marathon.

When I finally dragged myself to bed that night, I smiled at the thought of all the time I was going to be spending with Paul. I honestly hadn't been this excited about work stuff in...well, in forever.

Was I chasing a dream as far as my chances with Paul?

Maybe.

But I'd never been one to give up without a fight.

And I had a feeling he was worth fighting for.

"ROAD TRIP!" I crowed as I climbed from my car in Paul's driveway.

We'd hit it hard the last few days, and even earlier that day we'd done a lot of work. But it was late Friday afternoon and time for departure.

We'd separated after hours of working at Paul's house so we could each get cleaned up and packed.

Paul's car was close to needing an oil change, so we opted to take mine. I was driving the first half and Paul would nap so he could drive the second half. I was exhausted enough from the week of heavy-duty brain work, I knew there was no way I could drive all eight hours straight through, so I was glad to have a co-pilot.

"You are entirely too excited about an eight-hour drive," Paul grumbled. He looked completely drained and I thought I saw lines of tension around his eyes, even behind his glasses.

"You okay? You look…off?" I popped the trunk and took his suitcase. We both only had one suitcase and a carry-all type bag, so there was plenty of room. Even with the travel-size steamer Paul insisted on bringing. "We can't do laundry easily," Paul had said, "and packing enough shirts for every day would take too much room. If we have the steamer, we can freshen up shirts and pants. Just pack enough underwear and socks."

Paul sighed. "Yeah, I'm fine. Just tired. We did a lot of work this week and I think it's catching up with me. That's one of the downsides to aging." He gave me a look that said, "That's why you definitely don't want a man my age."

But all I could think about was how great we worked together, how much I adored his company, and how badly I wanted to kiss and touch him. I cleared my throat. "Well, we're stopping for drinks and snacks before we get on the interstate."

"I brought water," Paul said.

I wrinkled my nose. "Okay, but I need caffeine, snacks, and candy. We definitely have to stop."

Once we settled in and I headed toward a neighboring town that had a lot more choices as far as quick-stop type stores, I glanced at Paul. "Music? Audiobook? Podcast?"

He brightened a bit. "I've got some great educational leadership podcasts."

"Of course you do," I deadpanned. "Maybe some true crime?"

"Compromise? A few of mine then a few of yours?" he said with a tired smile.

"Deal." Glancing at him again, I couldn't hold back my concern. "You should definitely try to sleep a while. You look about ready to drop."

We reached the gas station and spent a few minutes gathering chips, nuts, candy, and drinks. Paul opted for coffee while I got the largest fountain pop available.

Once back in the car, we settled our drinks and snacks. I set the GPS for Indianapolis and Paul queued up his boring-as-hell podcasts and popped a couple pills.

"Headache?" I asked.

He sighed. "Yeah, hoping to head it off."

About forty-five minutes into the drive, Paul was asleep, so I changed the podcast to my favorite true crime episodes and settled in for another three hours of driving.

Thirty minutes before we were scheduled to stop—and I hated to wake Paul, but I was dragging and my eyes were drooping enough that I knew I was no longer safe to drive—Paul groaned into wakefulness.

"Oh God, pull over. I'm going to puke," he ordered in the most pained voice I'd ever heard.

I immediately pulled the car to the side of the road—as far off into the grassy area as I could because, damn, those cars on the interstate were scary fast when you were sitting still.

Paul flung open his door and stumbled from the car, retching and heaving miserably as he went. When he dropped to his knees in the grass, I scrambled over the console—knowing it wasn't safe to open my door into oncoming traffic—and joined him on the grass.

"Are you okay? How can I help?" I rubbed his back as Paul shuddered and dry heaved.

"Migraine," he whispered harshly. "I'll be okay. Just give me a minute."

I stared at him as if he'd grown two heads. He definitely didn't look okay. "I'm right here. Just let me know what you need."

Within about five minutes, Paul's retching had stopped and he let me help him into a standing position. But he held his head and moaned.

"Do you have medicine?" I asked as I helped him into the car. I knew people who got migraines, but I'd never seen anyone in the midst of dealing with one.

"Yeah, in my bag. Prescription pill pack." He kept a hand over his eyes and rested his head against the seat while I went to rummage through his bag.

"How many?" I asked when I came back to the passenger side.

"Just one. Probably too late to help a ton." He took the pill from me and swallowed it down with his cold coffee and a wince. "Must have come on while I was sleeping. I was stupid to think it was just a headache. I should have known that exhausted feeling meant bad news. I usually get enough warning with visual auras that I can take the prescription medicine and keep it from getting too bad. But if it starts in my sleep, I miss the perfect window."

"Are you still sick to your stomach?" I knelt at his side and placed a hand on his knee. Honestly, I was really worried.

"No, luckily once I puke, I usually have no other stomach issues. I slept through the visual disturbances, got the vomiting out of the way, now it's just the extreme light sensitivity and severe pain in my head." He lolled his head to the side. "I'm one of the lucky ones. By tomorrow, I'll be a little drained and my head will be sore, but mine don't often last more than the one bad day and the one recovery day."

"Lucky," I scoffed. "Right." I stood and checked the time. "I hate to say this, but we probably need to find a stop for the night. You're out of commission and I'm way too tired to get us through four more hours safely."

"Sorry," Paul whispered weakly.

I knew immediately how bad he must have been feeling if he didn't even balk at having to get a room for the night. "Okay, let's drive another thirty minutes up the road and see what we can find. You need anything?" I had enough adrenaline coursing through my veins to drive another thirty minutes for sure, but I'd crash hard once I had us safe and sound in a room.

"Just gotta keep my eyes closed and hope the pill

starts to help at least a little. Right now, it's like an axe is being pounded into my skull." Paul kept a hand shielding his eyes.

"Here," I reached around to the backseat and grabbed a towel I'd recently used to sit on when my trunks were wet, "would this help?"

Paul took the cloth without even looking and draped it over his face. "Yeah, that's great. Thanks. Really sorry to mess up the trip like this. I don't get them often, maybe six to twelve times a year, but they pretty much knock me out when I do."

"No worries. I'm going to take a couple minutes and find a good hotel up the road, then we'll be on our way." I watched the traffic and waited for a tiny lull before rushing to my door and jumping into the seat. Grabbing my phone, I turned off the podcast that had continued to play, and searched for a decent hotel. "We're in luck. There's a Holiday Inn with great ratings just up the road."

Paul made a garbled noise I took as approval.

Easing the car into traffic, I set the GPS for the hotel and kept one eye on the road and the other on Paul. I would be concerned for any friend in his situation, but the fact that I'd so easily and quickly come to care for Paul as more than just a colleague and a friend had me a lot more worried about his condition.

We pulled into the hotel about thirty minutes later.

"Hey," I placed a hand on his knee, "I'm going to go in and get a room. You just hang here, okay?"

Paul grunted.

Luckily, the hotel wasn't packed and I easily secured a room. As much as my horny, immature side wanted to accept the free upgrade to a king-sized one-bed room, I declined and opted for two double beds. I didn't want to make Paul any more uncomfortable than he already was. Plus, he was sick and there would be nothing going on but sleeping whether we had one bed or two.

I went back to the car and drove around to the side where our room was located.

"I'm going to carry our stuff in. Stay put, I'll be back." I rummaged through the trunk and managed to get all of our bags in one go.

Our room was just down a short hall and I sighed in relief when it was fresh and clean. Sometimes you never knew what you were going to get with a hotel room.

Dropping our bags, I rushed back to the car. I opened the door softly and roused Paul. "Hey, you ready to get inside?"

Paul groggily nodded. I reached to unhook his seatbelt and helped him stand. Seeing the man—

who was normally so strong and full of confidence —sway and moan in pain really threw me for a loop.

I kept my arm around him and let him lean on me as we walked slowly toward the room. Once inside, I kept all lights but the small desk lamp turned off. Gently helping him sit on one bed, I pulled the blankets down on the other. "Here, let's get your shoes off. You need to sleep."

Paul put up little resistance as I removed his shoes, but as I tried to help him stand and move to the turned-down bed, he paused. "Gotta pee. Need to drink more water too."

"You go to the bathroom, I'll go get some water from the car." I hated to leave him, but he was right that he needed to hydrate.

By the time I returned, Paul had stripped to his boxers and I nearly swallowed my tongue as I cracked open the lid and handed him the water.

"Do you need more medication? Something to eat?" I asked as he drained the water in long swallows.

"Tomorrow, I'll likely consume enough carbs to take down an elephant," he said wearily. "But tonight, protein and Gatorade would be the best."

"Perfect, I've got both of those. See, stopping for drinks and snacks was a good idea." I rifled through the quick-stop bag and found a stick of beef jerky and a bottle of Gatorade.

Paul accepted the items, but I quickly noticed he struggled to open either of them.

"Here, let me help." I yanked open the jerky before popping open the plastic bottle.

"Makes me weak as a baby," Paul muttered before sitting gingerly on the edge of the bed and eating his snack. "Hate this so much. Tomorrow will be better."

"No worries, just take care of you. I'll be good to go after some sleep, so you can continue to rest as we finish the drive." I paused. "Unless you think it would be better to go back home?" I really didn't want to lose out on the conference and time with Paul, but I'd understand if he needed to get back home.

"Nah, by tomorrow, I'll be almost back to normal. We should get to Indy."

I nodded—relieved that not only would he feel better but also that we'd continue our trip—as I turned down the blankets on my bed. "You want to shower tonight or in the morning?"

"Morning, gonna crash now," Paul mumbled as he took one last swallow of Gatorade and snuggled under his blankets.

"Okay, sleep tight. I'm going to shower. I'll get up

and get us some breakfast in the morning. I'm thinking we leave between nine and ten?" I slipped my shoes off and rummaged in my bag for new boxers while I reminded myself to take the laundry bags the hotel offered to use as dirty clothes bags on the remainder of the trip.

"Should we leave earlier?" Paul asked in the sleepiest voice I'd ever heard.

"We'll play it by ear. If we're awake, we can leave earlier. If not, we'll shoot for nine-thirty." I clicked off the little desk lamp and placed a hand on Paul's exposed shoulder. "Do you want anything to cover your face? Cool cloth? Anything?"

Paul reached up and patted my hand. "You're too good to me, thank you. You've been great. No, I'm good. Just hoping to sleep the worst of it off."

I gave his shoulder a squeeze and headed to the bathroom. I knew he'd be sound asleep by the time I got in bed and I prayed the sleep would ease his pain.

When I finally did crawl into bed, I took longer to fall asleep than I would have thought. I lay there, staring at Paul's silhouette in the dim light from the window, and marveled at my feelings toward him. He wasn't just a guy I wanted to hook-up with. He wasn't just some casual fling that would eventually wear itself out.

Paul was so much more than that to me. I wanted to earn his smiles. I wanted to be the one who helped ease his pain. I wanted to be the one he came home to each day. Way back when I was his student teacher, yeah, I'd just wanted sex. And I was honestly grateful nothing had ever happened then. But now? Now I wanted more. So much more.

And I was stuck falling for a guy who insisted we could never be anything, let alone more.

I must have finally fallen asleep because when I cracked my eye open the next time, the sun was shining through the crack in the curtains.

Paul was sitting up in bed looking at his phone, his hair wet from a shower.

"Good morning," I croaked. "Is the light a problem this morning?"

He turned a soft smile my way. "No, light is no longer an issue. My head just feels like it was beaten to a pulp, but no more axe pounding pain." His stomach rumbled. "And I'm starving. Bring on breakfast."

I rolled from the bed and stretched, not meaning to put on a show, but not the least bit disappointed when Paul's eyes strayed to my waistband and below. "Let's pack up. We can load the car and then grab breakfast. Just gonna brush my teeth."

Thirty minutes later, we were dressed in the

traveling clothes we'd worn the day before, the car was packed, and we settled in for a very nice little continental breakfast.

"You sure you don't want to stop at a restaurant?" I asked as I buttered an English muffin.

"Nah, this is free. We'll stop for lunch. Or we can actually get to Indy, get checked in, and then find lunch." Paul had a bagel, a muffin, and two donuts.

I eyed his plate with a smirk. "Enough carbs to take down an elephant, huh?"

He blushed. "Yeah, I crave them after an attack. I'll have to try to eat healthy after this crap meal."

We enjoyed our breakfast in comfortable silence and easy chit-chat before checking out and heading toward our final destination.

SEVEN

PAUL

I FELT a bit guilty not driving on the second half of the trip, but Jamison was well-rested and ready to go, so I took him up on his offer to drive so I could rest my head.

I'd been getting migraines since I was in high school. I knew others had them so much worse than I did, but that didn't make it any easier when an attack knocked me out. I was always glad that my issues usually only lasted a day or two.

As one of Jamison's true-crime podcasts played on, I snuck a look at him. He'd been the epitome of gentle caregiver when I was sick the night before and my heart had done some sort of swivel in regards to the man I'd previously been dead-set against anything happening with.

Something had changed between us last night.

Jamison had been so helpful and caring, and I'd been truly grateful having him there with me.

Yet, nothing had changed. He was still way too young, still a colleague, still someone I was basically competing with for a job. Whether he was adorable, caring, attentive, and hot-as-hell or not, I couldn't forget all the reasons nothing could happen between us.

So why was I letting my head play around with how much fun he and I could have during the week-long conference?

No.

We were there as professional educators to learn and help make our districts better. Nothing more. Any other thoughts had to be a residual effect of the migraine and proof that I was not thinking clearly. Despite the fact that I wasn't one to deal with unclear thinking or lack of good decision making after an attack, the migraine from the day before had to be the reason I was stupidly giving even the slightest leeway to the fantasies competing for stage time in my head.

I dozed for a bit while Jamison seemed completely absorbed in his podcast. At least sleeping allowed me to shut off my brain for just a bit.

By the time we arrived in Indianapolis, I was feeling nearly one-hundred percent better and I was excited about all the week held for us. I was possibly within ten years or so of retirement, but that didn't mean I wasn't enthusiastic about learning how to be a better educator and leader.

I had a feeling the week was going to be great.

Until I found myself standing in the lobby of a very nice hotel, my face slack, jaw dropped, as the apologetic—yet very polite—hotel employee assured me that there were no other rooms and the suite with a king-sized bed was the only thing available.

It seemed that, despite checking in early, another conference was also in town and all of the rooms were booked solid.

Jamison smiled and patted the counter as he stood close enough to me that I could feel his warmth and breathe in his fresh, clean scent. "We understand. At least we have a room. We'll need two keys, please."

I mumbled thank you as we finished up the transaction and headed toward the bank of elevators. As I stared at the keycard I realized we'd just been assigned to share a bed for a week. Heaven help me, I was strong and insistent, but even I wasn't sure I could avoid a temptation like waking up in the same bed as Mr. Young-Perky-Sex-on-a-Stick himself.

"It's not a huge deal. I'm sure I can sleep on the couch," Jamison offered.

"Nah, no one is going to be on an uncomfortable —possibly not the cleanest—couch for a week." I cleared my throat and hefted my bag. "A king bed is huge; we'll have an entire continent between us."

"It's nice we got a suite," Jamison said, trying to shed a positive light, as the doors to our floor slid open.

"Yeah, no more dwelling on what isn't right, let's just focus on the fact that our trip is paid for, we're here to learn a lot, and we have a place to stay." I slid the keycard into the lock and waited for the beep. Maybe if I kept up the mantra, I'd eventually believe it.

The room was very nice. If the one bed had me all jumbled up, that was just something I'd need to get over. Jamison and I were adults and professional colleagues, we could totally keep to our side of a bed and not bring awkwardness into the situation.

"Well, we've got the rest of today and all of tomorrow. What do we want to do with our time?" Jamison's face looked so excited and hopeful, I couldn't help but feel the same.

"I say we unpack, go get some lunch, and explore the city," I suggested.

"Perfect."

We ended up walking farther than we'd planned,

but the day was so nice and the city so welcoming that we just kept going as we took in the sights.

We eventually stopped at a restaurant called The Eagle and had the best food I think I'd ever eaten. We both got fried chicken and the spicy hot honey was just the right touch. Jamison got herbed fries with a side of aioli and I got horseradish mashed potatoes with herbed chicken gravy; we shared and I'm not sure which side was better because they were both delicious. The homemade biscuits with blackberry jam and honey butter were to die for, but then again, the iron skillet corn bread with maple butter was as well.

By the time we rolled ourselves from the restaurant, Jamison and I couldn't help but laugh at how damn good the food was and how badly we'd stuffed ourselves.

"So much for eating healthier," I groaned.

"Wanna hit the zoo? We could get a ride there and then walk from the zoo back to our hotel when we're done." Jamison was clicking around on his phone.

"Yeah, walking the zoo is probably a good idea after that huge meal. If I went back to the hotel now, I'd just want to nap."

"Well, we could walk to the zoo, but it would end up being almost a fifty-minute walk. Figured our time is better spent walking around the zoo rather than just making our way there."

We ended up in an Uber and the driver dropped us at the zoo in just under fifteen minutes.

"Do we want the dolphin show?" Jamison asked as he studied the schedule the ticket booth operator had placed in front of him.

The hint of longing I heard in his voice made me smile. "Of course. And the butterflies too," I said.

"I think that's included?" Jamison asked the employee and then made his ticket purchase.

By the time I caught up with him, he was at a display where a sea lion was barking and eating fish thrown by a keeper.

"Look at him. He's so cute." Jamison smiled.

"And loud," I marveled. "Sounds like some of the kids on recess."

We both laughed.

"Penguins first?" Jamison pointed toward the Arctic exhibit.

I nodded. "Lead the way."

We spent a few moments admiring the colorful fish and sting rays before turning the corner to find ourselves immersed in the frozen tundra. Jamison morphed into a big kid and I couldn't help but smile at his goofy laughs as he watched the penguins hop and dive into the icy water.

About twenty minutes later, we left the penguins and entered the shark touch exhibit.

Jamison and I both took turns following the employee's directions and got to touch a couple sharks, but the look he gave me told me he was thinking the exact same thing as me.

We washed our hands and exited the building.

"Oh my God," Jamison exclaimed. "How is it that grown adults can't follow directions? No wonder so many of the kids weren't listening to the right way to do it, most of those parents—hell, I hope none were teachers—weren't listening to a damn word the lady was saying." He huffed. "Sorry, that type of experience gives me anxiety."

"I hear ya," I said with a frustrated grunt. "Most of those adults needed to be asked to leave."

We wandered to the macaques and watched the tiny primates run and climb and act generally hilarious before making our way to see the giant walrus.

Jamison checked his phone. "I think we can see the lemurs, but then we should probably find seats for the dolphin show. They say it fills up quickly."

I smiled and bumped his shoulder before even thinking about what I was doing. "Don't want to get stuck in the splash zone."

"We don't?" Jamison asked, completely seriously.

My eyes went wide. "Well, you're welcome to sit down there, but I'll be sitting where I'm guaranteed to be dry."

He laughed. "I'm joking. As a kid, I would have begged to sit there. But now? I'd prefer not to smell like fishy water all day."

We spent a bit reading interesting facts about the lemurs before stepping into line for the dolphin show. Once we had a seat, Jamison's knee bounced so much I couldn't help but place a hand on his leg. "You okay?" I removed it quickly, but not before the warmth of his body traveled through my touch.

He winced. "Yes, I just love dolphins so much. I actually wanted to be a dolphin trainer when I was little. Then I thought about a marine biologist. But I'm kinda scared to death of deep open water, so I opted out. But I absolutely adore watching dolphins. I'd rather see them in the wild, but this will be great. I used to think I wanted to do one of those swim with the dolphins excursions, but I've heard some really bad things about those businesses, so I'll settle for seeing them from a boat or maybe a paddle board if the water is clear enough and not too deep." He pointed to one of the holding tanks. "I hate that they are kept confined here, but this zoo and a lot of others are working hard toward conservation and working with the animals in the most natural setting possible. Some of the dolphins they have would have died in the wild, so I guess being here is better than nothing."

A few moments later, the show began and I found myself entranced. Not so much in the show—yeah, it was great—but in watching Jamison's face as he learned facts and got to see the dolphins do what they were born to do with their jumps and clicks and tricks.

When the show ended and we made our way to the underwater viewing area, Jamison watched the mammals swim around and under and over like a little kid.

"Hey, gonna run to the restroom and get a drink. Meet me outside by that little restaurant." I had the strangest urge to lean into him and kiss his cheek. Instead, I hightailed it to the restroom.

Fifteen minutes later, I stepped out of line with the biggest lemonade they sold and took a long sip just as a smiling Jamison emerged from the dolphin pavilion.

"Want a drink? No straws due to safety, but I'll drink from the lemur side and you can have the dolphin side." I handed the cup his way.

He grinned and took a long drink. "Thanks. That's good. Okay, where to next?"

We spent the next forty-five minutes learning

about and looking at reptiles, meerkats, snakes, and orangutans.

"Oh my God, look at the baby," I cooed as a group of school-aged children moved away from the glass just a mother orangutan swung from a rope and sat facing us with her baby clinging to her.

"Aw, it's like she brought him over to show us," Jamison whispered.

If our shoulders pressed together and my breath caught in my chest, it was only because of the tight space and my adoration over seeing the adorable little baby.

"Since we definitely don't need to eat, maybe we hit the plains area while a lot of the kid groups are wrapping up their visits and heading toward the exit," Jamison suggested as we left the orangutans.

We spent several moments enjoying the giraffes, zebras, lions, and white rhinos. I definitely didn't smile and want him to keep holding my arm when Jamison yelped in fear as the wobbly suspension bridge to see the rhinos jostled us to and fro.

We laughed at the kids trying to race the cheetah, competed to see who could spot the real cheetahs resting in the grass, and made our way to the elephants.

"They're so majestic," Jamison said. "And they

just seem so friendly and smart. I hate that they are treated so poorly and killed around the world."

We spent some time reading about the elephants.

"Oh, we should get pictures. At East, we always had a board of staff and student pictures. Our zoo trip could be the start of a new board as we hang up our East Bumblebees and West Wasps and become Valley Hill Yellow Jackets." Jamison gestured for me to stand where three elephants were in the background.

"Fine, but you're in the pictures, too," I said. I had no issues with pictures if it meant our students could learn and see us as real people. Building relationships with our students was the most important—and best—part of my job.

"Here, I'll take one of both of you," an elderly lady said. "Pictures are always better when you take them with people you love."

I'm pretty sure that Jamison and I both had shocked looks on our faces, but the lady took the photo and handed the phone back to Jamison.

We thanked her and headed out of the Plains area in awkward silence.

"So, the birds?" Jamison suggested.

Okay, we were ignoring the lady's comment. Great. We had a history, we found each other attractive, but Jamison and I definitely didn't love each other.

But you easily could fall for him. Hell, you're in the midst of falling for him right now. No reason to pretend otherwise. And you could definitely love him if you allowed yourself.

Jamison waved his hand in front of my face. "Earth to Paul."

"Oh, huh? Sorry, what did you say?" I knew my cheeks were pink.

"Want to go see the birds?"

"Flamingos, yes. Macaws, yes. Getting inside those cages with the little birds flitting all over the place? That's a hard no from me." I shuddered. "But I'll watch and take pictures if you want to."

And that's exactly what we ended up doing for the next thirty minutes. I got some great pictures of Jamison with birds on his head and shoulders as he held out the little cup of food for the lorikeets.

"Not a fan of the little birdies?" he teased.

"No, they kinda freak me out. I mean, I have bird feeders and I like to look at them, I just don't want to be trapped in a small area with them." I grimaced.

"Fair enough."

While we headed toward the macaws, we glanced up as the noisy flock flew overhead. "Oh wow, so colorful," Jamison said as he pointed up toward the squawking streaks of color in the sky.

We followed the birds and spent several minutes watching them and reading about them before Jamison gasped.

"We missed the sloths!" he gaped at his map.

After turning around and waiting in a line that I likely would have scoffed at if not for having Jamison with me, we got to walk through and have a little one-on-one time with the slow, sleepy creatures.

"Okay, now we can head toward the jungle, but I couldn't be here and miss the sloths." Jamison took a final drink from the cup of lemonade and handed it back to me. "Sorry, almost gone."

"You want more?"

"Nah, we won't be here much longer."

"Okay, where to now?" I asked.

"I mainly just want to see the tigers and then the gift shop before we hit the butterflies." Jamison studied the map.

The tigers were absolutely amazing and gorgeous, but it made me sad to see them in cages. "I'd like to go on a safari and see them in their natural habitat someday."

"Oh my God, that would be amazing," Jamison agreed. "You should definitely put that on your bucket list."

"I'll do that. If you put the dolphins on yours."

"Deal." Jamison stuck out his hand to shake and I laughed off the electric current that traveled between us at the touch.

"Gift shop?" I suggested.

"Of course. It will be overpriced, but I always like getting a souvenir." He led the way to the crowded little shop.

We made our way through the crowd of shoppers and pointed out magnets and t-shirts and mugs as we dodged strollers and children and harried parents.

"Hey, if we get separated, let's just meet in about twenty-five minutes outside," I suggested as an idea took root in my mind.

"Good idea. Can probably use the bathroom here or over at the butterfly conservatory." Jamison gave me a smile as he rolled his eyes at a goofy t-shirt.

Once I'd made my way to the opposite end of the gift shop—glad that both ends displayed the same items—and made sure Jamison wasn't watching me, I scoured the shelves of stuffed animals for the two items I'd decided I wanted to buy. "Aha," I muttered when I found the plush yellow and black insect I'd hoped I'd find. Lucky for me, the gift shop sold a lot more stuffed animals than just the ones they had in exhibits. After few more minutes of sneaking around to find the other item I wanted, I grabbed the toy and made my way to the farthest away checkout line while making sure Jamison wasn't nearby.

I caught his eye from way across the store and gave a little wave as I kept my purchases hidden in front of me. He smiled and waved back. It looked as if he was standing in line as well, so I hoped I'd be able to buy my items and hide them in a bag before he meandered my way.

A few moments later, after an impulse buy of six butterfly-shaped chocolates made its way into my bag, I rolled the top of the bag down and exited the gift shop. When Jamison joined me with a bag in hand, we both laughed.

"Souvenirs are fun," he said with a sheepish smile.

"Ready for butterflies?" I gestured with my chin toward the conservatory.

"Yep. I've been to this zoo once, but didn't get to see the butterflies—I think they were closed for the season. Hopefully we'll get to see some good ones." Jamison took off toward the building.

"I bet you were a fun kid to take on field trips," I said.

Jamison smiled broadly. "Why?"

I shrugged. "You are always excited about learning, you're enthusiastic, but you follow the rules—mostly," I amended the comment as that blow job on school grounds came rushing back to me and shrugged, "I just think teachers probably always wanted you in their group on field trips."

"You may be right. I always loved trips as long as we were moving and learning." Jamison held the door open for me. "You know what drives me insane as an adult? When I see teachers giving their most challenging students to unsuspecting parents. I don't like to see a teacher pawning a challenging student off on someone who doesn't know the kid; to me, if the teacher or assistant or other employee has a good relationship with the student, it's best to keep the student with one of those people. Do you go on field trips?"

I nodded. "I do as often as I'm able. Love the apple orchard and pumpkin patch. Skating reward trips are fun. The museum trips don't often have a lot of extra room, but I try to drive separately and at least meet up with the classes for lunch if I can." I pressed my lips together. "Kinda wonder if field trips will be halted this year due to funds. And we'll likely lose a lot of the time we previously might have had for going on trips."

"Yeah, I was thinking the same thing. Maybe Betty will work her magic with money for at least each grade to take one trip." Jamison stopped in front of a brightly colored piece of artwork. "And we can always cover for each other so at least one of us gets to go have fun with the kids." He glanced my way. "And I know it's not about us getting to have fun. It's about letting the kids see us as real people and building relationships."

"Wow, it's almost like you had an amazing mentor teacher all those years ago," I teased even as I fought the urge to put my arm around him and pull him close.

"The best," Jamison said with a grin.

We made our way to stand in the line and listen to the instructions. The employee allowed us to stow our bags in the little lockers before it was our turn to enter the butterfly habitat.

Jamison immediately began to wander the little pathway around the butterfly habitat. "Oh my God, these plants are to die for; they'd look amazing in my yard. You know, if my yard was a tropical habitat." He made a slight yeeping noise. "Look at the tiny blue one," he whispered as he pointed toward a little butterfly that danced through the air. "Let's go upstairs and take a look around before walking the paths down here."

We spent about an hour with the butterflies as Jamison read about every single plant and butterfly possible.

"I always love when classrooms have butterflies; so much fun for the kids to watch them eat and grow and make their chrysalis. Last year, a Kindergarten class invited me to their release party and so many of the kids cried to have to say goodbye to their little friends." Jamison stood close to where several butterflies were slowly beginning to emerge from their cocoons and watched with an excited look on his face. "Seriously, watching them never gets old."

"No, it doesn't," I answered gruffly, but my eyes were mostly on Jamison.

"We need some pictures with butterflies," he announced.

"Sure, we'll just ask them to hold still for a few quick pics," I teased.

We ended up finding a few butterflies sitting still on plants and were able to sneak a few selfies with the insects in the background.

"Oh, come here," Jamison whispered. "I think we can both get in on this one."

A large black and orange butterfly was sitting peacefully on a leaf just above our heads. We moved slowly and pressed our heads together and snapped the photo with the winged-beauty in perfect shot. Almost as if in slow-motion, another butterfly fluttered over and landed right on the side of Jamison's head, its wings brushing against my hair.

We both gasped and held our breaths until it flew away.

"Please tell me you got that," I whispered.

"I clicked about fifty times, surely I got at least one good one. That was too perfect." Jamison pocketed his phone. "We can pick the best ones back in the room."

"You want to see more or are you ready to head out?"

"Can't get any more amazing than what we just saw, so I say we end on a high note."

After going through the process of making sure no stowaways escaped as we left, we grabbed our bags and headed toward the exit.

"You want to get a ride or just walk?" I asked.

"We can see our hotel from here, I'm thinking we can easily walk."

The walk back to the hotel took us to the White River Canal where we took a few more pictures and enjoyed the artwork.

"I haven't been here for it, but I've seen pictures. They turn the canal water green on St. Patrick's Day and blue for the Colts." Jamison gestured toward the manmade waterway.

"I've seen that. You can also do paddle boats. It's a fun little area; it goes on up a bit, I think. But I'm too tired to walk the entire thing."

"Agreed. Do we want to go out for dinner or order in tonight?" Jamison asked.

I rubbed the back of my neck. "Ugh, I think I need a nap and some medicine first."

"Another migraine?" Jamison asked, concern immediately etching his features.

"Luckily, no. Just a tension headache. My neck is achy."

"So, we'll rest and get rid of your headache. Then do we want to get dinner and drinks at the hotel restaurant?" Jamison asked as we walked into the hotel lobby.

"Yep, that works. Then we can work on our schedules for the week." I punched the elevator button.

When we reached the room, I dropped my bag on my suitcase. "I think I'll take a hot shower to ease my neck muscles and then maybe sleep a bit."

"Take some medicine first so it can start working," Jamison advised.

Twenty-minutes later, I pulled on a pair of pajama pants and a t-shirt. After hanging my towel on the door hook, I wandered into the large, open room.

Jamison was standing at the little kitchen nook area and greeted me with a smile. "Better?"

I gave a little shrug. "Probably wouldn't notice it

as much, but the migraine makes me a little more sensitive to pain for a couple days."

"Sit down." Jamison pointed to the desk chair.

"Why?" I eyed him suspiciously.

He huffed. "Just do it. I'm not going to bite."

Maybe I want you to.

I sat down in the chair with a pretty good idea of what Jamison was about to do. One part of me wanted to opt to spread out on the bed so he could straddle me. The other part of me wanted to run out of the room and avoid any and all temptation.

You're sharing a bed with him for a week. Do you really think you can avoid what's between you for that long?

Ugh. Why couldn't Jamison have been a man I had zero attraction to? Or a woman? Any other person on my staff or in my district and I could have easily laughed off sharing a bed, joked about being a blanket-hog, and had a fun, non-awkward week of educational conference learning.

But, no.

I was forced to share a room, a bed, with Jamison fucking Powers.

"Dude, no wonder you have a headache, you're tense as fuck." Jamison rubbed his thumbs into my muscles as he spoke. "Does that hurt or feel good?"

I made an involuntary whimpery moan when he worked a particularly tight spot. "It's one of those good hurts if that makes sense. Like it's painful, but you know it's going to get better?" I hissed as his hands continued to massage my neck and shoulder area.

"Oh, I know exactly that type of feeling," Jamison murmured.

Shit. Was he talking about...fuck. I'd walked right into that one.

I ignored the comment. Jamison's touch was magically easing the tension in my neck, but the tightness was making its way southward and causing a real issue in my flimsy bottoms. "Ah, um, that's good. Thanks. That really helped." I stood and made my way quickly toward the bed, hoping he wouldn't notice the tent in my pants. I sat down, my back to him and took a deep breath. "Thanks for that and thanks for all the help last night. You were really good with all the migraine shit. Douglas always got annoyed and acted like I purposely got the damn things just to get out of doing things with him." I scoffed. "Because feeling like death is always my first choice."

"That would really say something about him if you took a migraine over being around him." The bed dipped as Jamison sat on the opposite side. "I hated seeing you feel so bad, but I definitely wasn't annoyed with you."

"You were great and I really appreciated your help." With the situation in my pants under control, I cuddled down on my side of the bed. "Maybe an hour nap? Then dinner?"

"Sounds good. I'm down for drinks, but I don't want to be shitfaced or out super late." Jamison got under the blanket and shifted into a comfortable position. "I may have come to class with a hangover a few times way back when, but I can't do that anymore."

"Can't? Or won't?"

"Both." Jamison laughed. "One, we're representing our district and Betty trusted us to come here and act professional. Late night drunkenness wouldn't look good. And it's the same for me back in Valley Hill. Plus, I know you'll laugh, but I'm not getting any younger. Those damn drunken late nights are killer to recover from anymore."

"Just imagine how hard it is for me," I drawled. "If you take a day or two, I'd take a week. I'm good with wine, a good beer or cider, or a couple mixed drinks. But shots are a thing of my past for sure."

"Agreed." Jamison was quiet for a bit. "You know, I used to think I'd hate getting older, but I don't. I know thirty-five isn't old—and before you say anything, I don't think fifty is old either—but I'm enjoying getting older and I hear it mostly just gets better. I don't miss that immature, cocky kid I used to be."

"There are definite perks to getting older. I mean, the aches and pains aren't great, but the rest isn't bad." I wanted to roll to my side and face him, but I didn't trust myself. "And you weren't a bad kid. Cocky, sure. But most teens are. And you were one of the best student teachers I've ever had. Confident, enthusiastic, and ready to take on the world. That's not a bad thing."

"No, and it served me well. I just appreciate the years since then giving me a chance to learn and get to know myself more." Jamison cleared his throat. "Wow, I guess naptime turned into bare your soul time. Sorry. I set my alarm. One hour."

"Never gonna complain about a good heart-to-heart," I said lightly before closing my eyes and letting sleep overtake me.

When Jamison's alarm went off, we both roused and stretched.

"Feel better?" he asked with true concern.

"Yeah, I really do. Between the shower, the medication, the magic hands, and the nap, I'm good to go." I stood and went to rummage through my bag for clothes.

"My magic hands are at your service," Jamison teased.

I coughed and escaped to the bathroom.

"You can change out here. Not like I'm going to jump you," he hollered.

I ignored the thought that maybe I wanted him to jump me and dressed quickly in casual jeans and a button-up before exiting the bathroom.

Jamison gave me the once over. "Nice. You always look so put together. Sometimes I feel like I'm just a kid trying to look like a grownup."

He of course looked amazing in a pair of slim-fit jeans, a black t-shirt, and a fitted jacket. His black dress boots—which would have looked ridiculous with the outfit on me—finished his look perfectly.

I slid on my shoes and pocketed my wallet. "Keys?"

We both flashed our keycards and headed toward the door.

Just as I pulled the door open a crack, Jamison's arm came around me and shoved it closed. "What's wrong?" I asked.

He lowered his lips to my ear and I fought the urge to shiver. "Nothing is wrong. Everything is wrong. Heart-to-heart I guess." He sighed. "Look, I'm not going to purposely put you in an uncomfortable situation and I won't force you into something you don't want." Jamison's nose teased against the side of my head. "But I think if we're both honest, there's no not wanting going on here. I'm not that immature kid from so long ago. I don't want just a quick fuck and run. I can accept that you're not interested in a relationship, but I don't want to waste this perfectly good week. We had the gift of time handed to us on a silver platter and I don't want to watch it disappear without taking advantage of it."

Letting out the breath I'd been holding, I shifted just enough to face him. The warmth of his body, the minty scent of his breath, and his strong presence had my fiery blood pumping hard and fast. "So, you think a week together is enough? And then we can just walk away?"

A flash of something crossed Jamison's face. "I don't know that forever would be enough, but if a week is all I can get, I'll deal."

My heart clenched. Forever? Damn it all to hell. I find a guy who wants to talk forever and I have to turn him down? "And then we walk away? Go back to being just colleagues trying to save a school?" I knew even as I spoke the words that it was a terrible idea.

First, the kid was talking forever and we barely knew each other.

That's not true and you know it. You have more history with him than almost anyone else in town.

"If that's what I have to agree to, then so be it." His lips ghosted over mine.

"I'm not sure I can make that deal. I need some time to think about it." *You idiot! You want him. He's offering a week of sex and then you walk away. No one has to know.*

It was the walking away part that had me worried. Once I had a taste of him, would I be able to let him go? What's the other option? Avoid it and spend the rest of your life wondering what could have been?

"Our days are numbered. Don't take too long," Jamison whispered before dipping his head and capturing my mouth. The memory of that slight kiss from so many years ago didn't hold a candle to the demanding heat of his mouth and tongue as he devoured me.

Fuck. There was no way I could turn this down.

But fuck me sideways, how in the hell was I supposed to give in to the wants and desires that had been building between us over the years, get everything I'd ever wanted, and then just walk away?

I broke the kiss. "Give me until the morning to decide? And if I say no, please know that it's not because I don't want this." I cupped his cheek and feathered a kiss over his lips. "It's just because I don't trust myself to be able to do the right thing at the end of a week."

He nodded. "I know we're both planners and like to know what's happening ahead of time. Maybe we both need to let loose a bit in this situation. Enjoy the here and now and let the future fall where it may."

Danger! Danger!

I had to make sure he understood. "The future can only ever be the way it has to be. I can't bend on that. We are colleagues. There's way too much history between us, too much of a past power difference, too much age gap. We can't ever be more than co-workers." I held his chin between my thumb and finger. "If we do this week thing, I have to know that you understand it ends the day we leave here." My brow rose as I waited for his answer.

"I understand."

EIGHT

OH, I understood.

I understood that I was in deep and grasping at whatever life preserver Paul wanted to throw my way.

I understood that there was no way in hell I'd be able to spend a week living out fantasies I'd been having since I was in college—and honestly even before that—and then just walk away.

However, I also knew there was no way Paul would let go and give in unless he was sure I could agree to the rules.

So, I agreed to his rules.

Was I stupid to think he'd fall so hard for me after a week that he'd throw his damn rigid rules about us out the window?

Yeah, I probably was.

But, if he agreed, I had a week with Paul. A week to indulge desires. A week to make him see how great we could be if he'd just loosen that tight grip he had on what he thought was the right thing to do.

At the end of the week, I'd likely be heartbroken, but I'd have the memories and that would have to be enough.

Don't think that little romantic bitch deep inside isn't holding onto hope that a week will be all it takes to make Paul fall in love with you and you'll spend the rest of your life living happily ever after.

I chuckled as we stepped off the elevator. Yeah, so maybe it was a false hope, but I was a big boy. I knew what I was getting into. Happily ever after or heartbreak? One of them awaited me. But I had a dream-come-true week with Paul to spend first.

"What?" Paul asked as we neared the restaurant.

"Nothing. Just thinking about our situation. The history between us. When I was sixteen, I had the biggest crush on you. When I was twenty-one, it had shifted from that teen puppy-love to an all-consuming adoration and constant thoughts of sex. Then when I came back and ended up as your employee, all of my feelings had to be back-burnered because of the power difference—once again. When I got the principal position, I thought maybe. But through it all, no matter what our ages or positions,

I've always admired and respected you and I'm glad to call you a friend."

"And that made you laugh?" Paul pressed.

I cleared my throat. "No, the fact that less than ten minutes ago I basically offered you my body to use in whatever way you see fit for a week and now we're having dinner and drinks made me laugh."

Paul snorted. "Yeah, I can see it. But, like you said, no matter all of that history—actually, because of our pasts, we can work around the awkwardness. I spent so long avoiding you and convincing myself you annoyed the hell out of me. But, when I actually let myself be honest, I love spending time with you. Whatever this week brings, I don't want to lose the friendship. Even if all we can be is…"

"Professional colleagues, I know, I know." I gave him a wink and stepped toward the host stand. That history and basis of friendship was what I was counting on to pull Paul's head from his ass and make him realize we could be colleagues, friends, and partners. Plenty of couples had personal and professional lives that overlapped.

As the waitperson led us to our table, I solidified my decision. As long as Paul agreed to the week, I was going to spend it cementing myself into his life. I needed him to recognize that I wasn't that kid with a crush anymore. I was a grown man who wanted him—as a friend, a colleague, a partner. I wasn't into playing the field any longer. I wanted long-term and commitment. A week of fantastic sex and spending nearly every waking minute together was the best plan I had to make Paul wake up and realize we could have it all.

An hour later, after we'd enjoyed a delicious meal, we sat at the little corner table sipping the last of our wine.

"This is good. We should get a bottle for the room," Paul mused. "It's fun when food is covered and all you're paying for is alcohol."

"Definitely. This one is good." I took a final drink. "Oh, I just had the perfect idea. Since we have all day tomorrow, we should hit up at least one of the wineries around town."

"Wineries over the Indiana State Museum or Children's Museum?" Paul raised a brow.

"We're educators. We're here to spend a week in conferences. I'd rather spend our Sunday enjoying the city and wine." I shrugged. "Among other things."

Paul's cheeks pinked and he drained the rest of his wine.

"But I'll do the museums if that's what you'd rather do." I shifted so that my knee nudged his leg.

He cleared his throat. "No, wineries sound like a

good idea. Most won't open until noon and some likely aren't open on Sunday; we should do some research before. But that means we can have a lazy morning." As he spoke the words, Paul's eyes met mine and held.

"Lazy morning?" I said dumbly. "Oh, like plenty of time to laze around in bed—doing whatever one might do in bed—and get ready to go without being in a hurry?" I bit my lip.

"When you've got time for a lazy morning, it means you can stay up late." Paul's eyes flashed. "Doing whatever one might do in bed late at night."

"Sleep?" I batted my lashes and grinned as my hand found its way to Paul's knee.

"If that's what you want." Paul reached for the bill.

By the time we reached the elevator, I was nearly jumping out of my skin. We rode the empty car to our floor and I all but ran to the room. Opening the door, I walked through the doorway and turned to ask Paul if his words meant what I thought they meant.

But he was on me, pressing me against the wall and claiming my mouth in a kiss I swore was hot enough to set off the fire alarms. His fist gripped the hair at the back of my head as his hips rocked against mine.

When we finally broke apart, our breathing ragged, Paul pressed his forehead against mine. "I'm going to hate myself at the end of this week, but I must be some sort of glutton for punishment because I can't say no." His hand cupped my face as his thumb traced my bottom lip. "You've lived in my fantasies ever since that kiss in the parking lot. I hate that I can't give you more than this, but if we can agree to the parameters, I want this week with you."

"Mmm, when you talk rules and parameters it gets me all turned on," I teased. I wasn't going to get fixated on the rules or the end of the week or what would happen in the future. "Top or bottom?"

"Top."

"Always?" I cocked his head.

"I want to, but bottoming doesn't work for me. The few times I tried were disastrous; I can't let go enough to enjoy it." Paul scowled.

"Maybe just haven't found the right person to loosen up with," I said before sucking his thumb into my mouth. "But I love bottoming, so no worries."

Paul seemed relieved.

I made a note to gauge him as this week went on. There was nothing I'd like better than being the man Paul finally let loose with. The idea of topping him—

of Paul letting go enough to let me in both physically and emotionally—was heady stuff and I wanted it.

But only if Paul wanted it as well.

And that likely wasn't going to happen in a week.

And a week is all you've got.

I pushed the thought aside and bit Paul's thumb. "What do you want?"

"You," Paul growled.

"Well, you've got me." Pretty sure the man had had me for well over ten years. "Now, what do you want to do with me?"

"Want to take my time with you. Can we start slow?" Paul leaned in and kissed my neck.

"We can start whatever way you want. Bed?"

Paul paused. "Are you sure? We're completely different people; what if what we want is too different? What if you don't like…"

I took his hand and placed it on my rock-hard cock. "Does this feel like I don't like anything we've been doing?"

Paul cupped the bulge in my pants. "No, I just, Douglas always said…"

"That's the last time I want to hear his name this week. He was a fool and didn't deserve you." I dipped my head slightly and feathered a kiss over his lips. "Will we possibly do this and find out that it's a total bust? Sure, there's always that possibility. But I think it will be a lot of fun at least giving it a shot. Now, get out of your head and get into this bed." I grinned against his mouth and yelped as he walked me backwards until we fell onto the mattress.

The weight of Paul on top of me, the way he fit so perfectly between my legs, and the hard heat of our erections pressing together were a sensation overload of epic proportions. And I never wanted it to end.

Paul's lips found the sensitive skin of my neck and I whimpered as he licked and sucked. "This is a lot," he muttered. "Like I've just been handed a whole box of gifts and I don't know where to start first." He propped up on his elbows and gave me what appeared to be a nervous smile. "It's been a really long time and I'm scared I'm going to fuck this up. If we only get a week, I want it to be the best."

I pulled him down into a searing kiss, the heat between us taking my breath away. "I could very easily come in my damn pants right now, pretty sure you're not fucking anything up."

"There's so much I want to do and so little time," Paul murmured as his lips broke from mine and trailed along my jawline to my ear.

"There's no quota, no requirements. We do what feels right. I mean, I'm not suggesting we get in deep with any kink play at this point," I teased and breathed a sigh of relief when Paul chuckled. "But I have absolutely no problems with mornings and nights filled-to-the-brim with the same-old-same-old or something different every single time." I rocked my hips up to meet his. "But speaking of filled-to-the-brim, I'm completely down for that. I've got prep supplies, condoms, and lube—but I also get tested regularly—so if anal is something you're okay with, we're set."

"I get tested, too. All good." Paul cocked a brow. "You brought all of that? Were you planning this?"

I shrugged with a little smirk. "I keep them in my overnight bag as a precaution—they've been replaced more than they've been used. But I'd be lying if I said I wasn't hopeful this would happen. Hell, I've been hopeful this could happen since the day I became a colleague rather than an underling."

Paul grunted a laugh. "And I've been doing everything in my power to avoid any situation that may even hint at how much I wanted this."

"Can we get naked and go from there?" I ran my hands up and down his back.

Paul nodded and rolled from the bed. As he stripped, he kept his eyes on mine as I did the same. I'd never felt so exposed and so appreciated in my life as the dim glow of the desk lamp filled the room.

He looked as if he wanted to consume me—and fuck did I want to be consumed.

As he tossed his clothes to the small couch, I took in his gorgeous body. The smattering of salt-n-pepper hair that covered his body begged for me to rub my hands all over it. His perfect dick—cut and longer than I'd imagined—bobbed proudly from a trimmed thatch of hair. I licked my lips and scooted toward the edge of the bed.

"Can I?" I asked, gazing up at him, my mouth nearly touching his leaking tip.

Paul nodded. "Yeah, but I don't want to come yet."

I cupped an ass cheek and pulled so that his thighs were flush with the bed. Fondling his balls, I teased my tongue around his head and savored the flavor of his pre-cum. "I love a good face-fucking—just for future reference. Hard and deep, wet and hot, cum dripping from my lips."

Paul's hips bucked. "Fuck, Jamison, I said I didn't want to come yet."

I smiled up at him. "Sorry. Just wanted you to know that you can fuck my face hard and I'll love it." I wrapped my fist around his hard dick and stroked. "Not gonna lie, the idea of taking this gorgeous cock deep in my ass has me all kinds of turned on. Glad we have a week ahead of us." I opened my mouth and took Paul's shaft to the back of my throat. Fuck. His flavor and scent filled my senses and I knew I'd quickly become addicted.

"Shit, Jami," Paul groaned as his hand cupped my cheek.

For the first time in our entire history, he'd called me Jami instead of Jamison. Did it mean something? *Yeah, you idiot. It means his cock is in your throat and he slipped up using the nickname almost everyone else in the world uses for you.*

But I wanted it to mean more.

Paul thrust his hips a few more times as he used my mouth, but pulled out and fisted his cock. "Gotta stop or this will be over way too soon."

"We've got all night and a lazy morning," I quipped, but I scooted toward the middle of the bed as Paul joined me.

"I'm not as young as I used to be. Twice in a night is about all I can be counted on to get it up—and recovery time is a must." He winced. "Sorry, downside of…"

"I swear to God, if you call yourself old, I'm going to make you watch me jack off and then go to sleep with no more playtime."

"Damn, that's harsh." Paul chuckled. "I was just giving you a heads up."

"It's all good. I can't go one right after another most times either."

Paul was stretched out on his side next to me. His eyes roamed up and down my body as his hand trailed over my chest, my navel, my thighs. "You're gorgeous," he murmured.

My cock jerked and leaked onto my stomach as his hand cupped my balls and his mouth connected with a nipple. "Fuck, you're not gonna be the only one done way too quick." I hissed as Paul teased my nipple with his teeth and began to stroke my shaft.

"You're so thick, I could never take this," he said as his thumb massaged my slit.

"You could. It would be so good. You could let go for me, let me show you how good it could be." I closed my eyes as the friction of his fist and the image of my cock sliding into his ass filled my head. Paul's hard length rocked against my hip and I noticed he didn't protest about the idea of bottoming for me. But at that moment, we had more pressing issues. "Suck me."

Paul groaned and shifted to take my thick cock between his lips.

"Oh fuck, that's so good." My hips thrust up. "Won't last like this."

"Wanna make you come with just my mouth, but not now," Paul said as he popped off and moved to settle himself between my legs. "Think we can get off like this?" The thrust of his hips made our hard cocks rub together.

"Definitely," I gasped and rocked up to meet his hips. "Kiss me."

Paul wrapped one arm behind my back and one arm around to grip my neck as his mouth captured mine. Our wet, hot lips and tongues fell into the same rhythm as our rutting cocks.

"Wanna suck you off. Wanna tongue your hole and slide my cock deep into your ass." Paul's words were a promise against my lips as he thrust against me. "But right now," he panted, "wanna watch you come."

I reached between us and took both our cocks in my fist. With a whimper of need, I began to stroke.

Paul moaned. "So good."

Our thrusting became harder, the sexy noises filling the room became louder. I pulled Paul to me for a kiss just as my cock exploded over my hand, painting thick ropes of white onto my stomach. Paul followed, his tongue dipping to meet mine as his orgasm shuddered through him, his cum mixing with mine.

When we'd come down from our high, I grabbed a tissue from the table next to the bed.

"Was that…" Paul started.

"If you think that was anything short of earthshaking…" I warned.

He let out a sigh of relief. "Yeah, I thought so too."

"Showers? Sleep? See what the morning brings?" I suggested.

Paul agreed and I let him have the shower first.

By the time I was out, Paul was spread out on the bed with his notebook and the conference materials.

"I forgot we wanted to plan a schedule. We don't have to do it all tonight. I was just looking at it." He adjusted his glasses as he sat there in just his underwear looking sexy as fuck.

"It's all good. I'm tired, but not sleepy if that makes any sense." I glanced around the room and rubbed my stomach. "We should have gotten dessert to bring back. I want something sweet."

"Oh, I have something." Paul got up from the bed.

I went to stand next to him like an excited kid waiting for a cookie as he riffled through his souvenir bag.

"Shit, where is it? Wait, this isn't my bag," he said. "What did you buy?" he turned a quizzical eye my way.

I picked up the other bag and looked inside. "This isn't mine. What did you buy?"

Paul dumped the contents of one bag onto the bed.

I did the same.

We laughed as we took in the sight before us.

Butterfly-shaped chocolates.

A dolphin.

A tiger.

And two yellow jackets.

"I thought getting the yellow jacket for your new office was a nice thing to do. And a dolphin, of course." Paul shrugged sheepishly.

"And I thought a yellow jacket for your new office was the perfect touch. Along with a tiger, of course." I picked up the black and yellow insect and the dolphin Paul had purchased for me. "They're exactly what my office needs. Thank you." I wrapped my arms around his neck and kissed him. The feelings flowing through me were far above what I should have been having for a man I only got to spend a week with.

Maybe his gifts meant that he could eventually allow this to become something more.

Paul pulled back. "I guess when we're back to reality and this is all just a distant memory, at least we'll have these as reminders."

My throat felt tight. The end of the week was going to absolutely kill me. "I don't think I'll have any trouble remembering," I choked out. "Now, about this chocolate."

A brief look of regret crossed Paul's face, but he smiled at my redirection. "Impulse buy, but I'm glad I picked it up. Wanna split it?"

"I never turn down chocolate. Unless it has coconut." I shivered. "I hate coconut."

Paul popped open the package and handed me a butterfly. "Agreed."

About an hour later, after we'd done a preliminary plan of which presentations and workshops we wanted to attend, we cleared the bed and settled down.

For a few awkward moments, as we shifted and got comfortable, we were silent.

"Is this the most massive mistake of our lives?" I asked.

Paul turned solemn eyes and a sad smile my way. "Quite possibly."

"What changed your mind?"

"I guess I'd never given a thought to something temporary, something we could have for the moment and mutually agree to walk away from." He shrugged. "It's probably an epically bad idea, but I'm allowing the selfish side of myself to take over even just for this short time." His lips twisted into a soft smile. "I think I'd rather have an amazing week with you than keeping it the way it was. Believe me, I've had well over ten years of avoiding and denying. Touching you and allowing myself to feel is worth it."

"Even come Sunday when we're both gutted?" I asked, but then frowned. "Or maybe it will just be me gutted. Maybe you're better at walking away than I am."

"No, we'll both be in the same boat. It's going to suck. But even letting ourselves have this week— even when we know it's going to hurt—feels like the right thing to do. I've never broken any of my rules the way I have with you, but I'm not regretting it. It's like I've been given this week-long pass to live out fantasies and I don't want to turn it down." Paul wrinkled his brow. "Which is so weird. Never in my wildest dreams would you have been able to convince me that I'd give in and take part in a fling." He stretched his arm out and touched my hand. "But it seems that years of attempting to avoid you have caught up with me and I'm helpless against the pull."

"I'm sure my killer smile, winning personality, and tight ass all helped," I teased.

"I'm positive they did," Paul answered with a chuckle. "But honestly, it's more just you being you."

"You called me Jami," I whispered. "You've never

once called me Jami, even though almost every single other person on the planet does."

His cheeks pinked. "I've always kept to Jamison for two reasons. One, I really like the name. Two, and likely the biggest reason, it seemed like if I kept to the more formal name maybe I'd be able to keep that wall between us. People you're close to call you Jami; I needed to keep you at arm's length so I stuck to Jamison." He pressed his lips together and turned to his side to face me. "In my head, you're Jamison so that I don't mess up." He swallowed. "But in my heart, you've always been Jami."

Sniffing and clearing my throat, I asked, "We sticking to our continent between us plan?" I smoothed my hand over the soft mattress.

"We only have a week, might as well enjoy it." Paul seemed relieved to leave the deeper conversation. He scooted toward the middle of the bed and pulled me close.

I curled into his warmth and let myself be held. "I loved hearing Jami on your lips." I tipped my head up to kiss him. "But I love that you're pretty much the only person who calls me Jamison. So, feel free to call me either."

Paul smiled. "Noted." Then he laughed lightly. "Do you remember when I caught you behind the bleachers with what's-his-name?"

"Tim Olsen?" I snorted. "Yeah. By the way, he's married to a woman and has three kids. He's a dentist. Never hold out hope that the guys who only want you for head behind the bleachers will ever be honest with themselves."

Paul shrugged. "I don't know. Maybe he's bi or pansexual."

I started to protest then paused, my breath leaving me as if I'd been punched in the gut. "Damn, you're right. That was very narrow minded of me. I'm supposed to be the staff advisory to the student council and working to make things more inclusive. Yet I just...wow, that was bad. Thanks for calling that." I wrinkled my nose. "I guess I had enough guys want me on my knees or bent over, but they never wanted more than that, that I automatically assumed and that's just wrong. Hell, for all I know, Tim is bi or pan and his wife knows that."

"It's okay. You slipped up. The main thing is that you recognize it and fix it. Then move on. Like with everything in life, we mess up. That's expected. But acknowledging our mistakes and striving to do better next time is the main thing." Paul kissed the top of my head.

"Wait, we got way off track. What were you going to say about catching me behind the bleachers?" I ran my hand from his waist to his upper thigh.

"Just thinking about names. Do you remember what you said to me after Tim had tucked and run?"

I bit my lip and tried not to laugh. "I think it was something like Later, Dick Power."

"I believe it was See ya, Dick Power. But close enough."

I laughed. "I think you called out something like 'That's Mr. Powers.'" I squeezed his thigh. "Come on, as a teen, the name Dick Power was awesome. He's got the big dick power. Hell, even Dick Powers was great. Oh, you know him, he's got those dick powers." I let my hand roam to cup Paul's cock. "And I gotta tell you, I've been looking forward to testing out those dick powers for years and years."

His hips thrust against my hand. "Yeah, well. Dick Powers wasn't the best name to grow up with, nor was it a good one to have as an educator. Paul was much easier." He wrapped an arm around me and stroked my back. "I'm down for the Powers team each showing off our dick powers for the next seven days."

I groaned. "I think that can definitely be arranged." God, how could something between two people be so easy, so natural, and feel so right? Being with Paul felt like we were an actual couple, together for years, settled and comfortable.

As I snuggled into his chest, two emotions

battled for space in my head. Elation over being with Paul in a way I'd always wanted to be. He was an amazing man and I got to be in his life.

And extreme regret.

No, regret wasn't right.

Fear.

Fear of how badly it was going to hurt to walk away from this.

Paul was a strong, confident, and stubborn man. I had a sinking feeling it was going to take more than a week to change his mind. Even as his hand stroked up and down my back and he pressed a kiss to my hair—signs that he, too, was enjoying our time together as more than just a weeklong hookup—I knew getting him to give up his rules, reverse his decision, allow us to become something very likely wasn't going to happen.

You'll just have to persuade him.

A week was all I got.

Doesn't mean that you can't continue to prove to him how great you are together.

I sighed and cuddled deeper into his arms.

Yeah, maybe it would take longer than a week. But I had nothing but time and every reason in the world to convince this man that we could be more.

I WOKE EARLY the next morning, evident only by the tiny sliver of light coming through the heavy curtains, warm and cozy in the arms of a man I could see myself waking up with every single day.

Or at least for a week.

As I shifted slightly, I couldn't help but notice Paul's hard cock pressing against my ass. Deciding that we could start our lazy morning early, I rocked backwards and grinned when Paul grunted.

"You're a wicked tease." His sleepy grumble sent heat through my veins.

"We've got a long, lazy morning, an amazing bed, and all the right tools for wicked teasing. I couldn't help myself." I pressed my ass harder against his cock.

Paul's hot lips found my neck and I sighed as his tongue teased. "Wanna get us both off. Shower, sleep some more, and then suck you off."

I moaned as my cock got impossibly hard. "I like the way you think."

"Take your pants off," Paul demanded as he shifted to pull his underwear down.

After wrestling my boxers down my legs and kicking them off, I groaned and savored the press of Paul's hot cock against my ass.

He took hold of his cock and guided it between my legs. As he began to thrust, his pre-cum coated my balls, taint, and crack. It wasn't as slick as a good helping of lube would have been, but it would suffice. Paul reached around and took my dick in his fist. "Gonna make you come."

I whimpered as he began to stroke me in the same rhythm as his cock slid between my legs. "Fuck, that's good. Want your cum on me."

We moved together, savoring the heat and friction, for several moments. Soon, the thrusting and skin-on-skin was too much and I felt my balls draw up tight as Paul increased his speed and continued to stroke me.

His other hand moved to pinch my nipple. Paul's tight fist jerking me, his fingers tweaking my nipples, and his cock sliding hard and fast against my taint and balls all worked together to send me into a crashing orgasm.

Paul's hand, slick with my cum, milked me as his cock pulsed and coated my balls with his release. "Fuuuuuck," he groaned.

I sighed when he released my cock, his dick still throbbing between my legs. "I could very easily get addicted to these lazy mornings," I mumbled. *But you can't get used to them.* "Shower? I believe you mentioned something about more sleep and sucking me off?" I made light of the situation as quickly as I could. No reason to dwell on what we both knew was down the road.

"Mmm," Paul hummed into my neck. "If we weren't a mess, I'd say skip the shower. But, we've still got hours to sleep and whatnot."

I wiggled my ass against him. "Pretty sure I'm very interested in this whatnot you speak of."

I'd taken a shower with my share of men over the years and it wasn't always all it was cracked up to be. Movies, porn, and romance novels made showering together seem sensual and sexy. All-to-often, showering together was just awkward, wet, and cold when hot water couldn't be shared easily.

But stepping into the double-headed shower with Paul seemed as if we'd been showering together for years.

Because of course it did.

Awkward would have made things easier in the long run.

But Paul's soapy hands washing me, his fingers massaging my head, and his slick cock pressed between my ass cheeks as he stroked my dick was the most sensual, sexy shower I'd ever shared with anyone.

I returned the favor and washed Paul's hair. "Have I ever told you how sexy your hair is?"

"Turning gray is old, not sexy," he grumbled with

his eyes closed as the water rinsed suds from his hair.

"Nope. You've got that perfect salt-n-pepper, distinguished look going on and it gets me hard just thinking about it." My hands caressed down his chest before I took hold of his dick in my soapy hand.

Paul's head fell back against my shoulder and he thrust his half-hard cock into my fist. "And when I'm a lot more salt than pepper?"

"Sexy silver fox." My words were gruff against his ear as I fought off a pang of regret that I wouldn't be by his side when he was more salt than pepper.

"You live in a fantasy world," Paul grumbled.

I turned us and pressed his chest against the tile and nestled my now-hard cock between his cheeks.

Paul tensed for a moment, but the tension eased as I wrapped my arms around his chest and slid my dick up and down his crack while kissing his ear. "If thinking about you spreading me open and sliding your cock deep in my ass is a fantasy world, so be it." I nipped at his ear. "If imagining showing up to school and town events on the arm of the sexiest man in Valley Hill is a fantasy world, I'll own it." I gripped his hips and thrust my cock between his legs before leaning in and teasing his ear with my tongue. "If the thought of rimming your hole until you're begging for my cock, fingering your ass until you're primed and ready, and then filling you with my thick shaft is a fantasy world, I don't want to live in reality."

A whimpering moan escaped Paul's mouth before I turned him around and devoured his mouth. Taking both our cocks in my hand, I began to stroke and rub my thumb over our slits. "Can't wait to take this gorgeous cock in my mouth and choke on you as you come down my throat."

"Fuck, Jami," Paul gasped as he tensed and exploded in my hand.

Watching him come apart at my touch sent me over the edge and I joined him as my orgasm pulsed through me.

We spent several moments kissing and caressing before a final rinse—thank God for an amazing hot water supply. Quickly drying off and running towels through our wet hair, we climbed into bed. Our warm, damp, naked skin clung together and I sighed as Paul took me in his arms and kissed the back of my neck.

"Sleep a couple more hours?" he asked.

"Mmhm," I agreed and drifted into the most comfortable sleep of my life.

I WOKE a bit later and smiled to myself as I enjoyed the warmth of Paul's arms wrapped around me. Shifting gently, I maneuvered myself under the blankets, careful not to kick him in the face with my legs as I got into position.

I nuzzled my nose against his neat thatch of hair, savoring the unique scent of him mixed with the citrusy hotel soap. Pressing my lips against Paul's plump cock, I smiled as he shifted in his sleep and moaned. I fondled his balls and stroked his shaft, enjoying as he hardened slightly at my touch. Flicking my tongue against his slit, I swirled around his head like I was licking a lollipop.

I knew the moment Paul woke up and realized what I was up to. He spread his legs and thrust his cock between my lips with a chuckle.

"Is this my wakeup call?" he asked as he took me in his fist and jerked me slowly. "You are a wicked man, Jamison Powers." His lips feathered over my head as he spoke.

Popping off Paul's cock just long enough, I thrust my hips. "Suck me while you fuck my face."

His hot mouth consumed my shaft and I slicked a finger in my mouth. With my wet finger, I teased his taint and pucker as I took his cock back between my lips.

Paul mimicked my move and I gasped as his slick

finger teased my hole while he bobbed his head up and down my dick.

"Oh fuck!" I rocked my hips and groaned as Paul gripped my ass. "Want your cum down my throat, hard and fast," I begged.

Paul picked up his pace, his mouth and tongue devouring my cock as his hips pistoned, thrusting his cock deep to the back of my throat. As a tingle traveled down my spine and my balls drew up tight, I groaned. "Fuck, gonna come," I warned as my orgasm exploded through me, my cock throbbing my release between Paul's lips.

When Paul's moan vibrated against my dick, I gripped his ass and pulled him hard and fast as my lips and tongue worked his shaft. With a teasing press against his taint, I sucked him deep and nearly came again as Paul's hot cum shot against the back of my throat. When his dick finally stopped pulsing, I let him fall from my mouth and moved so we were face-to-face.

I licked his cum from the corner of my mouth with a wicked smile before flicking my tongue out to catch a drop of my own jizz from his chin.

Paul groaned and cupped the back of my head to pull me close before he devoured my mouth. Our flavors mixed on our tongues and my cock made a valiant effort to rise again.

"Best wakeup ever," Paul whispered against my mouth.

"Agreed." *We could have the rest of our lives with wakeups like this if you'd just let go and allow us to happen for real.*

Paul's stomach rumbled. "Breakfast?"

As if answering a mating call, my stomach gurgled as well. "Want to get room service? Go downstairs? Or walk somewhere?"

"The next several days will be early wakeups and probably continental breakfast. Since we're doing the whole lazy morning, let's order room service, shower, and then watch a movie or something until it's time to go." Paul's warm hand ran up and down my back, moving lower and pausing to cup my ass, before he tipped my chin for a final kiss.

My heart clenched with sadness that this perfect moment would never see the light of day—would never be our reality—and I began to roll away.

"Hey," Paul caught my wrist and pulled me close. "I need you to know—if our circumstances were different—this would be exactly what I'd want. You are exactly what I'd want. We're like the kings of impossible situations, but that doesn't mean what I feel for you isn't real." He kissed me, slow and deep.

"I know you mean for that to help, but it actually just makes everything worse. The fact that you're willing to throw this into the trash heap of impossible situations instead of fighting for me, fighting for us, declaring that the struggle to make this work is worth it, hurts more than the nearly two decades of you avoiding me." I pressed a kiss against his head and rolled from the bed.

Closing the door to the bathroom, I opted for a solo shower as I berated myself for even suggesting that I could possibly walk away from this man. A week would never be enough.

Hell, a lifetime with Paul wouldn't be enough.

My heart hurt already. By Sunday, I had a feeling I'd feel like my heart and soul had been run over by a cheese grater.

After showering and dressing for the day, we ordered breakfast and settled in on the bed. "God knows why I'm willing to put myself through this," I whispered against Paul's neck, "but I can't seem to give it up. Like, I know the more I enjoy this and get attached to what we have, the more it's going to hurt to lose it. But not getting to experience it seems just as bad."

Paul sighed against my head. "I know. I feel the same."

"Tell me again why we can't just go back, tell the town we're a couple, and continue fighting to save the school district?"

He chuckled.

"No, I'm serious. I just don't get it."

Paul huffed a little sigh that sounded like irritation. "We've discussed this. There's too much working against us. You were my student for one. You've been my student teacher. You've been my employee. And now we're basically competing for the same position. How would it look?"

I shrugged. "I don't know. I guess I still don't get how it would look."

"Like I'm abusing my power over you," Paul answered in frustration.

"You have no power over me, let's make sure that's very clear." I moved out of his arms and sat cross-legged to face him. "You have had no power over me since the day I accepted that principal position. Are you seriously suggesting that the board and the town will think you're fucking me to...God, I don't even know what you might be thinking...like your dick powers may be so amazing that I'll give you the damn job as long as you keep servicing me?" I snorted—partly because it was ludicrous and partly because it was funny. "You're fabulous and I adore you, but I can assure you no cock is good enough to make me give up on my career and watch an entire district fail."

Paul rolled his eyes and adjusted his glasses. "I'd

never suggest that. Like it or not, no matter how many years have passed, the rumors would begin flying. Did I abuse my power over you when you were an impressionable young teen? Did I coerce you into doing my bidding as your mentor teacher or boss? Am I distracting you or controlling you now with sexual favors or promises?"

My hand slapped against the mattress. "And we'd both know none of that is true. Those are flimsy excuses and you know it." I shook my head. "We live as gay men in a small town. I'm sure we've both dealt with our share of gossip and rumors. What am I missing here? There's got to be something else."

Paul leaned forward and rested his elbows on his thighs. "What happens when one of us gets the principal position and one of us has to step down?"

"We deal with it. If we're in a committed relationship, we work through the struggles." I ran a hand through my hair. "I'd hope to God that we'd value us more than a damn job."

Paul shook his head. "I'm not far from retiring. I've never imagined working anywhere but Valley Hill. Other districts aren't going to hire me—at least not at my salary level—and I…"

Sudden realization dawned on me. "Oh my God, you're worried I'm going to win."

He looked up at me with a pained expression.

"You're young and amazing and they'd be stupid to keep me in the top position when you're ready, willing, and able to take over." Paul closed his eyes and sighed. "I don't know that I could take the humiliation of being bested by my boyfriend. And if we fell apart? It would look like I'd been played just so you could win."

My mouth gaped like a fish as I processed what Paul said. For several moments, I had no words. I began to speak more than once and snapped my mouth shut to continue my attempt at forming a coherent sentence. "Wow, that's a lot to unpack."

Paul chuckled humorlessly. "Believe me, I know."

"One glaring thing that stands out to me is that you've got major power and control issues. You have no idea how to let loose and not be the person in control." I reached for his hand. My heart did a little dance when he grasped my hand in his—he wasn't pulling away and that gave me hope.

"I didn't have siblings I had to share with. I've always been a take-charge type person. Over the years, I've gotten what I wanted in almost every area of my life and I've been looked to as the person everyone counts on and trusts and turns to." Paul took his glasses off and rubbed at his eyes. "The one time I had no control of a situation was with Douglas and he nearly ruined me. I'm sorry if the thought of letting go or giving control to someone else is terrifying."

"Okay, I can appreciate that. Honestly, I can." I scowled. "So, if we weren't competing for the same position—keeping in mind that a lot can change between now and the end of this coming school year—you'd be fine with us being together?"

He pursed his lips. "I'd still be worried it looked like I was abusing my power over you," he held up a hand to stop me when I began to protest, "but if we weren't employed by the same district and competing for a job, I guess it would be easier to push that part aside."

"So, I'll quit. I'll go to Sugar Creek." I wouldn't do that, but I needed to hear Paul's response.

"The fuck you will," he growled. "Valley Hill is your home as much as it is mine. You're not going to Sugar Creek any more than I am. I won't allow it."

"Allow it?" I cocked a brow.

Paul huffed. "You know what I mean. You're not giving up your position here."

"And neither are you."

He pressed his lips together. "Which brings us right back to impossible situations."

"No, I don't think it does." I shook my head and pulled my knees up to my chest. "I think it brings us back to two very strong-willed men—who could very easily fall head-over-heels with each other—who need to take a good hard look at their personal and professional lives and decide what's important." I nudged him with my foot. "And a sexy, silver fox who needs to learn how to let go—both in his career and in the bedroom." I raised a brow with a teasing smile. "I promise it's not the end of the world to let loose."

"Letting go is not something I've ever been good at. I'm sorry we got ourselves into this mess—we were selfish and stupid and I understand if we need to call it quits before we get any deeper into a very messy situation." Paul put his glasses back on and let his head thump against the headboard with his eyes closed.

I cocked my head to the side and thought about his words.

Would we be smart to just chalk what had happened between us up to a very poor lapse of judgement and move on as colleagues like it had never happened?'

Yes. Yes, we would.

Was I willing to do that?

Hell, no.

Paul and I had a fuck-ton of things to deal with and work through. A lot of what we faced was completely out of our control—and I totally understood how scary that could be. We were both determined to save the district and keep our jobs—and I'd be damned if I let either of us just give up on that.

I had to admit, it stung a bit to think that Paul was so hung up on being in charge and winning that he'd be willing to just toss us aside. However, as far as relationships went, all he'd had was that disaster with Douglas. So, he had every right in the world to have turned to his job for fulfillment—and likely no idea about how to marry his personal and professional life together successfully.

What the hell are you going on and on about?

I laughed at myself. Basically—with a lot more thoughts and words than were truly necessary—I'd made a decision.

Maybe a decision that Paul wouldn't agree with—but also, it was one that Paul didn't need to know about just yet.

We'd continue our week. Call it quits at the end. Go back to Valley Hill and work our asses off to save the schools.

And I'd be there in every way Paul needed me to be.

As a sounding board, a cheerleader, a shoulder.

As a friend, a colleague, and a partner—sure, that last one would maybe take more time.

And I wear him down—in a good way. I'd prove to him that we could be us while still running our school and saving our district.

There was no way of knowing which of us the board would vote to move to principal and assistant principal.

I'd be patient.

I'd let Paul realize that we were damn good together—better together than apart. And I'd be there when he was ready to admit that.

And I'd have a good time gently persuading him to give up control bit by bit.

Both at school and in the bedroom.

"Jamison?" Paul called my name as if he'd said it multiple times. "Do you want to just end this now before it hurts any worse come Sunday?"

I smiled and leaned in to kiss him. "Nope." I popped the p. "I want to eat our breakfast, plan our day, and spend the rest of this week having the best sex of our lives. Then we'll go back to Valley Hill and everything will work out the way it's supposed to."

Paul pulled back and narrowed his eyes. "And we can do the whole friends and colleagues thing without fallout?"

"Of course, we can," I whispered against his lips. "We're professionals."

A knock at the door announced our breakfast and I climbed from the bed to accept our food.

When Paul and I had started the whole week-long sexcapade, I'd had two hopes. One, a week would be all it took and he'd change his mind. Two, knowing that a week wasn't going to be enough, I'd thought we'd return to Valley Hill and he'd miss me so much that he'd change his mind.

I now knew neither of those were going to happen.

Paul was as stubborn as I was; it was going to take more to change his mind. It wasn't even about convincing him—he knew we were good together. It was more about showing him it was okay to let go, to maybe not have every single moment of your life held in a tight fist, to give up a little bit of that power he held so dear.

With a new understanding of our situation and a plan for making this work—yes, it would take time and patience—I dug into my eggs and French toast. Walking away on Sunday would hurt and would be hard, but it was just a bump in the road that would eventually become our journey toward happily ever after.

Good God, you're such a romantic sap. What if you can't make your plan work?

I smiled around a bite of bacon I'd snatched from

Paul's plate and gave a mental shrug. I was up to the challenge and the end would so very much justify the means.

Just don't go getting yourself another broken heart.

Nah, I was going to get my man.

NINE

PAUL

"So, there are two wineries right here close by, but only one is open today," I mused as I studied my phone. Jami's head was in my lap as he scrolled his social media.

A pang of sadness rippled through me as I thought of how perfect we were together and how we couldn't have anything outside of this week.

But at least I'd have the memories.

You're a dumbass my head grumbled. *Why settle for memories when you could have the real thing?*

I pushed away the thought. I'd make the best of an impossible situation and then deal with the fallout.

"Ohhhh." Jamison sat up. "A friend just posted that they spent yesterday in Brown County, Indiana.

There are lots of shops and restaurants and four wineries right in one little strip."

"That sounds promising. Brown County is south I'm pretty sure. If the drive isn't too bad, we could head that way for the day." I pulled up Brown County wineries and a quick check of the map showed we were about an hour away. "Up for a drive?"

Jami smiled and tackled me, his lips capturing mine in a way that always sent heat rushing through me. "I'm always up for anything with you," he whispered against my lips and rocked his hips against mine.

"You're insatiable," I teased.

"You love it," he quipped.

Yeah, I did. And I was going to miss it like crazy.

Spreading my legs, I let him settle his hips between mine as he took my face in his hands. "Tonight, as long as you're on board, I want to go further than what we've been doing."

I swallowed thickly. "Further, as in…"

"I want you in me if you're okay with it."

Nodding, I attempted to stop the rush of blood to my cock. "Definitely." I was totally okay with it. And if a tiny sliver of my head kept playing Jami's words about him fucking me on a loop? Well, I'd continue to ignore the curious desire that had me wishing I was the type of person who could just throw caution to the wind and let Jamison take over.

You know he'd never push you or hurt you.

I did know that. One-hundred percent. But sex with Jami had been amazing. I had a feeling that sex with him was going to get even better that night. No reason to let my issues with bottoming screw up a limited time deal. Plus, what if I did somehow let go enough to enjoy it? And then I'd be left knowing how great it was to bottom for a man I could easily fall in love with, but being helpless to do anything about it.

Don't be an idiot. You can do something about it. You can give up these ridiculous notions and excuses and...

I shut off the romantic, hopeful side of my brain. The last time I let myself believe I could have a loving relationship, I got crushed. Best to keep to the plan and do what it took to keep emotions out of it.

Yeah, right.

Once we started with the conference and got back to school, I'd slip easily back into principal mode and the whole colleagues only thing would be a lot easier.

Jamison gave me a smacking kiss and rolled from the bed. "It's not super hot today, but it looks like it could rain. You okay with a little water?"

I grimaced. "Can't say I love walking around in

the rain, but as long as it's not pouring or freezing cold, I can deal."

We dressed in casual shorts, t-shirts, and comfortable shoes and we each grabbed backpacks before we headed to the car.

Jamison tossed me the keys. "You get to drive this time." As he opened the passenger side door he paused. "Wait, did you bring your migraine medicine? Just in case?"

I smiled softly. "Yeah, I have it. Thanks for checking." My heart clenched at how sweet and thoughtful Jami was.

"So, I grabbed this audiobook from the library." Jamison waved his phone in the air. "I like audiobooks, but I can only really listen while I drive or if I'm taking care of the plants or going on a walk. I get distracted otherwise and miss the story." He bit his lip. "Anyway, it's a suspense, but it's also a romance. Like, a gay romance."

My eyes went wide. "I don't read much fiction— usually just books for school—but I like a good suspense. Pretty sure I've never read a romance, gay or straight."

"We don't have to listen to it. It could get awkward to listen to a sex scene while we're stuck in a car together." Jamison's pink cheeks were adorable.

"Turn it on. If it's not our thing, we listen to

something else." I started the car and backed out of the space. "Can you get the address put into my phone first? We can start the book once I'm out of this downtown area."

Jamison complied and after several stoplights and side streets, we ended up on I-465 which took us to US-31. Once we'd traveled south on 31 for a while, we were directed west until we reached SR-135, and then it was a straight shot to Nashville, Indiana.

With my phone on the stand so we could see the map, Jamison connected his phone to the speakers and started the audiobook.

An hour later, I knew that listening to gay romance audiobooks with Jamison was both good and bad. Good because we were really into the story and it passed the time. Bad because all I wanted to do was bend him over the backseat and fuck him crazy after listening to that deep, sexy voice read those sex scenes.

Jami paused the book and helped me find a five-dollar public parking spot.

When I turned off the engine, we both sat there in a bit of stunned silence.

"Okay, so that was…" Jamison trailed off.

"Kinda hot?"

He chuckled. "Definitely. But I love that it's a story. Like, it's not just sex—although, that was hot as hell. I was hooked on the story from the first word. Bodies buried in concrete? That's creepy and I definitely want to know more. We're not far enough into the book yet for me to have any real guesses as to who the suspect is, but I'm looking forward to listening to more." Jami turned a shy smile my way. "And I've got to say I'm already rooting for Drake and Liam to work out."

I frowned. "Drake made it clear that he's married to his job and not out at work. I don't think he'll ever come around to being what Liam wants or needs in a relationship." *Hmmm, a somewhat parallel storyline to your life, huh?*

"Nope, maybe I'm a hopeless romantic, but I'm going to keep hoping they work out. I mean, it's a romance, so I think it's like a rule that there has to be a happily ever after. Or at least a happy ending—a teacher was gushing about the romance books she reads and called it a happy for now." He shrugged. "That's what I'm hoping for."

"Romance doesn't always end in happily ever after," I groused. "Just look at our past relationships. Hell, look at our present relationship."

"It's fiction. Let go and enjoy the story." Jamison squeezed my leg.

"Yeah, well. Real-life definitely isn't fiction."

He leaned in and kissed my cheek. "I've heard tell

that sometimes real-life is even better than fiction."

"There you go living in your fantasy world." I harrumphed like an old codger and climbed out of the car. "But I'm into the story, so at least there's that."

He walked around to my side and stood close enough to whisper in my ear. "I'm into the story and very into creating some of our own sexy scenes like the ones in the book later tonight."

I shivered as his breath feathered over my skin. "Should we look into narrating the scene?" I teased.

Jami laughed. "Mmm, that voice. So sexy."

I kissed his cheek. "Okay, let's move that idea to the back burner unless we want to get arrested for public indecency."

"As if," Jami scoffed. "Paul Powers would never."

"Laugh all you want," I said. "But I know damn well that Jamison Powers would also never. Not these days. You love and respect your job too much to let that happen."

"True," Jami conceded as he rubbed his hands together. "Okay, where do we want to start?"

I grabbed one of the freebie maps from the man running the parking lot. "Looks like, from where we are, we can start with the Brown County Winery Tasting Room. It's just up here on the corner."

"Lead the way." Jamison smiled and we took off

walking.

Thirty or so minutes later, we'd spent a delightful time sipping several samples of wine and chatting with a charming older lady. I purchased a bottle of Vista Red while Jami declared I'd pry the Blackberry from his cold, dead hands.

Over the next two hours, Jamison and I laughed and chatted our way through Salt Creek Winery, Country Heritage Winery Tasting Room, and Cedar Creek Winery. We'd gathered bottles of wine such as Blue Velvet, Berry Tart, Plum, Red Raspberry, and Blackcurrant.

"So, it's easy to see that we both prefer sweet wines," I said as we hoofed our purchases back to the car.

"No other way to be." Jami stretched as we reached the car and he popped the trunk. "Now, I think we better get some food. Even though all we did was sample, we pretty much each just had two full glasses and I may be slightly buzzed."

"Food would be good." I pulled out the map. "We're close to HobNob Corner. Looks like good food."

Jamison studied the map over my shoulder. "Ohhh, can we do the OoeyGooey Cinnamon Rolls place before we leave? Take some back for a late-night snack?"

"Of course." I led the way to HobNob. My body thrummed at the thought of what other deliciousness our night together might bring.

"This is cozy," Jamison said as we were seated.

We laughed at the chicken salad option on the menu because, of course, it had celery. Jamison ended up getting the Rube Martin which was their form of a Rueben. I got the pot roast. Without even thinking—like an old married couple—we shared our meals so the other could try the food.

"Some of the best food I've ever had," I said as we finished. "I bet on a cold winter day the soup is to die for."

"We'll have to come back," Jamison said and then clamped his mouth shut. "But we'll be super busy. Wanna go check out the shops?"

I quickly took the distraction and grabbed the bill. It had been decided I'd pay for everything reimbursable so paperwork was easier in the end.

As we headed across the street, Jamison groaned. "Damn, I was hungry and definitely needed food. But the wine and food are now mixing together to do evil sleepy things to my head."

I laughed. "We'll walk it off. You like handmade soaps? Looks like a cool little shop there." I pointed to Bathology.

When we wandered into the store, Jami breathed

in deeply. "Oh my God, I've got to get soap here. It smells amazing."

Fifty-dollars and lots of sniffing later, Jamison proudly put his bag of handmade soaps into his backpack and we headed down the street. We ended up checking out a vintage bookstore, a sock store, several gift shops, and a couple garden places where Jamison's eyes lit up as he took it all in. He decided on buying a few plants, pots, and decorations.

As we passed a woodworking place, I had an idea. "We should get name plates for our offices."

"Perfect." Jamison smiled as we went to place our order.

"So, two plates, both with Mr. Powers?" the kid behind the counter asked after we described what we wanted.

"Yes, please." I glanced over my shoulder. "I'm going to run to the restroom real quick."

When I walked out of the public restroom, air drying my hands because of no paper towel, Jami met me with a smile. "They said we could come back in two hours and they'd have the signs ready."

"Excellent. We just pay then?"

"I went ahead and paid since it's not reimbursable. You can get me back later when you buy me a cinnamon roll." He bumped my hip.

We wandered along, checking out another book

store and several shops full of various items from pottery to crystals to paints to toys to beef jerky to coffee to candles and everything in-between. The town definitely had a little something for everyone.

"I think I'll get these two candles," Jamison mused as he sniffed a large jar candle.

"Sounds good. I'm going to move to the next stop, the scents are getting to me a bit in here." I stopped myself from brushing a kiss against his lips. That was something a couple would do. Jamison and I—no matter how easy things were between us—were not a couple and couldn't be.

A short time later, Jamison found me sitting on a bench outside a little shop that declared Lady Gray would read your palm for only five dollars.

"Oh, fun. Let's do that." Jamison pointed at the decorative sign boasting stars and moons and crystal balls.

"That stuff isn't real," I scoffed.

"But it's fun. Come on." Jamison pulled me into the store.

"Welcome to Lady Gray's. Would you like your palm read? Only five dollars," a tiny, pixie-ish lady with cute dark hair and huge brown eyes smiled at us from a table where she sat with tarot cards.

"Yes, please. He's first and he's paying." Jamison shoved me forward.

"Oh, am I?" I muttered.

"Palm reading and cinnamon rolls should cover the sign." He winked at me.

Lady Gray took the ten dollars and invited me to sit down. "Best if you don't hover," she said to Jamison. "You can sit on the bench."

Jamison blushed and took a seat. "Sorry."

Lady Gray examined both of my hands and I quickly felt at-ease even though I didn't believe in any of this mumbo-jumbo. As she ran her thumbs and fingers over my palm, I couldn't help but relax into the touch.

"You've found happiness," Lady Gray said softly. "Why do you push it away? The power you struggle to hold onto is not what you need. Only when you open up to happiness will you find the true power you so desperately seek."

A shiver traveled down my spine and I mumbled something along the lines of thank you as I stood from the table. Her words made no sense, yet they'd struck something in me. Something I wasn't interested in trying to sort out. A cheap, worthless palm reading wasn't something to base my future on or concern myself with.

"My turn," Jami crowed as he took his spot at the table.

I sat down and worked to ease the scowl that had

taken residence on my forehead. The woman was clearly a quack. Probably had a generic list of words and phrases she put together for each unsuspecting chump who handed over a fiver.

I watched as Lady Gray took Jamison's hands and studied them the way she had mine.

"You have plans. Plans that seem to be at odds with each other, but you trust that the two shall merge into beauty. You should follow your heart." Lady Gray looked up into Jamison's eyes and cocked her head. "You have found the beauty, but the journey to make it your own will be long."

Jamison smiled broadly. "You're amazing. Thank you." He tossed a ten-dollar bill on her table before turning to me. "You ready?"

I frowned as I gave Lady Gray a small wave and followed Jami out the door. "You tipped her? Why?"

"Because she's great."

"You believe all of that? She just makes stuff up. People hear what they want in the words she tells them."

"Nah, I think she was spot on." Jamison shrugged and shifted the bag in his hand. "Want to hit that coffee shop on the corner? I could use a caffeine jolt. We've got a few more shops to check out and then we can pick up our order and head back to the hotel."

I tried to push away the unsettled feeling Lady Gray's words had given me. "Yeah, sounds good."

When we walked into the coffee shop, Jamison breathed deeply. "Ahhh, my nose is in heaven today with all of the smells."

I chuckled. "And mine is nervously pleading for the soaps and candles to not trigger a migraine."

We took our place in line and studied the menu.

"Shit, will the soaps being in the room or even in the trunk cause you a problem? The candles should be okay as long as I don't open them." He twisted his lips. "If you're ever at my house, I'll try to remember not to burn candles."

"You're fine. The soaps staying in the trunk are probably fine. I don't think you got anything super flowery or heavy; those are the scents that usually do me in." I ignored the comment about me being at Jamison's house. We'd see each other daily and definitely have to work together, but it would likely be best if we weren't making house visits a normal part of our routine. Professional and on-site interactions were one thing. Being alone with Jami at his house? That would probably be a very bad idea. Best to avoid the temptation.

Jamison gestured toward the board. "What are you getting?"

"Just the Americano with cream and sugar. You?"

"Same. Do you want to split a piece of pie?"

"I thought you were full," I teased.

Jami smiled. "I was. And now I want pie. Any kind you won't eat?"

"I don't love fruit pies, but I can eat whatever."

Jamison ordered his coffee and a piece of sugar cream pie—the pie of Indiana—and I ordered my drink. After paying, we found a corner table to wait for our coffee and pie.

"So, we can look at the schedule again tonight. I know I want to hit at least one of the MTSS workshops and the one on effective PLCs." Jamison pulled his phone out and scrolled as he spoke. "I think there are some that we can divide and conquer, but a few are ones that we should probably attend together."

"Agreed. I think the first one is Discovering Your Leadership Strengths and Challenges. The brochure made it sound like that's part of the opening speech. I want to do the Developing the Collective Genius of Your High Performing Team along with Making Difficult People Easy." I said thank you to the waitperson who dropped off our drinks and dessert. "Our test scores—throughout the district as a whole—have always been pretty good, but there's always room for growth. So, we should hit at least a few presentations and workshops with a focus on tests."

"Yeah, but I don't want to spend too much time on testing. Gather a couple really strong ideas to share and implement in that area, but I think we'll be better off giving a lot of our focus to meshing the buildings together. Bringing three student populations and three staffs together isn't going to be without its challenges." Jamison sipped his coffee and gave a little sigh that I felt all the way to my core. Over a sigh? Damn, I was a mess.

"I agree with that. The older kids won't likely notice much disruption since they're in the separate wing. But the two groups of elementary students are going to need time to adjust. The only good thing is that both of our buildings are coming together in a new location; kinda gives everyone equal footing." I took a bite of the pie. "God, that's good. I haven't had sugar cream pie in forever."

Jami took a bite and moaned. "I should definitely make this sometime. I think it's fairly easy, I need to find the perfect recipe. This would be great to bring to staff meetings."

I chuckled. "You'd need to make a lot more than one pie for staff meetings."

He snorted. "True. I like to bake, but maybe I'll keep the pie making for just us and the office staff."

"But I do like the idea of treats at the staff meetings. I usually do donuts from Sweet Hole there in town; the owner gives a good discount since it's for the school. And I can usually get coffee donated." I savored another bite. "I won't turn down sugar cream pie in the office."

"The Sandwich Spot gives a discount, too. Good for staff lunches on professional development days." Jamison frowned. "I guess we probably need to see what kind of budget cuts we're facing before we start planning lots of lunches and treats." He raised a brow. "But I'm not against spending a bit of my own money to keep the staff motivated and happy."

"Same. A happy and enthusiastic staff is one of the best things in the world. I really think you'll be impressed with the group that's coming from West."

Jamison took a drink of his coffee. "The group from East is great, too. I really don't think we'll have issues with the staff coming together. Just the usual bumps over moving rooms and giving them time to set up. East and West both have great teachers and we have to remember that this issue isn't about our schools and students and teachers not being great. It's all about money—or the lack of money. We've been consolidated only because of low enrollment and not enough money to keep three buildings fully functional." He pushed the last bite of pie my way. "Sometimes I get down on myself thinking we're being punished, but that's not the way it is. If we can keep the test scores and performance at a level that continues to show growth, get the referendum passed, and get a mayor and city council who will work with the district to entice more families to choose Valley Hill as their home, we should be able to—hell, we'll have to—move back to separate buildings within a couple years if not sooner."

"Oh Lord, don't get me wrong, I definitely want to see that happen, but let's not indicate to the teachers that this move may be for just one year. We may get some who faint and some who mutiny over the thought of having to move again in such a short time." I stood, put my backpack over my shoulder, and gathered our dirty dishes to put in the tub on the trashcan.

"Good point." Jamison followed me out the door into the damp, gray day. "We can keep that part to ourselves here in the beginning."

The rain that had held off for most of the day began to sprinkle lightly as we made our way to a few more stores we hadn't seen yet. We both bought some magnets for our offices in a fun novelty store before making our way to a little pottery shop.

"Ohhh, I don't know what this is, but I like it," Jami exclaimed as he admired a piece of pottery.

"That's a vase," the shop person said. "It's

handmade. The three different heights allow for a tiering effect when you put the flowers in it."

"We should each get one. And one for both the front desk and the secretary. I'll make sure we keep them stocked with flowers." Jamison was already perusing the different choices of color and size.

"That's a good idea. Flowers always make for happy people." I picked a black and gray one for my office. "Since you know the secretary better than I do, you pick that one." My secretary from West had decided to retire a year early rather than move to the middle school with me. I'd miss her, but it made for one less awkward decision for staffing.

"Leo is a good kid. Young, but smart and efficient." Jamison picked up a teal vase. "I know he doesn't plan on being a school secretary forever, but I'm glad to have him working with us for now. He'll like this one."

"What about one for you and one for the front desk?" I showed him a yellow and black design.

"That one for sure for the front desk. Perfect yellow jacket colors." Jamison continued to scan over the choices. "I love the purple, but I think I'm going to go with the blue. I love the way the colors go from bright to faded."

We spent some time chatting with the employee who carefully wrapped up our vases and rang up our purchases. We split the cost and agreed to take turns providing the flowers when Jamison's garden wasn't blooming.

"I think it's probably time to pick up the signs," I said with a glance at my watch.

"How about you take all of this to the car and then swing around to the woodshop and pick me up?" Jamison suggested. "I'll have to show ID to pick them up since I paid."

I shrugged. "Sounds good." I took the bags from Jamison and headed toward the parking lot. "I'll be there in a few."

As I turned to go the opposite direction of the woodshop, I noticed a lot of people milling about outside—Jamison would maybe have to wait a bit to pick up our order. On impulse—which was something that I seemed to only do when Jami was involved—I detoured into the sock shop.

We'd visited the store before, but I wanted to get a gift for Jamison. After a quick browse of the store, I plunked six pairs of socks on the counter—buy five get one free worked out perfectly. Two pairs that said principal, two with jack-o-lanterns, and two with snowmen. I envisioned Jamison and I presenting a solidly united front as the admin team at the school. What better way to look like a team than matching festive socks?

"Will this be all for you?" the young kid behind the counter asked.

"Yes, thanks. Do you have a website for ordering as well?" I could always order us more socks for other holidays and such.

"Yeah, it's on the receipt." The kid was efficient and polite, even if he seemed bored with his job.

"This your summer job?" I asked as he bagged up the socks.

"Yeah, the hours let me get in morning and evening football practice. It's not glamorous, but it gives me money for a car payment and insurance." He shrugged and swiped my card.

"Summer a busy time down here?" I asked as I put my card back in my wallet.

"Seems like it's always busy down here, but yeah, summer gets pretty full. Fall is the crazy time though. People come for the leaves and crafts and all things pumpkin spice." He scoffed and rolled his eyes.

I smiled. "A tourist town for sure."

"Oh yeah," he agreed as he handed me my bag. "Have a good day."

"Thanks, you too." I rolled up the bag and shoved it in my backpack before rushing out of the shop and to the parking lot.

I moved Jamison's candles to the back of the

trunk and nestled his soaps right next to them. Then I put the bag of socks and our other sacks in a corner so they'd be out of the way of our luggage when it was time to head home.

Waving to the friendly attendant as I left the lot, I maneuvered streets of busy shoppers until I reached the woodshop.

Jamison stood with a large brown paper bag with handles. "'Bout time," he teased as I pulled up to the curb. "This bag is heavy."

"I left room for it in the trunk. Just put it toward the back or the side so there's still room when we have to get the luggage in there." I popped the trunk.

Jami climbed into the car a few moments later. "Did you want me to drive?"

"Nah, I'm good." I eased the car away from the curb and checked a street sign. "I think I can get us back to Indy, but we may need directions for getting through downtown."

"Oh! The cinnamon rolls." Jamison pointed toward a little shop. "We almost forgot!"

I found a spot to park and gave him a twenty-dollar bill. "I don't like nuts."

Jamison snorted. "The results are in and that is a lie." He leaned over the console and whispered in my ear. "You seem to love my nuts."

His words zinged right to my cock and I cleared

my throat while shifting in my seat. "You know what I mean, no nuts on the cinnamon rolls."

He chuckled and exited the car.

A few moments later, he returned with a much larger bag than I was expecting.

"Damn, how many did you buy?" I asked as I drove off.

"That place was sensation overload. Comfy cozy, scents galore, and soft music playing. I think the smell of cinnamon and icing put me in a trance. There were so many types to decide on. They were doing buy one get one free."

"Good deal." I eyed the bag with a smirk. "How many did you buy?"

Jami bit his lip sheepishly. "Three?"

I laughed. "So, we have six cinnamon rolls?"

He nodded. "Figured they could be dessert tonight and maybe breakfast the next couple days?"

"If we're spending all day in conferences, we should probably get healthier food in the morning—protein and fiber—but I can't see why the rolls can't be our late-night snack for a few nights."

Jamison smiled. "I know what else I'd like for my late-night snack." He waggled his brows.

I laughed and shook my head, determined not to drive the whole way with my cock fighting against my zipper.

An hour later, after pleasant chit-chat and only one wrong turn as Jamison navigated us toward the hotel, we climbed out of the car and stretched.

"I need a shower." Jami moaned as his shirt rode up to show an enticing stretch of skin. "I wonder if the sauna gets used a lot. We could sit in there to relax, shower, order some food, and spend the rest of the evening…"

I cocked my brow.

"Doing whatever feels right," he said with a wink and a shrug.

As we walked toward the elevator, I remembered the audiobook. "Dang, we should have listened to that book."

"Shoot. Oh well, we can listen on the way back home. And if we don't finish, you can always borrow it."

We took a short detour to see if the sauna area was crowded and lucked out to find it wasn't. After a quick stop in the room, we made our way back to the sauna. Most hotels had the sauna in the same area as the pool and hot tub—which always meant kids in and out or at least lots of people. This one was in the gym area which did have a few people on the machines, but was basically empty.

"A lot of people probably getting here tonight for the conference. Probably don't want to make a long drive and then come work out." Jamison opened the door to the sauna and I followed him in.

"Lucky us," I said and spread a towel on the wooden bench.

Jamison fiddled with the hot rocks and water before setting the timer. "Twenty minutes?"

"Yeah, I'll be too hot if we stay longer." I stripped my shirt and tossed it on one of the racks before sitting down on the towel and leaning back, my arms spread on the back of the bench.

I closed my eyes to enjoy the relaxing heat, but felt Jami staring at me. Cracking an eye, I looked at him. "What?"

He chuckled before pulling his shirt over his head and tossing it on the side. "Nothing. Just thinking about how different this little scene could be if we weren't on a work trip in a fancy hotel surrounded by lots of people."

I snorted and closed my eyes again. "This isn't a porno, Mr. Powers."

"Oh, but what a porno it could be," he drawled. "At least we have a private room."

I spent the rest of the time we sat in the sauna willing my dick to behave at least until we got back to the room. I was really going to have to get a grip on the way I reacted to Jamison once we were back at school.

TEN

JAMISON

"How about you shower, I'll order the food, and then I can jump into the shower," I suggested as we entered the hotel room after the sauna. I knew what I wanted to happen later that night and I needed a little bit of time to myself to prep.

"Sounds good. You doing room service or delivery?" Paul asked as he took off his glasses and cleaned them on his shirt.

"Delivery? If you're willing to go down and get it if I'm still in the shower."

"Yep. Where were you thinking? Something light? I don't think I can do greasy burgers or anything right now." He stripped his shirt over his head and I nearly tackled him to the bed—forget the shower and food.

"You know what I could really go for?"

Paul cocked a brow and waited.

"Some of that famous Powers chicken salad." I grinned. "Seriously, best stuff I've ever had. I never even thought of making it for myself and skipping the celery and nuts."

Paul laughed. "I'll bring some for lunch one day."

"You bring the famous chicken salad and I'll bring my famous sugar cream pie. We'll have the perfect lunch." I scrolled through my phone for food ideas.

"Famous sugar cream pie? How can it be famous when you've never made it?" Paul teased.

"Because I'm good at everything I put my mind to," I quipped.

Paul rolled his eyes. "Don't I know it." He headed toward the bathroom. "Holler at me when you've made a decision and I'll tell you what I want."

"Oh, I've made a decision," I called out as he closed the bathroom door. "I want you buried in my ass. Does that work with what you want?" I smirked at the moment of silence.

Paul poked his head out of the bathroom. "I was talking about food, you perv."

"My bad." I winked and blew him a kiss.

When the shower turned on, I flopped down on the bed with a long sigh. I was so majorly fucked. Paul and I had fallen into the easiest relationship I'd ever had. Maybe because there were no expectations beyond this week. Maybe because we were basically friends with benefits—colleagues with benefits?—and we weren't trying to impress like in the beginning of a real romantic relationship.

But that was the kicker. With the exception of knowing this magical week was going to end, everything about Paul and me together was real. We got along, we had a lot in common, we were just different enough to keep it interesting. The sexual chemistry was through the roof. We respected each other and seemed to enjoy spending time together.

If the end wasn't looming, I could easily see this relationship being a permanent, long-term thing.

And I had a feeling Paul could too, but he was too damn stubborn and tight-fisted to admit it and see where things could go.

Maybe Lady Gray was a quack, but I was clinging to the words she said to Paul. "You've found happiness. Why do you push it away? The power you struggle to hold onto is not what you need. Only when you open up to happiness will you find the true power you so desperately seek."

Would he ever give in to the happiness we'd found? Was I dumb to think that what we had was enough to build a future around?

I took a deep breath and remembered that I wasn't giving up on this thing between Paul and me just because our week together would eventually end. I had a plan. Lady Gray's words echoed in my ears. "You have plans. Plans that seem to be at odds with each other, but you trust that the two shall merge into beauty. You should follow your heart. You have found the beauty, but the journey to make it your own will be long."

Yep, I had a plan and I wasn't going to throw it away, no matter how much my heart might get stomped between Sunday and our happily ever after. I'm good at everything I put my mind to. And that was a truth Paul needed to be ready for.

I decided on sub sandwiches from a locally owned shop nearby and asked Paul what he wanted on his before placing the order.

An hour later, both of us relaxed from the sauna and showers, and our bellies full from some of the best sandwiches I'd ever had, Paul rummaged around and pulled out the chocolate butterflies.

"Want to split one? I don't want a whole one, but just need something sweet." He held up the package.

I nodded and held out my hand. "I'll give you something sweet," I teased.

Paul gave me the butterfly and rolled his eyes.

I put it between my teeth with a goofy smile. "Come get it," I mumbled around the chocolate.

A flash of desire mixed with humor crossed

Paul's face as he dropped the package he'd been holding and crawled across the bed to meet me. "You're trouble," he whispered gruffly as he leaned in to take the chocolate between his lips. He bit off his half of the butterfly and began to chew slowly, his eyes never leaving mine.

I let the chocolate melt slowly on my tongue before chewing and swallowing. "Come here," I said and wrapped my hand around Paul's neck and pulled him close. "I've wanted to kiss you all damn day." If I was distracted and horny after one day of not being able to kiss him, what was I going to be like when I didn't even have our nights to look forward to? I pushed the thought away and savored the warm softness of Paul's lips against mine.

"All damn day, huh?" Paul whispered against my mouth. "Here I am, what are you going to do about it?"

I reached up to gently removed Paul's glasses. "We're going to kiss for a while, suck each other for a bit, and then you're going to sit in that chair while I ride you. When you're about to come, you're going to finish with me bent over that desk, then drop to your knees and suck me off." I batted my lashes. "If that works for you."

Paul groaned and devoured my mouth. The sweet softness of moments before caught fire and turned to a fiery heat which quickly consumed us. Kissing quickly turned into stroking, sucking, and tonguing. And then I was rummaging in my bag for a condom and lube. As much as I wanted to take him bare—and I trusted both of us to be honest about our status—condomless sex with a man who swore this couldn't last more than a week seemed like a poor choice on several different levels.

"Sit in that chair," I demanded.

"Bossy." But he rolled from the bed, stroking his hard cock, and sat in the straight-back chair.

I tossed him the condom and licked my lips as he rolled it down his length.

Straddling Paul's lap, I reached between us to slick his cock and behind to spread lube into my ass. As I shifted and took his cock in my fist, pressing his plump head against my tight hole, a momentary pang of sadness traveled through me.

All things sexual with Paul had been amazing so far and I knew riding his dick and getting fucked over the desk would be as well.

But there was a wall between us.

For as open and easy as our relationship was in all other aspects, we both seemed to have walled off the part of our hearts that would allow for sex to be loving, intimate, more.

This was fucking. Period.

And I wouldn't expect a week-long fling to be more than that.

But I still longed for that intimate connection with Paul where we melded together both physically and emotionally.

As his cock breached my ass, I hissed at the brief sting of invasion.

"You okay?" Paul froze, a look of genuine concern on his face.

"Yeah, I'm good." I leaned in and kissed him, deep and dirty, as my body opened and took him in completely. I began to rock my hips, using my legs as leverage to slide myself up and down Paul's shaft. My cock bobbed between us, the friction from our bodies lighting me up. "Tell me when you're close," I demanded.

Paul thrust up over and over, his slick cock stretching me and brushing at the bundle of nerves deep inside me. "Oh fuck, close."

"Desk." I stood up slowly, wincing when Paul's cock slipped from my body.

Paul spun me around and kissed me, our hard cocks rubbing together, before he nudged me toward the desk and bent me over. "Spread your legs."

The cold wood and sharp edge of the desk bit into my skin as I bent at the waist, my chest flat against the desktop and my legs spread wide. I gasped as Paul spread my ass and slid back into me. He gripped my hips and began to thrust hard. Grasping at the sides of the desk, I held on tight as each hard, fast thrust of his hips brought me closer and closer.

"Fuck, I'm close," Paul grunted.

"Do it, come in me."

"Are you close?"

"Yeah, but don't wait for me," I said.

With a few more pumps of his hips, Paul tensed and his cock throbbed in my ass. After a few moments, he pulled me up so my back met his chest and he kissed my neck. "Turn around," he commanded.

I sighed as he pulled from my body, but I turned around and smiled softly into the warm, deep kiss he gave me. Groaning as Paul dropped to his knees in front of me, I took my thick cock in hand and smeared my pre-cum against his lips. "You going to finish me off?"

Paul nodded and took my length deep to the back of his throat. As he sucked me, he teased my balls and taint, letting his finger stray to my well-used ass. When he slid two fingers into me, I began to piston my hips. Watching my cock between his lips, feeling the stretch of his fingers in my ass, I tensed and shot my release deep in the back of Paul's throat, moaning as he swallowed everything I gave him.

He nuzzled his nose against my lower abdomen before standing to kiss me. My flavor on his lips zinged through me even though there was no way either of us was getting it up again anytime soon. "Let me get a washcloth," he murmured against my lips.

We took a moment to clean up and then fell into bed. Cuddled together, warm and sated, my heart hurt at what Paul was willing to throw away. Did I really mean so little to him? But then I stopped. I too was allowing myself to pretend that this didn't mean as much as it actually meant.

The sex with Paul was the best of my life, but it didn't match the connection I felt to him when we were just hanging out. The sex felt like a fling. No real connection, no intimacy, very impersonal as if two strangers were fucking in a bathroom stall. Not that it wasn't full of promise and potential—and it truly was physically amazing—but neither of us seemed able or willing to reach out and touch that intimate part of sex together. And who could blame us? It was already going to hurt to lose what we'd allowed ourselves to have. Why make it worse by adding in that extra layer of intimacy?

The friendship? Hell, even the working

relationship. Those two things felt connected, strong, and built on a solid foundation. I guess our history together allowed for that part to be easy.

So, I pressed a kiss against Paul's chest and cuddled close. There was no fixing the situation at that exact moment. Nothing I could say or do was going to change our current circumstances. We'd enjoy our week and return to Valley Hill. We'd get settled into a routine at school and I'd slowly wear Paul down while we continued to build our friendship and work relationship. I had no doubt that Paul and I would be successful in the school setting. I wasn't worried at all about our colleague or friendship status.

And I could only hope that our relationship outside of school and friendship would blossom— whether Paul wanted it to or not—and we'd eventually...no, Paul would eventually...figure out that we could have it all. We could be more and still have the rest.

I fell asleep clinging to the hope that my plans and wishes would be enough.

THE WEEK of the conference went very well. Paul and I attended some amazing presentations and

workshops—and even had time to gather freebies
and samples from the convention sales floor. We
agreed that we felt very prepared to pass the learning
on to our staff and take on the challenge of the new
school year.

We spent every morning of our week together
chatting easily over breakfast. Our days were packed
full of learning. We explored Indianapolis and
discovered several great restaurants. And our nights
were spent fucking each other's brains out.

Truly, the sex never got boring. It was fantastic. I
never pushed the subject of Paul bottoming for me
because the week-long fling wasn't the right time for
that. But we found ourselves extremely compatible
in bed and that lent itself to a lot of wild nights. By
the time the week came to an end, muscles I didn't
even know existed were sore and my knees were
nearly rubbed raw. I'd been grateful for the large
supply of condoms I'd brought for the trip because
we ended up with only two left after our week
together.

And then it was Sunday.

By some unspoken agreement, we got up early
and avoided any kind of physical contact. After
showers and packing, we loaded the car and headed
to Valley Hill.

With the awkward silence between us, I cuddled

into my heavy heart and fell asleep until Paul nudged me awake. "Hey, we're about halfway there. Want to get lunch and then switch?"

I yawned and stretched. "Yeah, sounds good."

We ended up at Applebee's where our comfortable chatter made a comeback. By the end of lunch, I felt fueled and ready to tackle the drive. Paul looked knackered, so I turned on the radio and kept it low. "Recline your seat and rest. I'll wake you if needed."

Paul fell asleep almost immediately and I let my mind zone out while I drove. A couple hours later, Paul stirred and sat his seat up. "We should listen to the book," he suggested.

I twisted my lips. "We won't be able to finish it, but you could borrow it from me later."

"Normally, I'd say it wasn't a big deal, but I have a feeling I'll need to know how this story plays out." Paul reached for my phone. "Want me to get it started?"

I nodded and soon the narrator's deep voice filled the car.

Over the next couple hours, Paul and I were treated to a building mystery of dead bodies showing up in concrete and two men falling head-over-heels for each other. Okay, that wasn't exactly accurate.

Liam had already fallen for Drake. Drake was the stubborn one who fought what he and Liam had going until he just couldn't fight it any longer—I liked to think my own story would play out similarly. Their time at the lake house was the perfect mixture of sweet and sexy; I almost worried my speakers would melt from the hot, deep voice reading the sex scenes.

We reached Valley Hill with about an hour of the story left and Paul groaned as I pulled into his driveway. "Damn, let me know when you finish—and no spoilers!—so I can borrow it."

As we climbed from the car, I glanced at him as we arrived at the trunk. "You could come over tonight or one night this week? We could finish it together?"

Paul frowned. "We both know that's not a good idea."

I pursed my lips and nodded. "Right." I gestured toward his door. "Can I at least pretend to help you carry stuff in so we can say goodbye properly without a neighborhood audience?"

Paul swallowed hard and, for one brief moment, I worried he was going to say no. But he gave a quick nod and hauled his bag from the car. "Grab that brown bag. The rest of our stuff we can split up at school tomorrow."

I followed him into his house. "So, you're going into the building tomorrow?"

"Yeah, you?"

"Yeah, I want to get in there and set up my office. There are going to be lots of teachers wanting to get in, so we need to meet with the custodial staff to see what their cleaning schedule looks like. May have to work around the fresh wax depending on which halls they've already done and need to do." I placed the brown bag on Paul's kitchen counter and turned to face him.

He'd dropped his bag in the hallway and stood leaning against the kitchen sink.

"Thanks for a great week." I ran a hand through my hair and gripped the back of my neck. "And I mean that. The whole week. Not just the sex."

Paul adjusted his glasses and smiled softly. "I know what you mean. I really enjoyed the whole trip; I guess I hadn't realized how badly I needed to get away." He took a step toward me. "I think we make a really great team and I'm looking forward to the rest of this summer and the school year." He chuckled. "I didn't think I'd ever say this, but I'm glad to be working with you. You're amazing at what you do and our school is lucky to have you."

I smiled. "Thanks. I feel the same about you." I moved close enough that I could feel the soft warmth of Paul's body. "I need you to know that what we have together means more to me than I ever thought it could. I know your position on us and I respect it—even if I don't agree with it. But," I reached up to cup Paul's cheek, "maybe I'm a romantic sap or just as stubborn as you, but I'm not giving up on us. I have every hope that we'll fall into an easy routine at school, proving that we are a great team, and you'll slowly realize that what we have together is too good to throw it away."

Paul started to protest, but I silenced him with my thumb against his lips.

"I know you don't want to throw us away. I know you think you're doing what's best for our careers." I stepped even closer, our chests flush together, our heartbeats melding together. "But I think Team Powers can have it all. The friendship, the work relationship, and more. I want more with you. I could so very easily fall in love with you," my voice broke on those words, "and it scares me to death, but I don't want to lose that chance." I leaned in and pressed my forehead against Paul's. "I'm not giving up on us. I'm not letting this be the end. I want you in my life whichever way I can get you, but I'm a selfish bitch and I want more than just friendship and work. I want every part of you; I want to give you every part of me." I nuzzled my nose against his.

"I'm sure this is pissing you off or scaring you or whatever—and I'm sorry if it seems like I'm going back on our agreement—but I have to be honest with you. I need you to know all of this so that, if some night you're thinking about me and wishing things could be different, you'll know they can be. I don't want you thinking that I'm on board with letting this thing between us die." I closed my eyes and brushed my lips across his.

For one moment, I thought Paul was going to remain solidly distant, but a short grunt slipped from his lips and he wrapped me in his arms, kissing me back slow and deep.

When we finally broke apart, Paul frowned. "I could easily fall in love with you, too, Jamison." He ran a thumb over my lips. "But we've discussed this. There's too much working against us for it to ever work out."

I shook my head. "No. You discussed it, I listened but never agreed. Your excuses regarding us are flimsy. Your fear of being demoted is unfounded. I think your only real fear—if you'd just be honest with yourself—is that you'll end up in a loving relationship and have it ripped away." I kissed him. "Well, hopefully this week proved it to you, but I'm not Douglas. Can either of us promise forever? No. But is what we've so easily built with each other worth the effort—even if there's no guarantee? I say yes. And I'll be patient while you decide if what we have is worth the effort, guaranteed forever or not."

Paul squeezed his eyes shut. "I don't know that I could ever live through that kind of betrayal and heartache again."

I tipped his chin. "Even if you and I don't have forever, do you really think I could hurt you the way he did?"

He gritted his teeth, jaw bulging, but shook his head. "No."

"So, why let Douglas and a potential ending keep you away from what could possibly be a lifetime of happiness?" I held him close, my forehead pressed against his temple. "We don't know what the future holds. For us, the school, our jobs, anything. But I do know I'd rather face the unknown with you than without." I kissed him. "I'm here. I'm not going anywhere. I'm looking forward to working with you. And I will not back down on us."

Paul shook his head. "You're so young. You shouldn't be waiting around for a messed up old guy to make a decision. Find someone who can give you what you want."

I smiled softly. "I did. Actually, I found him almost two decades ago. He's taught me so much over the years and I'm grateful to call him a friend and a colleague. This guy has gotten even better with age and he's exactly what I want and need." I brushed a kiss along Paul's jawline. "I just have to be patient while he comes to his senses and realizes he can let loose. I'll be there when he does."

Paul closed his eyes and sighed. "Impossible situations seem to be all I'm good at."

"Not true. And when you finally loosen your grip and let yourself see the very possible situation right in front of you, I'll be waiting." I turned to go and he followed. When I reached the front door, I turned back to Paul. "I do need you to know—no matter how much we both may want it, crave it—when you contact me to tell me you want me back in your bed, I need it to be because you've made up your mind. I won't be your booty call. We can't be no-strings."

Paul took a deep breath and drew me into a tight hug. "Your strings are so tightly wound around my heart, sometimes I wonder how it keeps beating. Definitely not no-strings."

With a quick kiss and tears stinging my eyes, I walked out of Paul's house. I made it to my bedroom before flopping down and giving in to the waterworks.

ELEVEN

PAUL

"I LOVE THEM," Jamison declared with a laugh as he pulled the three pairs of socks from the gift bag I'd handed him.

It was Friday after a long week of work and we'd met in my office for a working lunch.

"We can coordinate our sock schedule and wear them on the same day." I smiled before taking a bite of chicken salad sandwich.

"You got the same ones? That's perfect." Jamison took a bite of his sandwich and groaned—he still swore my chicken salad was the best ever—before reaching for a wrapped gift and handing it to me. "I got something for you, too. Well, it's pretty much for both of us."

I quirked a brow and tore open the paper. "Oh wow, this is perfect." The large wooden sign said

Team Powers with an expertly carved yellow jacket decorating the bottom right corner.

"Figured we both have our Mr. Powers signs for our offices, but the big sign can go on that little wall between us." Jamison smiled and gestured toward the door.

"Excellent. I think there's even a hook already out there." I stood and walked out of the office. Jamison and I each had our own office, with a connecting door in between, and there was thin wall between our main doors where the Team Powers sign would fit perfectly.

I hung the sign and stood back to look at it.

"That looks great!" Leo, our administrative assistant, said brightly as he came around the corner. "Let me get a picture so we can put it on the staff picture board."

I'd done a good job of keeping distance between Jamison and me throughout the week since we returned to Valley Hill—and it was killing me—but there was no way to get out of a picture with my colleague without looking weird.

Jamison grinned and took his place beside me.

"Squish together just a bit so I can get the whole sign," Leo instructed.

Feeling the heat of Jamison's body so close to mine did wicked things to my head. I had to stop thinking about him and get my head completely focused on school only.

"Those are great. I'll print them." Leo turned to go back to his desk.

"Oh, wait. Can you print the ones we got from the zoo?" Jamison pulled his phone out.

"Sure, just send the ones you want printed. I'll get them ready and start working on the board. Some of the old pics can stay, but I want updated ones, too, so these will be great." Leo returned to his tiny office across from ours.

"Dessert?" Jamison asked as we walked back into my office. "I brought sugar cream pie."

"Really?"

"If you were bringing your famous chicken salad, I couldn't be shown up. I had to bring my famous sugar cream pie." Jamison winked as he pulled out a covered pie pan.

"Famous, huh?" I teased.

"It's pretty good even if I do have to say so myself." He uncovered the pan and sliced two thin pieces of pie. "But, it's very rich so we'll start small."

I took the last bite of my chicken salad and tossed my plate in the trashcan before forking a small bite of pie. Popping the bite into my mouth, I groaned as the sweet, savory flavor melted on my tongue.

"Damn, I swear that's even better than the one we had at that restaurant."

"Mmhm," Jamison agreed. "I told you, famous."

I laughed. "I shouldn't have doubted your greatness."

We spent the rest of our Friday checking in with teachers who were in the building, updating class lists and schedules, and debriefing with Danika about the required state testing, district testing, and building testing.

"So much testing," Jamison muttered as we cleaned up the conference room table where we'd been meeting.

"Tell me about it," Danika agreed and headed out with a wave.

"I kinda have a love hate relationship with testing," I said. "On one hand, I hate how much time it takes away from instruction. I hate that so many kids are ranked and judged based on a single score rather than their whole person. I hate that some kids are bound to be poor test takers and then they're stuck with that score. I despise how test scores are one of the biggest ways we evaluate teachers." I took off my glasses and rubbed my eyes. "I do appreciate that we've moved to more of a growth model in testing. And the results can be very useful in addressing where a student struggles. Plus, test scores are one of the things we're lucky to do well in this district. If we had low test scores along with the money problems, we'd likely already be shut down completely." I winced and massaged my temples.

"Headache?" Jamison asked with evident concern. "Migraine?"

"No, just a tension headache."

Jamison stared at me for a moment and I could almost hear him offering to rub my neck and shoulders, but he swallowed and gave a nod. "Better take something for it before it gets worse."

He was right. And he responded exactly the way we had to respond to each other from now on.

So, why did it feel like I'd been punched in the gut? Why did I want him to offer to come over that evening and help me get rid of my headache?

"What are you up to tonight?" Jamison asked as if he hadn't just sent me into a damn tailspin of want and confusion.

"Huh?" I put my glasses back on and squinted at him. "Oh, not much. Maybe read a few chapters in some school books. Order in and watch a movie before crashing." As much as I didn't want to hear about Jamison's plans, I asked because it was the polite thing to do. "You?"

He shrugged. "Pretty much the same as you. Throw in wine and a swim, too." He smiled.

God, how badly I wanted to suggest we pop open a bottle of wine, enjoy a late-night swim—together—and cuddle on his bed to watch a movie before things moved into hot and heavy territory.

I gritted my teeth and forced a smile. "Sounds like we've both got a perfect night planned."

Jamison cocked his head and frowned at me. "I think we both know there's a much more perfect night option out there. You ready to make it happen?"

I coughed and glanced toward the door. "You know we can't."

"Won't." Jamison moved closer and poked his finger against my chest. "You won't. There's a big difference. Have a great night. See you Monday."

WHEN SCHOOL STARTED, I knew without a doubt that Jamison, Danika, and I—along with our entire staff—had gone above and beyond in preparing for the new year. The year started without a hitch and seemed to be running as smoothly as could be expected.

Our teachers and staff continually worked hard on standards-based lesson plans and behavior plans, keeping their rooms safe and welcoming to all students, and establishing parent communication routines.

Our class lists and schedules—lunch duties, special area classes, arrival and dismissal, and courses—had all been gone through with a fine-toothed comb and most worked out well. Only a few tweaks here and there were needed.

Our custodial crew had done an amazing job preparing the building. I missed Roy, but the new crew was great and very much appreciated. They kept the building looking good and running well.

Our enrollment for the district may have been down and not able to support the need for two elementary buildings and a middle school, but the consolidated building was already near capacity. Which, if I was being honest, kinda worried me. We wanted our Valley Hill enrollment to grow, but if it grew much this year, we'd be busting at the seams in the middle school building and that wasn't fair to the staff or students. But the bigger our enrollment got, the better chance we had to keep the district going strong and reopen the elementary buildings. Or at least one of them.

If either Jamison or I were chosen to go back to our old buildings, would I be more willing to consider giving in and letting something happen between us? Who was I kidding? Every damn day brought me closer and closer to saying screw it and giving in.

Between the two of us, Jamison seemed to be handling our necessary separation better than I was. Maybe he was frustrated and hurting on the inside, but he was doing a great job of covering it.

I, on the other hand, was seriously wondering if I was going insane. Every single little thing reminded me of Jamison. A scent, a flower, a piece of chocolate. A glass of wine, a joke, an innuendo. No matter the words or music I heard, I thought of Jamison. No matter the foods or candles I smelled, I thought of Jamison. No matter what I tasted or saw or touched, I thought of Jamison.

Every night, I had to force myself to put my phone in the bathroom to charge so I wasn't tempted to text Jamison over my nightly glass of wine as I wound down with a podcast or television show.

Every day, I had to fight the urge to walk through the connecting door between our offices, slam him against the wall, and kiss him senseless the way I'd been dying to since that last kiss in my kitchen.

The weeks that had passed since our time together had been absolute torture.

I kept telling myself that I had to stay strong and hold tight to my reasons and decision. I kept telling myself that Jamison and I staying apart was for the best and would be better for both of us in the long run.

But I missed him.

I missed him so damn much my heart hurt. I wasn't sleeping well. And I swore my body physically ached with how badly I needed him.

I missed our easy chit-chat. I missed dinners and movies and outings. I missed cuddling with him. And maybe it made me a complete perv, but damn it, I missed touching him, kissing him, fucking him. I couldn't erase his scent from my nose or his flavor from my tongue.

And I was slowly but surely starting to wonder if Jamison was right.

Maybe my reasons we couldn't be together were flimsy.

So what if we had a history? A lot of couples got together after knowing each other for a long period of time.

So what if he was younger? When he was sixteen, it would have been a real problem. But now? I wanted so badly to believe that it wouldn't be an issue.

My worry about being demoted to assistant principal truly was unfounded for the time being. No one in the entire district had any idea how this whole thing was going to play out. It would sting if I got moved down, but I was beginning to wonder if having Jamison by my side would help ease the sting. Not to mention, working with Jamison had turned out to be so easy, I wasn't sure it would even end up being so bad if he was named my boss.

Sure, the side of me that had gotten used to having powerful positions would cringe a bit at calling my boyfriend my boss—especially after being his superior for so many years. But would it be the end of the world?

Which would you rather deal with? Being happy with Jamison by your side and a change in job title? Or being miserable without Jamison by your side—maybe having to watch him go on with his life and someone else—but keeping the same job position?

I sighed and scrubbed a hand over my face as I attempted to pull myself from my thoughts when I was supposed to be working on a report that was due next week. At the end of the last school year, I would have had absolutely no issues choosing my job over a man. But now? Now that I'd gotten to experience Jamison and see what my life could be like with him by my side? Well, now the decision wasn't nearly as easy.

Really?

Okay, it was actually getting to be easier and easier with each passing day. Every day I woke up without Jamison in my arms; every night when I tossed and turned, trying to sleep, without Jamison curled beside me; the answer to those questions became clearer in my mind.

But I wasn't sure how to take the next step.

What if I told Jamison I wanted what he'd been offering and he said he'd changed his mind?

What if we started something and it ended as badly—or worse—than things with Douglas?

"Do you really think I could hurt you as badly as he did?" Jamison's words played through my head and I scoffed slightly.

No. Jamison was nothing like Douglas.

I thought about Lady Gray's words. She said I'd found happiness, but I had to let go and accept it. Was it possible that she could have been referring to the happiness I'd found—even for that short amount of time—with Jamison?

I snorted.

I didn't believe in that mumbo-jumbo.

Then why did her words give me pause?

Because you want something to validate your choice if you decide to open up and accept what you and Jamison could have together.

I took off my glasses and rubbed the bridge of my nose.

Would Jamison be on-board with a relationship

that wasn't advertised publicly at school? Most of the staff knew Jamison and I were gay, but I wasn't comfortable flaunting whatever was between us. And that wasn't just a gay thing; I had no issues with colleagues who were couples—we actually had a husband wife couple in the elementary and a lesbian couple in the middle school.

What? You think Jamison is going to want to walk the halls holding your hand or sticking his tongue in your ear?

I chuckled and rolled my eyes at myself. I was being ridiculous. Jamison was as much a professional as I was when it came to school stuff. He could be trusted to keep our personal lives separate from our professional lives.

I stared at my computer screen for several moments.

Had I just made a decision?

An epic decision that could possibly alter the pathway of my life permanently?

My heart pounded in my chest.

The part of me that always held tightly to power and control wanted to shake a fist and demand that I tighten my hold. Don't let go. Letting go is dangerous. Letting go brings about the unknown. Letting go may end up being something you can't reverse in the long-run.

But the part of me that easily admitted I could

fall in love with Jamison with very little persuasion was cheering excitedly. Letting go could be exciting. Letting go brings about new experiences you didn't even know you were missing. Letting go may end up being the best decision you've ever made.

I swallowed thickly.

It looked like I was going to take that step forward. Let Jamison know that I wanted the more he kept talking about.

I smiled and closed down my computer. The report could wait until Monday. I needed to contact Jamison. Maybe we could spend our weekend together.

And then my phone rang.

TWELVE

JAMISON

"OH SHIT, Betty, I'm so sorry. What can I do?" I heard Paul's voice as I paused at the entrance to his office.

He glanced up, face stricken, and motioned for me to enter and close the door.

We were over a month into the school year and things had been going very well as far as school stuff was concerned. Things between Paul and me? Well, that was a different—frustrating—story. I was being patient; truly, I had no other interests and it wasn't like I was wasting my time pining for Paul. But the man got an A+ in stubbornness and I wanted to grab him and kiss some sense into him.

"I've got Jamison here, can I put you on speaker phone?"

I sat down as Betty Short's voice filled the room.

"Hello, Jamison," she said in a voice that immediately told me something was wrong.

"Hi, Betty." I gave Paul a questioning look.

"As I was telling Paul, my husband is in the hospital. They believe he's had a heart attack." Betty cleared her throat. "The doctors say it appears to have been a mild one, but the tests they want to run should show the amount of damage and if any procedures need to be done in order to prevent something worse down the road."

"Shit, I'm so sorry," I said.

"You're in Sugar Creek?" Paul asked.

Valley Hill had an urgent care center, but not a large hospital.

"Yes. We'll be here at least a few days. Depending on the test results and what the doctors deem necessary to get Don out of the woods in terms of future issues, they've said they may go ahead and do the procedures—assuming he's well enough—which would mean we might be here longer." Betty murmured something to someone on her end. "But my sister has come to keep me company and Don is awake and alert. So, all is as good as can be expected on this end. I just wanted my Team Powers to be aware. I don't plan on being gone for long—and, of course, Stedman Oliver will act in my place—but I thought it best if you both knew. I have no doubt that you'll keep the new school running like clockwork even if I'm not there to stop in and pester."

"We've got it covered. You take care of yourself and Don. We'll be here when you're back," I said.

"And anxiously awaiting your pestering," Paul added.

I smiled.

We let Betty know that we could bring whatever she might need to the hospital and to call us if she needed a break, a cup of coffee, or just a visit. She assured us that she most definitely did not need those things and that she'd be back at work before too long.

After the call, Paul and I sat there in momentary silence.

"Well, this sucks, but I guess the fact that he's awake and alert is a good thing. Maybe the mild heart attack will lead them to fixing things that could have been super bad down the road." I shrugged. "Still sucks that they're dealing with it."

Paul nodded. "Yeah, it does." He blinked a few times and adjusted his glasses. "Hey, there was something I wanted to talk to you about."

An alarm siren sounded, piercing the air with its shrill warning.

"Damn it," Paul muttered.

We both rushed from the office to the main hall. Several teachers stuck their heads out of their rooms and a few students paused as if waiting to see what staff would do.

"Sorry 'bout that," the radio crackled in my hand. "Testing the alarm system. No need to vacate. Might go off a few more times."

I huffed, but tried to sound calm, cool, and collected when I replied. "No problem. We'll make an announcement. Let us know when the tests are done."

Paul had already headed back into the main office and picked up the phone to share the information over the loud speaker. "Just testing the alarm system. No need to vacate. But it might go off a few more times. Staff and students, remember to always take the alarms seriously; I appreciate the number of you I see on the cameras who were already heading to evacuate. Good job. You can disregard if the alarms go off anymore today."

I followed Paul back to his office and closed the door. "Not a huge deal, but wish they had let us know they were testing the system so we could have warned the staff and students."

Paul blanched. "I feel like Dwayne may have mentioned it to me in passing and I forgot to spread the news." He removed his glasses and ran a hand over his face. "Dropped the ball on that one."

"Like I said, no big deal. I think I'm mostly just crappy because it scared the bejeezus out of me." I placed the walkie-talkie back on its base. "What did you want to talk to me about?"

Paul looked at me blankly for a moment before a look of steely resolve filled his face. He took a deep breath and nodded. "I've been thinking…"

His phone buzzed.

"Paul, I've got Doctor Stedman Oliver on line 1 for you," Leo's calm, easy voice filled the air.

Paul rubbed at his temples and sighed. "Put him through."

The phone rang and Paul answered. "Doctor Oliver, what can I do for you? I've got Jamison Powers here with me and you're on speaker phone."

Stedman Oliver was a pompous ass and the one thing about Valley Hill I didn't like. He'd applied for the superintendent position at the same time as Betty Short. But the fact that he was an outsider with very little educational experience and Betty was a lifelong resident with her entire career in various educational positions within Valley Hill schools meant that he didn't stand a chance. Since no one else had put their name in for the position, Stedman was offered the assistant superintendent spot. He'd taken it, albeit begrudgingly, and spent his whole time basically salivating to take over the moment Betty retired. Luckily, the superintendent position was a board vote and not many seemed to like Dr. Oliver any more than I did.

"Good, good. Two birds, one stone," Dr. Oliver's voice boomed. "I'm calling with some devastating news."

Paul's brows shot up and our eyes met.

I frowned.

"Betty Short is likely going to be stepping down. Her husband has had a catastrophic heart attack and isn't expected to make it." Stedman cleared his throat. "I'll be coming into the school on Monday to meet with the two of you. We have some changes that will need to be put into place ASAP."

"Sir, I have to say, I'm a bit confused," Paul began. "Jamison and I just spoke with Betty not fifteen minutes ago. She reported that Don was awake and alert. Definitely didn't sound like a catastrophic heart attack—although we're concerned for Don and Betty for sure. I'd hope she'll take all the time she needs, but she didn't indicate any reason to think she'd be stepping down."

A long silence filled the air. "You spoke to Betty? She called you about this?"

The question held accusation and perhaps a hint

of a man-child feeling left out of something. Almost as if Dr. Oliver had perhaps heard the news second-hand and now was angry that we'd heard directly from Betty.

"Betty and I came into the Valley Hill district about the same time. We've been colleagues our entire careers and I'm lucky to call her my friend as well as my boss. Yes, she called to inform Jamison and me of Don's medical condition." Paul scowled and steepled his fingers under his chin.

"Familiarity and fraternization," Dr. Oliver growled. "It's unwarranted and uncalled for. There's a power structure in this district—as with all good organizations—and it is meant to be followed. The top of that structure has no reason communicating personal information to those below. Familiarity and fraternization are what bring businesses down. This entire district needs an overhaul in staffing. Once all-new people are put into place, I'll run things differently. Teachers, custodial staff, office personnel, no one in this district needs to have familiar relationships with each other. We're here to do a job. Period. Friendships, personal information, none of that is needed. And it won't be allowed under my watch."

"My watch?" I mouthed in disbelief.

Paul's eyes grew wide. "I beg to differ, sir. I

believe one of the reasons Valley Hill is as successful as it is is due to the strong relationships between staff members."

"Successful?" Dr. Oliver shot back. "If the district was as successful as you say it is, would you and Mr. Powers now be sharing a building and competing for the top spot? I told Betty it would be best to let you both go and get some new blood in there, but she's got a soft spot for both of you. Familiarity and fraternization," the man groused.

"With all due respect, sir," I began. "The school year started very strong and our plans and procedures are in place—as approved by Betty—and are running very smoothly. We're closing in on the end of September already. As you know, a strong routine and high expectations are one of the cornerstones to a well-run school; disrupting that now, when the students and staff have already been working hard to learn and adjust to the new year, could be unnecessarily detrimental. What changes are you proposing?"

"You'll be told of those when I say," Dr. Oliver growled. "Something has come up for me next week. I'll be in touch. And I'll be monitoring that school. Don't think that I'll go easy—I'm not Betty. I've got eyes everywhere." And with that, Stedman disconnected.

Paul and I stared at each other for a moment before blinking as if we were waking from a dream.

"What the actual fuck was that?" I asked.

"I have no idea. But I will definitely be passing the conversation onto the school board." Paul took off his glasses and rubbed his eyes. "Damn, I wish I could tell Betty. But she's got enough going on right now."

My lips twisted. "Yeah, probably best not to tell her right this moment. But I'd say the moment she's back at work, we let her know of Stedman's call. She likely already knows exactly what he's like, but she needs to be aware of how he's behaving in her absence. Do you think the board will approach him?"

Paul shook his head. "I know a couple of the board members. I won't go to the entire board in an official capacity. I'll share this little tidbit over coffee. They won't be able to act on it, but at least they'll know. If anything official comes of it, we can move on from there." He drummed his fingers on the desk. "And I know Betty is well-aware of his asshole personality, but she needs to know how much he's gunning for her job—even more so than I originally thought."

"There's that familiarity and fraternization," I mocked in a deep voice. "Oh, hey, what did you want to talk about?"

Paul's face paled. "Oh, um, nothing. It can wait. I think we need to take the weekend to relax and collect ourselves before the new week and whatever Doctor Oliver may throw our way."

I cocked my head. He wasn't telling me everything. "My pool and a couple glasses of wine are a great way to relax. Want to come over?"

He looked as if he wanted to say yes. His eyes shone with a mixture of desire and sadness, want and resignation. "Seems that all the talk of familiarity and fraternization would have reminded you that us spending time together outside of school isn't prudent."

I scoffed. "You're the one who basically told Stedman that our district is as good as it is because of our staff building relationships with the students and each other. And now you're going to use his words to keep me at arm's length? Classic." I stood and walked to the door. "Staff being friends and whatnot is great for them, just not for us, huh?" I yanked open the door and let it slam shut with a little more force than necessary.

Leo jumped. "You okay?"

"Yeah, I'm good. I'm heading out."

He glanced at the clock. "Early for you. Sure you're okay?"

"Yep," I bit out and stalked into my office to pack

my bag. It was only an hour early, but I had no more meetings for the day and my observations for the week were complete. I'd take home the work that needed to be finished and work on it throughout the weekend. I needed a change of scenery and a chance to clear my head.

Paul called my name as I walked out, but I needed to be a lot calmer before speaking to him.

By the time I got home, I was a ball of tension—definitely not calmer as I'd hoped. My head and heart throbbed with emotions.

Worry for Betty.

Anger at Dr. Oliver.

Hurt from being rejected again by Paul.

Damn, Stedman. I had a feeling that Paul had something he wanted to tell me and that call from Dr. Oliver threw him into a tailspin and knocked him off whatever course he'd been on when he told me he wanted to talk to me.

BY THE END OF OCTOBER, I was no less frustrated than I'd been since Paul and I were thrown together to share the building. Actually, I was a lot more frustrated if I was being honest.

School was going great—no issues there. The

staff and students were meeting and exceeding every single expectation and standard put before them. Sports and clubs were going strong. Beginning of the year test scores were good, but showed room for growth. Parents seemed happy with the new school setup—sure, they missed their home building, but they understood.

Paul and I were amazing as a team at school. The kids fed off our energy and we often found ourselves hanging with middle schoolers at lunch or playing with elementary kids at recess. We had daily check-ins with each other, weekly meetings with Danika, and weekly professional learning communities with grade levels. Paul and I had fallen into a seamless working relationship where there was no competition, no jealousy, and no real issues of which to speak.

All-in-all, we were the quintessential Team Powers just as Betty had hoped.

But nothing more.

Betty was due back at work within the week. Don had ended up having a quadruple bypass surgery. He was down and out for much longer than Betty had originally planned. But he was doing much better and Betty now felt comfortable leaving him with the home healthcare nurse.

Dr. Oliver had made a few rounds of the building

during the month Betty had been gone. He nitpicked about most everything, but really had no leg to stand on with his gripes because our school was built on standards-based instruction, positive behavior supports, and a growth model. All three of which had high levels of evidenced-based research as support; Stedman could gripe all he wanted, but our building was doing well.

The election was looming right around the corner. Things were tense around town for sure. It appeared that our old mayor—who was truly a nice guy, but had no skill for working with the district in making Valley Hill more appealing for families looking for long-term residency—was going to be ousted. The new mayor promised—if politicians could be trusted to make good on promises—to keep Valley Hill the same comfortable and humble midsized small town while making it an appealing and valid option for families looking for a new home. He assured that Valley Hill could return to its heyday —like back when my parents were settling in to raise a family—and he seemed excited to work with the district on increasing enrollment.

If the referendum passed—which would increase taxes by less than one hundred dollars a year—the district would be able to stay open. Those who were for the referendum argued that less than one hundred a year to keep our school district and avoid bussing our kids to Sugar Creek or elsewhere was completely worth it. If it didn't pass, the future of our town was grim if I was being honest. No school district would mean families would likely opt to move out. The referendum would actually be good for the entire town, not just the schools.

Even if we got enough votes, the consolidation would need to stay in place for at least another year —unless our enrollment grew more quickly than projected—but we'd be able to continue on our path without losing teachers and staff.

And then there was Paul.

Everything always came back around to Paul.

Paul who had grown even more distant since Dr. Oliver's call.

Paul who often seemed like he wanted to talk to me.

Paul who I'd stupidly gone and fallen in love with even when I knew it was quite possible he'd never love me back.

We'd spent the evening before at the Valley Hill High School Friday night football game. Together— presenting a strong, united front—but worlds apart. I'd caught Paul looking at me several times throughout the evening, but he always quickly diverted his gaze.

Today was Halloween and we'd been at a middle school football game earlier in the day. Now we were in the school parking lot preparing for a school-wide Trunk-or-Treat in the parking lot.

"Can you make sure these bags go to the two cars that just pulled in?" Paul asked as he pointed to two bags of candy and marked something on his checklist.

"Yep." I picked up the bags. "You want to pick a driveway and pass out candy tonight? This will be over in time, I figure we'll get quite a few trick-or-treaters in the neighborhood. I was thinking of having a little fire pit, some cider, and visit with the kids and families."

Paul glanced up at me as if I'd grown two heads, but his words surprised me. Instead of his usual adamant no, he blinked a few times and shook his head. "You have no idea how badly I want to say yes," he whispered gruffly.

"Then say yes." So what if there was a hint of begging in my voice. I fought the urge to reach out and pull him close, to hold him and tell him how much I missed him.

"I want to," Paul answered. "So badly. You're getting harder and harder to avoid and say no to."

"Well, that was my plan. It's taken a lot longer than I'd anticipated." I glanced around to be sure no one was within earshot. "I'll be home after trunk-or-treat is over. You know where I live."

Paul closed his eyes and breathed deeply. "And if I somehow push aside every bit of trepidation regarding this thing between us being a terrible idea and show up on your doorstep?"

"You better be prepared for the long haul. I'm not a booty-call, I'm not down with another fling. If you come to me, I need to know it means you're ready to open up to us happening." Another car pulled in and I grabbed another bag of candy.

"Would you be willing to keep it quiet at school?" Paul rubbed the back of his neck.

"No PDA at school. I'm pretty sure you know I'm okay with that. And I'm not planning to propose to you at a football game or in an all-school assembly." I smiled and hefted a fourth bag for the newest arrival. "But I'd expect us to be a real couple outside of school. Dinner, dates, hanging together."

Paul nodded. "Good to know. I have to be honest and tell you that I'm torn. I've been torn since we came back from Indy—these have truly been the longest four months of my life." He smiled softly at my huff—did he think these months hadn't been hard on me? "You're the best thing that's ever happened to me, but I'm also scared this thing between us could end up being the most devastating disaster of my life. I'm barely surviving without you, but I'm confident I'd never live through the heartbreak of finally having you and then losing you."

"I get it. I have those same fears." I moved closer, our bodies mostly shielded by the raised trunk of Paul's car. "But I'm so excited—so sure—that what we could have together will be beyond amazing that I don't even want to dwell on the fear part. You've seen that we work together very well—even with our personal issues these last few months, we've pulled off Team Powers without a hitch. I'd like to think you can trust me enough to keep work and home separate. I'm not asking for sex in your office— although, sex in an at-home office is totally on the table. I'm not asking to make out in the teachers lounge. Not even asking to hold hands as we skip happily down the hall."

Paul chuckled and made a mark on his checklist before picking up the final bag of candy from his trunk.

"Nothing at work has to change." I closed the trunk. "Even if something changes due to locations and schools and titles, we'll still be a great team. And having you to spend my time with outside of school sounds like a dream come true."

He studied me for a long moment and I could

almost see the wheels turning in his head. "I'm not saying no. Somehow with each passing day since we got back to town, my solid reasons and valid excuses…"

I snorted and Paul rolled his eyes.

"…the reasons and excuses I felt were very solid and valid," he amended, "have gotten harder and harder to hold onto." Paul adjusted his glasses. "I'm still having some worries about people thinking I took advantage of my years of being your superior."

I growled. "You are no longer my boss. We are equals. The only place you top me in any way is in bed—and if I have my way, that will be switched up from time-to-time."

Paul's eyes went wide.

With a laugh, I assured him, "But that's a conversation for another time. A lot of people around here don't even know that we have such a long history. I'm not a kid anymore—I haven't been a kid in a very long time."

"Stedman Oliver will fire me if he ever gets Betty's position," Paul mused. "Probably fire both of us."

"Wait, is he the reason you've pulled back? What were you going to talk to me about that day he called?"

Paul's cheeks pinked in the brisk fall air—rumor

had it that we were in for a very early and very bad winter—and he shrugged. "Just that I was working on coming to some decisions."

I cocked my head and studied him with narrowed eyes. "No. You weren't going to tell me you were working on making some decisions. You'd made up your mind." I scoffed. "And you let that douchebag asshole derail you? Paul, I need better. I can't be constantly wondering if the slightest disapproval from someone is going to make you run."

Paul adjusted his glasses. "I know. And that's where I am right now. I was ready. I was going to tell you I'm all in. But then Oliver called and I panicked. I need to be sure that I can withstand the strong wind of disapproval from folks like Oliver when it comes to how our relationship affects our professional lives. It's only fair to you."

"Couple things and then we should get this party started. One, Stedman Oliver won't be voted into the superintendent spot—the board doesn't like him, you've said so yourself. Two, if we have a true relationship, everything from our jobs to our hobbies to our highs and lows will affect the other—because we're a couple, a partnership, a team. We'll withstand the Stedmans of the world together, and we'll weather any storm that comes our way." Glancing around to make sure we weren't the center of attention, I brushed my thumb against the back of his hand. "More than anything, I just want the chance to stand by your side, support you, grow with you, and love you."

Paul's breathing hitched. "I think I'd like that. Can you give me a bit more time? I know I've been unfair asking you to wait this long."

"First, you didn't ask me to wait. You told me it was pointless and to move on. Second, I have nowhere else I'd rather be and nothing else I'd rather be doing. Come over to sit on my driveway. Or come over to sneak in my backdoor." I snorted out a laugh at the unintended innuendo. "I'll be there."

Paul gave a nod. "I want to. I just have to convince myself it's okay to take that step."

"I get it. Because once you take that step, there's no going back. I'm in this for the long haul and I need you ready to travel the same road." I gave him a small, hopeful smile and turned toward the cars awaiting their donated bag of candy.

We spent the next two hours visiting with families, passing out candy, and enjoying the last little bit of sunshine on the chilly day.

"Mr. Powers, you're not dressed up!" a little boy dressed like a pirate shouted.

Paul and I both yanked up a leg of our jeans to show our Halloween socks.

"We're dressed up like principals in Halloween socks," Paul assured the little guy.

"That's silly." The kid laughed.

"Lame," a middle schooler teased when we gave him the same answer a few moments later.

"Oh, and what are you?" I pressed with a grin. Middle schoolers were always a mix of costumes to the extreme and just enough effort to count as dressed up so they could get candy.

"I'm a football player." The kid smirked and gestured to his uniform.

"Uh-huh, convenient that you walked off the field and straight to the candy. Leave some for the little ones." Paul nudged the kid.

"For real though, my sister is home sick so I said I'd come gather some candy for her. She'll let me have the kinds she doesn't like," the big, tough football player said. And just like that, I remembered why I loved kids. Each age and stage had their pros and cons. The fact that this kid gave up his time to gather candy for his sister—just to get her discarded pieces—showed what a huge heart he had. He often gave teachers trouble, had been known to get into a tussle here and there, and struggled to keep his grades up to stay on the team. But his goodness shone through at that moment and it warmed my heart.

"Here, pick something for her and take a piece you'd like," Paul said as he thrust a bucket toward the kid.

"Thanks," the kid said and took a tiny bag of gummy bears and a Snickers before heading to the next car to collect his treats.

"Think he likes the Snickers or the gummy bears?" I mused.

"I'm thinking he's a gummy bear person." Paul watched the kid walk away. "Reminds me of you."

"What? Why?" I frowned.

"I didn't know you at that age, but at sixteen you were cool, cocky, sure of yourself. You maybe didn't have the same issues as Shawn, but you weren't without fault. Your true self—that big heart and smart mind—was easy to see. I think he's going to do great things someday."

I watched Shawn swagger farther down the line as he collected candy for a sick sister and had to agree. "Yeah, I can totally see it."

THIRTEEN

PAUL

I TOOK a quick shower after the trunk-or-treat at the school. I'd actually planned to turn off my porch light and go to bed early with a cup of hot tea and a movie in hopes of forgetting my sorrows.

But the conversation with Jamison earlier in the day had changed my mind.

I originally thought it was a terrible idea to go sit on his driveway and pass out candy. His invite to sneak to the backdoor had sounded so much better.

Until I got home and pictured myself walking down the street, lurking in the shadows, and slipping through his backdoor in the dark of night.

I wasn't a damned horny teenager just looking to get off.

A grown man looking for a relationship—okay, looking was maybe the wrong word...maybe slowly accepting the relationship being offered—didn't go sneaking around and hooking up on the sly.

Jami deserved better.

I snorted.

Jami demanded better.

We'd had our fun tryst in Indy. But that was over now. If I wanted the same thing Jami wanted, it meant being real and honest. No more secrets, no flings, no avoiding the spark that continued to grow between us.

So, after pulling on a worn pair of jeans— probably the most casual pants I owned outside of sweats—and a Valley Hill yellow jackets t-shirt, I grabbed my backpack and headed to the kitchen.

Within minutes, I had stuffed my bag with leftover candy from the school event, two chicken salad sandwiches I'd planned on eating for lunch the next day, and a bottle of wine.

At the very last minute, I rushed to my room and threw in my toothbrush, underwear, and condoms. A fluttery feeling tickled my stomach as I recalled our conversation about getting tested regularly. I wondered if going bare was something Jamison would be interested in. Shrugging to myself, I zipped up my bag. That was a conversation for later, but I was definitely on board.

Another thought zinged through my head as I

pulled on a zip-up hoodie, pocketed my phone, and locked the door behind me. Jami had mentioned switching things up in bed. Despite my past experiences with bottoming ranging from blah to disastrous, I found myself very interested in trying it with Jami.

No one else had ever been able to get me to let loose and give someone else control. No one else had ever been able to get me out of my head.

Only Jami had that kind of power over me.

And that both excited and terrified me.

As I headed down the street looking like a kid going to a friend's sleepover, I waved to the few people out and about. Part of me wanted to run and hide, afraid they'd know exactly where I was going and they'd ring up Stedman Oliver and report that I was most definitely planning on familiarity and fraternization with someone way too young for me.

The other part of me told my worries to shut the fuck up and be confident in my decision. Jamison was right. We were amazing together in and outside of the bedroom. We had a chemistry that served us well as leaders in the school and as...what were we outside of school? Friends? Yes, but it was more. Lovers? Again, yes, but still it was more. Would Jamison be willing to label us partners? Boyfriends?

I adjusted my glasses with a huff. Relationship

stuff was for the birds in a lot of ways. But I knew deep down that what we had was worth it.

Jami was worth it.

When I was close enough to see Jamison's driveway, I noticed two camp chairs, a portable fire pit, a cooler, and a big bowl.

A smile played at my lips knowing he'd planned for me to be there.

Then my smile was wiped away when I realized maybe he'd been frustrated when I said I couldn't come and he'd invited someone else.

Stop. You're being an idiot and looking for reasons this won't work. Just stop. He told you he would wait. He told you he wanted you and only you. March your ass up there and take your place beside him where you belong.

Where I belonged.

My heart clenched and a warmth traveled through me as I recognized the absolute truth of that statement. Next to Jami was where I belonged.

We'd stood beside each other for nearly two decades—yes, our roles were very different during those years, but they were a huge part of who we were now—and I was ready to take my place beside him again.

Where I belonged.

As I stepped onto Jamison's driveway, he came

around the corner of the house with a thermos and two mugs.

And froze.

For several long seconds, we just stared at each other.

Then a wide smile filled Jami's face and he made his way toward me.

"Wasn't sure you'd make it. Hoped," he said with pink cheeks and gesture at the little setup.

"Wasn't sure I'd make it either," I said, my words suddenly thick with an emotion I couldn't name.

Jami put the thermos and mugs on top of the cooler and sat down, indicating I should do the same. "What changed your mind?"

"You. Our history. The spark between us." I hung my bag on the back of my chair and sat down. "The fact that I'm a better person when I'm with you." I took off my glasses and pinched the bridge of my nose. "The fact that I'd rather be scared but happy with you than barely existing and miserable without you."

Jamison smiled. "It took you a while—damned stubborn, that's what you are—but I'm glad you're here."

I swallowed thickly and put my glasses back on. "As I walked up here, I was struck with the thought that beside you is where I belong. It's where I've been throughout so much of our past. It's so weird how we kinda existed in each other's periphery for so many years, crossing in and out of each other's lives. Even when we were far apart, I felt you—despite trying to ignore it. And now, standing beside you seems the most natural place for me to be. Almost like our past has come full circle." I grimaced. "I don't know if that makes any sense."

Jami reached over and patted my hand. "It does. Like our paths were destined to meet here and merge into one—if you were to look at our paths over the past twenty years, they've crossed several times. It wasn't until now that they were meant to come together."

"Yeah, that's exactly it."

"So," Jami bit his lip, "are you staying tonight?"

I threw a glance over my shoulder to my backpack. "Let's just say that I plan on plenty of familiarity and fraternization."

He cackled. "I like the sound of that. But first?"

"Candy," I said with a smile as I tore open a Snickers and waved at a little fairy princess walking toward us. "Oh, I brought chicken salad sandwiches. For a late-night snack? Brunch tomorrow?"

Jami grinned and opened the cooler so he could arrange the two baggies I'd brought among his waters and sodas.

"You planning on some heavy drinking?" I teased.

Jamison blushed. "I may have gone a little overboard. Maybe some of the kids will want a drink?"

We spent the next hour complimenting costumes, saying hello to families and students, sipping cider that Jami had doctored up with cinnamon whiskey, and enjoying the warm glow of the fire pit.

"You are the only person on the face of this planet who could ever get me to drink whiskey in the presence of students," I muttered as I took another sip of the warm drink.

"First, I'm hoping to be the only person on the face of this planet to ever be able to get you to do a lot of things," Jami quipped with a waggled brow. "Second, it's not like you're taking shots in front of kids. This isn't Principals Behaving Badly."

I snorted.

"You're sipping warm apple cider from a mug. If there happens to be a splash of cinnamon whiskey to enhance the flavor, no one has to be the wiser. Plus, it's after school hours and you're not on school property." Jamison cocked his head. "If you were out at a restaurant, would you skip the wine for fear that a student would see you?"

I thought about that for a moment and shook my

head. "No, I usually order wine with a meal if I'm at a nicer restaurant. I guess it doesn't cross my mind in those situations because the chances of seeing a student are much lower."

"Well, I guarantee that no one knows what you're drinking. And even if they had their suspicions, we're on my driveway and we're not intoxicated. Let's finish off these last handfuls of candy with the group heading toward us. I'm ready to go inside." Jamison swirled the candy in the bowl as he drained the rest of his cider.

By the time the stragglers arrived—older kids who didn't likely have the earlier bedtime a lot of the little ones who had come earlier did—a cold rain had started to fall.

"Gah, I don't like rain," I grumbled as I pulled my hood up. "Makes it hard to see in glasses."

"Put the empty mugs and thermos in the cooler. Can you carry that to the deck? I'll put the chairs away. Fire pit will need to cool off, I'll get it in the morning." Jamison began to fold up the chairs.

I put the items in the cooler and walked toward the backdoor with my bag slung over my shoulder. The moment was so perfectly mundane, but also a huge turning point. Tonight with Jami meant there was no turning back. We were in this for the long haul.

The nervous energy traveling through my body both scared and excited me.

I placed the cooler on the kitchen floor and began to unload it. Thermos and mugs to the sink, sodas, waters, and chicken salad sandwiches to the fridge.

What if what we'd started in Indy was so good because it was taboo and temporary? What if once we were together for real, no time limits, no sneaking around, the magical spark that had been glowing between us for—well, for years if I was being honest—was suddenly snuffed out?

"You in here overthinking things?" Jamison asked as he walked into the kitchen, sliding the glass door closed behind him.

"Maybe," I muttered as I hefted the cooler to the counter, positioning it over the sink so the drain valve could pour out overnight.

Jami ran a hand through his damp hair and gave me his killer boy-next-door smile.

My stomach flip-flopped with a million butterflies. More like boy-next-door-who-will-totally-bring-you-to-your-knees-but-looks-completely-innocent. The guy was simply gorgeous, stunningly charismatic, and unnervingly confident. He was also stubborn, determined, and patient—and I was grateful for that.

But those were things most people who knew Jamison would know and recognize about him.

Did they know the other side of Jamison? The sexy, sensual, oh-so-talented-with-his-mouth side? A fist of jealousy clenched me. I didn't want anyone else to know that side of my man.

My man?

Was that too much? Too fast?

"Paul?" Jamison waved his hand in front of my face. "While I don't want this to be the secret, off-limits, one-week-only thing we had last time, I need you to know that you're not stuck here. You're not required to stay. You can leave anytime. I want to give this relationship a chance, but I don't want you looking like a caged animal planning its escape."

I reached for his hand and gave it a squeeze. "Sorry. It's not that at all. I'm just on a major overload right now. Too many thoughts and feelings."

"Do you want to just go watch a movie or something?" Jami brought his other hand up to cup my face.

"Maybe? Did you ever listen to the rest of Buried Secrets? We could cuddle up and finish that, see where things go later?" I was completely on-board with the night and us, I just needed a moment to reset my brain and my heart.

"Perfect plan. Showers, audiobook, and then wherever things go is fine with me. More than anything, I just want you in my arms." Jamison stepped closer, his breath a whisper against my mouth.

"Just in your arms?"

"My arms, my bed, my life. Let's be real, I want you anywhere and everywhere I can get you." Jami wrapped an arm around my waist and pulled me flush against him. "Can you tell me what's got you so overloaded right now?" He nuzzled his nose against mine.

I took a deep breath and closed my eyes. "I want to be here; it feels right. I kinda think my head is on a bit of a short-circuit because it's been so accustomed to running my reasons and excuses for this not to work on a continual loop. The fact that I'm now accepting that those things were just fear talking and I'm ready and willing to take this next step with you is all just a bit much for my mind to wrap around. I'm a creature of habit and I was well-settled into my routine of No, I can't be with Jamison for all of these reasons, so doing a complete one-eighty has thrown me off a bit."

"And that's all?"

My cheeks heated. "I was thinking about the side you present to everyone and the side I know of you

—and I was hit with a bit of jealousy about other men who maybe know that side of you. Which then compounded my overload because jealousy is new for me and I feel so grateful to know that side of you —to know every side of you." I took a deep breath and blew it out slowly. "Yeah, so...overload." I leaned in and kissed him. "But I want to be here."

"And you're sure? I don't want to think that I pushed you into something." Jamison pressed his forehead against mine.

"I'm sure. You know I'm not one to let myself get pushed into things."

"Did something specific change your mind?"

I shifted to snake my arms around Jamison's neck. "The memories of our time together. The way we worked so well together told me that we could be even more. A crazy jealousy I didn't even know I had when I thought of others getting to know you the way I do. A heavy blanket of sadness when I thought of my future without you by my side." I leaned in and pressed kisses along his jawline. "Mostly? I realized how much I longed for our easy chit-chat and comfortable silences, our outings and lunches— all of the things we've had since this whole thing started—to continue. I didn't want shopping, meals, movies, trips, and laughing together to be things we only got to do when work called for it. I want all of that in our personal lives as well. I want all of you, not just the work version."

Jamison's mouth feathered against mine, seeking, questioning.

My hands caressed the back of his head as I groaned and chased his lips.

When our mouths came together, a mixture of cinnamon apples and longing, it felt as if everything that had been askew in my life recently shifted into place—there was no more struggle, no more denial, everything was exactly as it should be.

We broke apart, breathing heavily, smiling against each other's lips.

"You take the hall bathroom. We both do quick showers and meet in my room." Jamison nuzzled his nose against mine.

I had a feeling he wanted a little time to himself to prep and I totally respected that. While I wasn't planning to bottom that night—but weird how much the thought intrigued me these days—I knew I'd want some time to get myself ready if that was in the cards.

"Sounds good." I kissed him lightly. "See you soon."

Thirty minutes later, hair and skin still damp, we crawled into Jami's bed in just our boxers. He put his iPad between us and pulled up the audiobook. As the narrator's deep voice filled the air, I reached over to pull Jamison closer to me.

The quick and easy way he cuddled into my chest made my breath hitch. How had I gone so long without this in my life? How had I thought I could give this man up?

By the time the story finished, I was a strange mix of emotional and horny. The love between Drake and Liam was so strong and gave me all the feels. And the sex between them had been hot.

Which had me having a whole different type of feel. Like a hard and throbbing feel.

"Did you like it?" Jamison asked, his hand stroking across my chest.

"Loved it," I croaked like a damn pubescent teen.

"It was a good story. I kept thinking I knew who the killer was, but then I'd get thrown off the path from time-to-time."

"I know it's just a book and completely fictional —I feel stupid even commenting on the characters because they aren't real—but I liked how Drake changed throughout the story, but he was still the same person too. If that makes sense. Like, he was still interested in his career and helping others. He was still kinda gruff and grumpy. But I liked how he finally accepted that he needed Liam in his life." I ran my hand up and down Jami's arm.

"Hmmm, yeah, I liked that part too. Sounds like someone I know," he teased.

I growled and rolled Jamison to his back. "Joke all you want, but it was hard for me to finally let go and admit how badly I want you—need you—in my life." Jami's hands came up to cup my face, our underwear covered dicks came together, and I dipped my head and kissed him. A zing of want and need I'd never felt before sparked between us and I knew without a doubt that where we were heading now was going to make our week in Indy look like a pathetic trial-run.

Sex with Jamison before had been amazing.

Sex with Jamison now was going to be epic.

I could feel it.

What had changed?

You changed.

Had I? Yeah, I had. Instead of insisting on temporary and walking away, I was open to an actual relationship and making this thing work. By accepting how badly I wanted Jami in my life—and acting on it—I'd torn down a wall between us that I didn't even know I'd built.

We kissed—hard and fast, slow and soft—for several minutes. Our hands roamed, hips rocked, and dicks leaked through our cotton boxer briefs while straining to be released.

"Fuck," Jami groaned when he broke the kiss. "I need you, want you to fuck me."

I slowed our movements, brushing a hand through his messy hair and stroking his cheek. "I want that, too. But I don't want a quick and messy, cold and impersonal fuck. Want more than that," I whispered gruffly.

"I want it whichever way gets your cock in my ass the quickest and keeps it there the longest," Jami quipped, biting at my bottom lip before soothing the sting with his tongue.

Rolling to grab my bag, I pulled out a condom and tossed it on the bedside table.

"Lube is in the drawer," Jamison said, but frowned as he glanced toward the condom.

"What's wrong?" I asked as I settled back in beside him.

"I've never once asked this of another sexual partner, even Matt and I used condoms always, but what are your thoughts on not using them?" Jamison propped up on his elbow and trailed a finger from my throat to my naval.

"I get tested regularly and I plan on this thing between us being monogamous."

"Same for me. My latest tests were clear. As for the monogamous part, that's completely what I want." Jami leaned down to lick my nipple which caused my dick to jerk. "But if you ever get to a point where you want to try something different, I'm open to talking about it."

I growled again and rolled on top of him. "The thought of sharing you with another man kills me— never something I'd really thought about, but it seems I'm definitely a one-man type guy." I rocked my hips into him, loving the way he spread his legs for me and whimpered against my mouth.

"Fine by me," Jamison panted. "Thoughts on the condoms?"

"If we're both on the same page, I say it's all good." I pressed my forehead against his. "This feels like a really big decision—like a serious commitment —are we at that point in this relationship?"

Jamison's serious eyes bore into mine. "I have to be honest—and you let me know if it's too much— but I'm definitely at that point. This thing between us isn't just dating to me. It feels like so much more. Maybe it's because we've known each other for so long, maybe it's because there's some crazy, strong connection between us that makes things so very different from all the other guys I've dated." He gripped the back of my head and pulled me in for a kiss. "But you're it for me—my person, if you will— as long as you're at that same point."

I let loose a breath I didn't know I'd been holding

and gave a hoarse little chuckle. "Didn't know I'd been waiting to hear that," I said with a smile. "But damn if that doesn't make me feel better." I kissed him. "Yes, I'm at that point."

The last little bit of hesitation I'd been feeling unraveled as Jamison surged up to capture my mouth in a soul-searing kiss. The deep, dark secret longing of my heart that wanted nothing more than to know Jamison and I both wanted forever soared as I shifted to kiss from Jami's jaw to his throat. As I made my way farther south, I stopped to tease his nipples, dip my tongue in his belly button, and press kisses along his shapely V-lines. Swiping a lick against his leaking head, savoring his salty essence, I moved to bury my nose in the thatch of hair at the base of his cock as I hefted his balls into my hand. As I gently fondled him, I grabbed a pillow and shoved it under his hips.

The shift in position allowed Jami's legs to open more as he pulled them toward his torso. The movement opened him just as I'd hoped and I nuzzled my nose against his taint, nudging his balls and pressing a soft kiss against his most intimate spot.

When Jami gasped, I smiled against his hot, soft skin and swirled my tongue around his hole. As he rocked his hips, begging for more, I continued to tease until I could take it no longer. Moving to my knees, I leaned over and grabbed the lube before settling between Jami's spread thighs. As I slicked my cock and worked a lubed finger, then two, into his ass, I licked my lips to see his rock-hard cock dripping pre-cum against his stomach. Pressing the plump head of my cock against his pucker, I slid in slow and deep, loving how he opened for me inch-by-inch until my balls rested against his warm skin.

"Oh God, so good," Jami panted, "so fucking good."

His arms reached for me and I dropped to my elbows, our chests plastered together, to kiss him as I began a long, slow rhythm of thrusting into him over and over.

"Fuck, Jami," I ground out, breaking the kiss and pressing my forehead against his as I paused the movement of my hips. "You're so fucking tight and hot, I'm not going to last long."

"Keep going. Want your cum in me. Want it dripping from my ass when you suck me off." Jami kissed me again and rocked his hips in invitation.

I began again, pulling nearly all the way out and then sliding hard and slow back in, as our tongues matched the same pace.

"Talk to me," I demanded, wanting to hear Jami's dirty words as I owned his body.

"You fuck me so good," he groaned out. "Can't wait to feel your hot cum fill my ass. You going to let me fuck you some day?"

When my hips faltered and a deep moan sounded from my chest, Jamison smiled a wicked smile.

"I'll take that as a very definite yes." His hands ran up and down my back, nails bringing goosebumps to my flesh. "Someday soon, I'm going to spread your ass and press kisses against your pretty hole. Gonna rim you until your tight little pucker is wet and ready. Then I'll press my hard cock against your hole and slide deep inside your tight heat. You'll gasp at how my dick stretches you, but you'll love it."

Jami's words had me on edge, I was right there, ready to tumble over and I thrust deeper and harder as he whispered in my ear.

"I'll fuck you so good, you'll scream my name just as my hard cock throbs and shoots my hot cum deep in your ass," Jami finished his little story with a gasp as he bit down on my earlobe.

With absolutely no hope of containing it, I moaned as my orgasm rolled through me. My cock throbbed as it released spurt after spurt deep in Jami's body. "Fuuuck," I groaned as I tried to catch my breath. After a few brief moments, I slipped from

Jami's ass as I captured his whimper with my lips. "Your turn," I whispered.

I maneuvered to take Jamison's hard dick between my lips as I rolled from on top of him to my side. Pulling him to lay on his side as well, I gripped his ass and encouraged a hard and fast rhythm.

"God, love to see your lips stretched around my cock," Jami said as he ran a hand through my hair and thrust his hips. "You want my cum? Want to swallow me?"

I nodded and hummed around his cock as he pumped his shaft deep into my throat. I'd never wanted a face-fucking as much as I wanted this one.

"Fuck," Jami gasped. "Gonna come." He tensed as his salty load exploded on my tongue.

I gripped his ass and took everything he had to give me before swallowing, wiping the dribbles of cum from the corner of my mouth, and letting his spent cock slip from between my lips.

I shifted up the mattress until our faces were level.

Jami had a blissed-out smile on his lips, his eyes glassy. He pulled me close. "Kiss me, wanna taste," he demanded.

I gave him what he wanted. My lips brushed his softly before plunging my tongue inside to meet his.

Our flavors mixed as our tongues danced and a full-body, well-sated exhaustion poured over us. "Sleep?"

Jamison nodded, his eyes already closed. With a smile, he spoke. "Hey, Paul?"

"Mmhm?" I mumbled as I brushed his hair from his forehead and caressed his cheek.

"Not just the sex—but that was earth-shatteringly-good—but I'm pretty sure I'm in love with you. Like in love as in I love you." He gave a goofy, sleepy grin as his eyes fluttered open to study me.

"Pretty sure, huh?" I teased. "Well then, I win. Because I'm one-hundred percent positive that I'm completely, head-over-heels in love with you. And I have been for quite a while."

"Glad you finally figured it out." He kissed me. "And I love you, too. Pretty sure, sure, positive, I don't care which words. I just love you."

I nuzzled my nose against his. "Love you, too," I whispered.

For the first time in a very long time, I fell asleep feeling completely content, happy, and in love. Everything was right in my world as long as Jamison was by my side.

FOURTEEN

JAMISON

IN THE WEE hours of the morning, I found myself awake and wanting more. The slow and sensual sex from earlier in the evening had shown me that the invisible wall we'd had between us had been torn away—I'd found that intimate connection I'd been craving.

But waking in the silence of the night, Paul's arms wrapped protectively around me, I wanted hard and fast—I wanted everything with him. Rolling in Paul's arms, I kissed him awake, rocking my hips into him until his cock took notice and got with the plan.

"What do you want?" Paul asked in a sleep gruff voice.

His words washed over me in a wave of emotion as I realized this was real, we were real, and Paul wanted nothing more than to give me what I longed for.

"Hard and fast, you behind me. Fuck me dirty," I whispered as I nibbled at his ear.

"Fuck, Jami, you're going to be the death of me. I'm an old man," he teased.

"But at least you'll die happy," I retorted as I shifted to my stomach and lifted up on my hands and knees. "No stretching, just fuck me. Lube if you want it, but I know I'm still slick from before."

Paul grunted and I knew he loved the idea of his cum still being inside me.

I heard the snick of the lube bottle right before the slick head of Paul's cock pressed against my hole. I dropped to my elbows, spreading my legs farther apart, and moaned as my body stretched to welcome Paul's invasion.

When his warm balls rested against my taint, he paused as his hands gripped my hips. "You okay?"

"I'm good. Go hard. Bruise me, slap me, I want to feel you all day tomorrow." I pushed my ass back and gasped when his cock hit me deep.

Just when I thought Paul was going to protest, going to refuse to be rough, he started to move. With a delicious bite of fingers digging into my skin, Paul set a punishing rhythm. The burn of my muscles as his shaft forced me open was exactly what I was craving and I whimpered as the pain morphed into pleasure. The sting of Paul's hand slapping against my ass nearly pushed me over the edge.

"You gonna come for me?" Paul demanded with another smack of his palm against my skin. "You want my load?"

"Fuuuck, yeah," I groaned, burying my face in the mattress. "Give it to me. Then jack me off with your cock still deep in my ass."

Paul grunted and returned to gripping my hips and railing me in. A few strokes later, his cock began to pulse as his hot cum spilled into me.

He wrapped an arm around my chest and pulled me upright, my back to his chest, as he panted in my ear and his dick continued to throb in my ass. "Wanna feel your ass clench around me when you come," he whispered and began to stroke my leaking shaft.

Between his cock still stretching my hole, his words and kisses against my neck, and his perfect grip stroking me, I had no chance of staving off the orgasm that rolled through me. My cum coated Paul's hand as my head fell back against his shoulder.

When we finally came down from our highs, Paul grabbed a couple washcloths so we could clean up. Then we cuddled back under the covers.

"So, I think we need quite a few more rounds of practice, but it seems as if we may be pretty compatible in bed. Soft and slow, check. Hard and fast, check." Paul nuzzled my neck.

"Lots more practice needed, but I think we can rest assured we fit," I murmured before falling into a happy and sated sleep.

I WOKE with a warm hand stroking my morning wood and a hard cock pressed against my well-used ass.

"Can this be my wakeup call every morning for the rest of my life?" I teased.

"I'm down for it," Paul growled in my ear. "I think making you come is my new favorite pastime." His fist continued a slow slide on my shaft. "I'm not sure I've ever had so much sex in my entire life."

"It's the horny honeymoon phase." I turned my head to offer my mouth.

Paul devoured me, his tongue dipping between my lips, lapping at me as if I was his favorite flavor of all. "Well, I love it. Are you too sore?"

"Can't do a repeat of last time, but I'm good to go if you're gentle." I pushed the blankets off our naked bodies. "Take me like this," I demanded, bending my leg to open myself to Paul's cock.

"You are so fucking hot," he whispered against my shoulder as he draped his body half over mine and pressed his swollen head against my hole. "Tell me if it's too much."

A biting sting forced a gasp from me, but the discomfort faded as Paul's hand came around to fist my cock. "It's good. So good. Make me come."

"Fuck, you're so tight and hot. Slick with my cum." Paul thrust his hips in a slow and steady rhythm. "Tomorrow, at school, when I see you wince as you sit down, I'm going to know it's because my cock ruined you."

"Fuuuck," I moaned at Paul's dirty words and my balls drew up tight. "I'm close. Come in me, wanna feel it hot and deep."

Paul kept his gentle thrusting, but increased his pace. Soon, his rhythm faltered and he grunted as his release spilled into me.

With one last stroke of Paul's fist on my shaft, I lost myself as my orgasm washed over me.

"Holy fuck," Paul whispered gruffly as we both caught our breaths. "I love you for so many reasons and I'd spend the rest of my life loving you even if no sex was involved, but damn, that's so fucking good.

I'm sure I sound sappy or dramatic or cliché, but I swear no sex has ever been this good."

"Agreed. What we have is so different—so much better, so much more—than what I've ever had with anyone else."

Paul growled and wrapped me in a tight embrace as his lips captured mine and owned my mouth. "I don't like thinking of you with anyone else."

I smiled into the kiss. "No worries, you've ruined me for anyone else. You're stuck with me forever."

"Not a punishment," Paul answered.

When he was quiet for a moment, I cocked my head. "What are you thinking?"

"Just that we can't sleep over all the time if we don't want people at school knowing." He frowned.

"We agreed no PDA at school. But we said our personal lives outside of school were free game. I don't know that we should start playing house right away, but sleep overs are definitely on the table." I nuzzled his nose. "Dinners out, dinners in, movie nights, working weekends if needed, weekend getaways, shopping trips, I want all of it. Don't get hung up on people at school. I won't ask to hold your hand, kiss you, or jump you in the building, but outside of school? It's on."

Paul chuckled then narrowed his eyes. "Were you serious about wanting to top?"

My breath hitched. "I want it. I like to top from time-to-time, but I love bottoming, especially for you. But I'd love to take you, make you see that it doesn't have to be a bad experience." I leaned in to kiss him, my tongue probing gently. "But I won't push you into anything you don't want. You let me know if and when you're ready. I promise I'll make it good for you."

Paul bit my bottom lip, sucking it between his teeth before breaking away. "I want it. With you. I trust you and I want to give it a chance."

"Pretty sure my ass hung out the closed sign after this latest round, so we'll see where things go next time we're together."

He chuckled. "I'm sorry your ass is sore. Is it weird that I feel strangely proud of that?"

"Ohhh, Mr. Powers is a sadist. Who knew?" I teased.

"Since there's no school on Tuesday, what if we spend Monday night together. Then we can distract each other all day Tuesday as the election results trickle in."

The school was a polling location. In the past, we hadn't closed on Election Day, but the races were pretty tense—both locally and nationally—this year, so it was decided that we'd be best off to keep the kids away from any potential issues that might arise.

"I think that sounds like a great plan. Monday we can do dinner and a movie. My place or yours?"

"You come to mine. I'll order in. You pick the movie."

"Tell your ass to prepare itself." I winked. "Let's shower and get some food. I'm starving."

Paul's stomach rumbled and he blushed—whether from the noise or my comment about preparing his ass—but he nodded and rolled from bed.

We showered, went through the drive-thru at a local coffee shop for a late breakfast, and spent the rest of the day lazing around the house.

I'd never in my life felt so right.

I wasn't exactly sure what had flipped the switch in Paul, but I wasn't questioning it. I was grateful he'd finally decided to give us a chance. Knowing we were both on the same page as far as where we wanted the relationship to go was a huge comfort and I was looking forward to the future.

With Paul by my side.

I had a feeling Team Powers was only going to get better with each passing day.

"I ORDERED CHINESE, IS THAT OKAY?" Paul asked as he wrapped me in his arms the moment I walked through his door on Monday night.

"Perfect." I sighed into the embrace and melted as his mouth captured mine in a seeking kiss. "Mmm, missed this," I murmured against his lips. "Today was…"

"Ridiculously hard?" Paul asked. "I wanted to touch you all damned day. And not even sexually…"

I raised a brow in mock offense.

"Okay, not just sexually," Paul amended. "I caught myself wanting to reach for your hand a couple times, and I nearly kissed your cheek in the cafeteria."

"That would have gone over well in front of a hundred middle-schoolers," I deadpanned.

"Right. I know." Paul huffed. "I thought it would be easy to keep my hands to myself—hell, I've found you attractive for years and years and it's never been a problem—but I quickly learned today that once I've had a taste of you, I can't help but be greedy and want more."

"Well, you've got me." I kissed him. "So, I was thinking of some logistics. Not to ruin any kind of mood, but I definitely can't bottom tonight—someone ruined my ass. Are you up for it tonight or want to wait for tomorrow?"

Paul froze.

"Or not at all. Sorry, didn't mean to insinuate it was a given. You always have a choice." I cupped his face.

"I've been imagining it tomorrow. Election results making us nervous, we need a break so we stumble to bed, you take my mind off things..." his words trailed off as pink crept up his neck.

"I like this plan. So, tonight can be blow jobs or frot." I finally took a moment to toss my overnight bag in the hallway somewhere near Paul's room.

"Or both?"

"Or both," I answered with a grin. "I've created my very own sex monster."

Once the food arrived, we settled in on the couch and Paul turned on the television while I plated the meal.

"Ugh, all the local channels and national channels are all-election all-the-time," he grumbled.

"Movie? Or we can start a series?" I handed him a plate of food.

"Comedy? Drama? Action? Romance?" Paul clicked to the guide.

"I'm up for whatever." I took a bite of an eggroll. "Oh! I saw Betty coming in right as I was going into my PLC meeting with the seventh-grade team. I never got a chance to ask you what she wanted. Everything good?"

Paul smiled. "Yeah, she's good. Don is doing well. The home health care nurse has been able to cut back the hours that she spends at the house." Paul scooped up some noodles and chewed. "Betty caught wind of Stedman Oliver's phone call and subsequent visits."

I snorted. "Caught wind, huh?" I teased knowing full-well that Paul had made a couple well-placed comments to the right school board members over coffee.

He smirked, quite proud of himself it seemed. "She is not happy. She was actually a bit pissed at me for not telling her directly, but she calmed down when I reminded her that she was dealing with some pretty serious personal life issues at the time and it didn't seem like the right thing to do to run tattling to her about Oliver."

"I don't envy him," I said around a bite of rice.

"Same. She shut my office door and ranted for a good thirty minutes about how his pompous ass had overstepped so many boundaries. She was planning to go speak with him after she left the school, so I'm sure his afternoon didn't go as he'd planned." Paul grinned. "I feel kinda like a drama-whore, but I can't help but love that she found out and now he likely got his ass handed to him. It's never been a secret that Betty wasn't a fan, but she'd always been professional. I have a feeling—while still being professional—the gloves came off today. I wouldn't be surprised if the man resigns."

My brows shot up. "Who would take his place?"

Paul shrugged. "I'm not sure. I'd guess there are procedures in place. Not like Betty needs the help, but I'm sure there's someone who would step into the assistant superintendent spot."

"I'm just glad she now knows what a snake in the grass he is. I didn't like how quickly he swooped in with plans to go against all she's worked so hard for in the last several years."

We ended up talking throughout the entire meal and never even noticed that we'd totally skipped picking a movie or show.

"Want to pack this stuff away and head to bed?" Paul asked.

"It's like seven o'clock. Is that what time the senior citizens go to bed?" I loved to give him a bit of good-natured teasing.

Paul growled. "Laugh all you want. I was thinking of turning on a movie and spending the rest of the evening cuddling with a certain hot young thing. But if that's not going to happen…" he trailed off.

"Who is this hot young thing? Should I be

jealous?" I teased as we gathered up the food and put the leftovers in the fridge.

Paul grabbed me by the waist and pushed me into the corner of the counter. As he nuzzled my neck, his hands found their way under my shirt to rub my back. "He's gorgeous." He nibbled at my ear. "Fucks like a dream." Pressed a kiss against my jaw. "Has a cock I can't stop thinking about." Bit the sensitive skin where my shoulder and neck met. "Sucks me off like a pro." Feathered a kiss over my lips. "But the best thing about him is that he's quickly becoming my best friend. He's super smart, funny, caring, and one of the best colleagues I've ever had."

I moaned as Paul's hard cock pressed into mine. "So, what you're saying is he's the total package and I should definitely be jealous?"

Paul laughed. "Mmhm." His hand cupped the back of my head. "Maybe we should take this to the bedroom and you can try to convince me you're as good as him."

We laughed and kissed and couldn't keep our hands from roaming as we made our way to Paul's room.

By the time we fell asleep, two orgasms apiece between us, I was convinced I'd never in my life had so much fun with a boyfriend. We never ran out of things to talk and laugh about. And if we weren't talking, we found plenty of other things to do with our mouths.

The struggle to get to where we were hadn't been easy—and had been very slow going—but it had been completely worth it. We were the poster boys for good things come to those who wait.

FIFTEEN
PAUL

I WOKE to a very playful Jamison stroking me and pressing kisses against my skin as he made his way to my cock. I hissed as his hot mouth engulfed my length. "Good morning to you, too," I murmured as he sucked me deep. "Not tired of that after last night?" I ran my hand through his hair.

Jami hummed and I felt it all the way to my core. "If I wasn't still a little sore, I'd slick this gorgeous cock and ride you for the next hour." He took me back in his mouth and stroked while he sucked.

"Awfully bold of you to assume I've got an hour of staying power," I teased, my balls already drawing up tight as the small of my back tingled.

Jamison laughed—which went straight to my heart; seriously, who would have ever dreamed I'd have the type of relationship where laughing during oral was an acceptable and adored thing?—and increased his speed.

Several moments later, as my orgasm washed over me, I couldn't help but smile at Jami's sleepy eyes as they gazed up at me. When he'd swallowed everything I'd given him, I shifted position on the bed and gestured for him to straddle my chest. "Nice and slow, fuck my face like you're going to fuck me later," I instructed, smiling at the way he groaned at my words.

I took his thick length between my lips, loving the flavor of his skin and pre-cum, the brush of his balls against my chin, and his unique scent. As Jamison braced his hands on the headboard and slowly thrust into my mouth, I watched his face and imagined what it would be like later when he took me. My ass clenched—somewhat in nervousness, but mostly in anticipation. I knew Jami would never hurt me—but more than that, I loved him and trusted him in a way that I'd never loved and trusted in the past. Not even with Douglass. Jamison made me whole and I wanted to give all of me to him—even if bottoming was never going to be something I wanted to do all the time, I wanted to experience it with Jami. And I'd finally learned—at least with Jami—that I could let go and not be in such tight control all the time.

I gripped his ass as he tensed and unloaded in my mouth, his orgasm making his arms shake as he rode it to the end. Swallowing him down and accepting the kiss he offered as he shifted positions to lay on top of me, I smiled. "I love you. I think this should become an Election Day tradition."

"Mmm, love you," Jami murmured. "Election Day, Christmas, New Year's, Valentine's, Easter. Let's get a calendar of traditional and obscure holidays so we can make sure we do something special," he waggled his brow, "for each one."

I laughed. "I don't know. Seems a little creepy to plan sex around Parents Day, Siblings Day, Children's Day...and those are now a thing, I saw them on my calendar in the office. Fucking you senseless just because it's Grandparents Day seems a bit wrong."

Jami chuckled. "Okay, okay. But major holidays and always Election Day."

"Always." I wrapped my arms around him and held him close. The fact that we were so easily discussing yearly traditions made my heart soar. Maybe we took a long time to finally find our way to each other—yeah, I knew a lot of that was because of me—but maybe it was so we'd both be at the right point in our lives where we could easily want a long-term relationship. A flutter in my chest reminded me that I wanted even more than long-term, I wanted forever. I wasn't ready to tell Jamison about it just yet, but I had plans to make our relationship permanent when the time was right.

Jamison groaned. "We need to get ready so we can go vote. I need to grab something from the office, too."

The last thing I wanted to do was get out of bed and go stand in line, but there was no way I was missing my chance to vote.

Three hours later—thank God I'd brought a backpack of water and snacks—we made our way from the voting booths in the gym to our connected offices.

"Oh hey." Leo glanced up from his desk. "Did you guys get to vote? The line wasn't bad when I got here."

"It was three hours for us," I grumbled.

"Should have been here earlier," Leo said.

Jami and I glanced at each other and I swore Leo probably saw the mischievous grin and pink cheeks. Nah, three hours wasn't bad if it meant a morning in bed with my guy.

Leo cocked his head and eyed us both for a moment before smiling and gesturing toward the big yellow jacket sign at the front of the office. "Go stand there with your I Voted stickers. I'm taking pics for the board. The students need to see their adult role models voting." Leo took the picture. "Get one in front of the Team Powers sign, too."

When pictures were done, Jami grabbed what he needed from his office.

"Don't stay too late," I told Leo. "Be sure to enjoy your day off."

"No worries, I have a date later. Just wanted to get these spreadsheets done while the office was quiet." He glanced between us again. "You guys have plans today?"

Before I realized what I was doing, I nodded and brushed my hand against Jami's. "Anything and everything to avoid election coverage while still keeping up with outcomes."

When Leo bit back a smile and Jamison coughed, I cleared my throat and jerked my hand away to adjust my glasses. "Housework, reading, take a walk, bike ride, do some school work, that type of thing." Shit. Could Leo see what was between Jami and me? Fuck. Of course he could. I'd touched Jami's hand. Right in front of Leo. Had he seen it? Maybe he'd thought it had been an accident.

I took a deep breath. It felt like the whole world had just seen what I did. Huh. It didn't even bother me—okay, maybe it bothered me just a bit if my pounding heart was anything to go by. But overall, I was okay. The world hadn't ended. I wasn't planning to make any grand announcements, but things between Jami and me were so great, I couldn't see how others wouldn't recognize it. And that was okay. Plus, it was just Leo. Not like I'd kissed Jamison in front of an all-school staff meeting.

Leo gave a nod as if to say Yeah, right, but he was professional enough not to call me out. "Well, that sounds like a...delightful day. Enjoy." He gave a wink and turned back to his work.

Once outside, as we climbed into my car, Jamison laughed. "You did really well under pressure there, Mr. Powers."

"Shut up," I grumbled. "I was just trying to make conversation, I didn't realize I'd possibly insinuated more when I made the anything and everything comment. Was it really that bad? Was I super obvious? Could the hand thing come across like an accident?"

Jami took my hand. "Nah, a lot of people wouldn't have picked up on it. Leo is gay and he knows me fairly well. So, I think he picked up on whatever vibe is between us and put two and two together."

"And I sealed the deal with my rambling and inability to be smooth," I groused.

"And possibly the hand touch," Jami teased.

I huffed. "So stupid. But it just comes so naturally now."

"Are you mad? I promise Leo won't go around telling the entire school. I can even tell him it's important to keep it completely quiet."

I gave his hand a squeeze. "No, I trust him to be professional. A month ago, this was my worst fear. But now?"

Jami raised a brow.

I shrugged. "Now, I guess I've moved a bit into the why should I even care category. It feels like there's no way I can completely hide what you and I have—even if we're standing three feet apart in the office, there's a current of something between us. Or maybe that's just me. Do you feel it?"

He smiled and caressed my hand with his thumb. "I definitely feel it."

"I'm guessing others can sense it. Maybe not everyone, but the ones who know us well and the ones who are more in tune to that type of thing." I pulled the car into the garage and killed the engine. "And I don't know how to hide what's between us—aside from me remembering to keep my damn hand caresses to myself. I mean, I'm still on the side of no PDA at school or school events. But I can't stop the vibes we give off." I leaned over and kissed him. "And it doesn't even bother me. I mean, it kinda does because I don't like not being able to control something. But I'm so in love with you, I don't even care."

"Who are you and what have you done with the real Paul Powers?" Jami teased against my mouth before his tongue licked and made its way to dance with mine.

I broke the kiss a few moments later. "We should have picked up lunch. Want to order delivery? We can watch a bit of the news while we eat." I nuzzled my nose against his. "And then I think I need a shower and some prep time."

"Election Day, who knew it could be so damn sexy?"

We made our way inside and I let Jamison order sandwiches, soup, and salad for lunch. While we waited, we turned on the local news and watched for a bit.

"It's going to be a while before we get any news on the mayoral race. Switch to a national channel." Jami got up to answer the door when the food arrived a little while later.

With a sheepish look on his face, he returned to the living room and put the food on the coffee table.

"What's wrong?" I asked.

"Well, you know how you're feeling a bit more comfortable with people knowing about us?"

"Yeah…"

"Um, that was Todd Christopher. Who knew he was old enough to be delivering sandwiches, huh?"

I winced. "Todd Christopher as in the son of Mrs. Christopher in the English department and grandson of Gene Christopher on the school board?" I took off my glasses.

Jami grimaced. "Yeah. Didn't even think when I went to answer the door. To be honest, the kid looked kinda confused. Like he knew who I was, but he wasn't connecting why I was answering the door at your house. He may not even put it together."

"At least you had clothes on," I muttered. "Hell." I ran a hand over my face. "There's no way to keep school and personal life completely separate. We're too involved in school and the town. It's not like we're associated with a huge school in a huge town where actual anonymity could be a possibility. I guess it could be slightly worse if our town was even smaller, but we're going to be recognized even if we go a couple miles out of Valley Hill from time-to-time." I put my glasses back on. "We're off school, not on school property. Nothing wrong with friends —or boyfriends—ordering lunch and watching the news."

Jamison beamed. "Boyfriends, huh? I like the sound of that. Like really like the sound of that." He walked closer and wrapped his arms around my neck. "Is there anything wrong with boyfriends ordering lunch, watching the news, and then spending the rest of the day rimming and fucking each other's brains out?"

The sound that escaped me was a mix of laughter and a groan. "God, you're so bad."

"Mmm, but it will be soooo good," Jami whispered against my ear. "Let's eat before I decide to skip food altogether and just go straight to dessert."

We spent the next thirty minutes enjoying our lunch and watching the news as preliminary election results began to roll in. Jamison and I had spoken enough about our political views in the past to know where we stood on the national election, so our chit-chat turned to discussion of the local race.

"I really like Mayor Smith, he's a good guy. But he's not been great for Valley Hill and our schools. He's a people person and he likes to visit and keep the folks in town happy, but he doesn't have that big picture skill. He's been complacent and we really need a mayor who's enthusiastic about growing the town and our schools, not just keeping us from drowning," Jami said before taking a big bite of salad.

"Agreed. I think Smith has served his time. I'd

say served it well, but the way he's not kept up on bringing new families and businesses to town has been really detrimental." I spooned up a bite of soup. "Valley Hill needs this new Sharp as mayor. I've listened to him speak, heard him talk about his plans. I think he can really serve Valley Hill and help us save our schools if he stays willing to work with the school board."

As we finished up our food, Jamison reached for the remote and clicked off the television. "And with that," he said with a wink, "we're done with the news for the rest of the day. We'll check in on the mayor and the referendum tonight."

"What will we do for the rest of the day? Won't we get bored?" I did my best to keep a straight face.

Jami laughed. "Go take a shower. Do you have supplies? I brought some just in case."

"I'm good. I bought some special just for today." My cheeks pinked but I realized there was no one on the face of the earth I'd rather be talking to about prepping than Jami.

"Aw, my little Power Planner." He grinned then cocked his head. "Hmmm, are you also a Power Bottom? Only time will tell."

I kissed him hard. "I'll meet you in the bedroom in thirty."

"I'll be waiting." Jami smacked my ass as I headed to the shower.

Thirty minutes later, I walked into my bedroom and smiled. "Someone's been busy." The entire room was bathed in soft pink and blue light—thanks to some silk scarves and wraps draped over windows and lamps—and candlelight danced, making shadows on the walls.

Jami shrugged. "It's so bright outside. The light in here was way too harsh, so I softened things up a bit." He grabbed a bottle of lube from his bag and placed it on the side table. "The final perfect piece."

I snorted. "So, this is where the awkwardness starts." I moved toward the bed. "In the heat of things, with dirty words and naked bodies, it's easy to be all for trying something again." I hesitated at the edge of the bed, holding the towel around my waist. "But now it seems so planned and cold."

"I hear you and I understand," Jami said as he climbed onto my bed and held a hand out for me, his own towel falling away to reveal his gorgeous body.

I laughed. "Was that planned?" I took his hand and joined him on the bed.

"No, I swear. But it was perfection." Jami took the towel from my waist and tossed it to the ground. "There's no plan here. No script. No requirements. We kiss and touch like always. I know what I'd like to do to you and if you're on board, we'll make it happen. If not, we do whatever feels right."

My body shivered at his warm touch and the chill in the room. With our knees in the middle of my bed, our bodies came together, arms snaked around each other, lips and tongues meeting in a sensual dance that eased my nerves and told me everything was going to be perfect.

I shifted to lay on my back and pulled Jami on top of me. "Talk to me. Tell me what you want to do."

Instead, Jami kissed me, our thickening cocks rubbing together as my hands trailed down his back to grip his ass. When he finally broke the kiss, Jamison smiled down at me. "Oh, I have grand plans."

I moaned and rocked my hips up into his.

"We're going to make out until neither one of us can catch our breath." Jami leaned in and spent several moments kissing me. Our tongues licked, seeking and hot, until we broke apart, panting.

I smiled against Jamison's mouth. "And then?"

He hummed and brushed his lips along my jawline until he reached my ear. Nibbling and sucking the lobe between his teeth, Jamison murmured, "Then I'll make my way down to spread your ass open. I'm going to lick that pretty pucker of yours, tongue fuck you until you're sloppy wet and open for me. I'll finger you until you're begging for my cock."

I groaned and fisted my cock. "Get to it then. No more talk," I demanded.

Jamison laughed. "Bossy bottom," he teased, but he pressed kisses against my neck before moving to lick the tip of my dick. "You want to be on your back or stomach?"

"Back, want to watch you," I answered. No question there. I lifted my hips for the pillow Jamison shoved under me. Heat flushed through my body, both from the open position and the desperate desire coursing through me, and I spread my legs for him.

Lust flooded Jamison's face and he bit his lip as if holding himself back from a feast. "You're so damn gorgeous," he whispered as he dropped to feather kisses along my thighs, my balls, my taint.

And then he was there, giving me something I'd never trusted another man to give me. Jami's warm breath against my most sensitive skin sent shivers through me. When his soft tongue licked a path from the top of my crack to my taint, I whimpered.

"You like that?" Jamison murmured. "Like my tongue on you? Want me to lick you open, fuck your tight little hole?"

I made some sort of noise, possibly a grunt,

possibly a gasp, and pulled my legs toward my chest, offering more of myself to him.

"Words, Paul. I need words. Do you want me to keep going?" Jami paused with his hands on my ass cheeks, pupils blown, full pink lips glistening as he waited for my answer.

"God, yes. Fuck me with your tongue," I begged.

Jamison moaned and dipped his head, his tongue flicking out to tease my hole. His hot, seeking tongue continued to work its magic, and I writhed beneath his touch. Jami probed his tongue in and out of my ass, the ring of muscle softening and giving way more and more with each warm, wet thrust.

"Look at you, so sloppy wet and open for me," Jamison purred. "You ready for my fingers or want to stop with this?"

My heart soared at how Jami knew what I needed. Knew I needed to call the shots. I was nearly out of my head with want and desire at that moment, but the fact that he let me be the one making each decision showed me once again I could trust him with my body and my heart.

"Fingers," I gasped. "Want them." My entire body longed for his touch.

Jami leaned over and grabbed the lube, the snick of the cap filling the room. "You're really wet and open, but if this hurts, you let me know. I'll stop no questions asked." He smeared his slick fingers against my hole, his eyes never leaving mine. "You hear me?"

I nodded, my throat thick with emotion. Between the love I felt for this man, the unfamiliar feeling I got from his protectiveness, and the extreme desire coursing through me to finally feel him inside, I wasn't sure which way was up. But I knew he'd never hurt me. "I'll stop you, but I want it. Please, Jami, give it to me."

A gasp sounded from my throat when his first finger breached my rim.

Jamison paused, concern in his eyes.

"I'm good. Feels good." I wasn't lying. The initial sting had almost immediately given way to a pleasurable stretch. "Want more."

The second finger took my breath away and—after a deeper stretch and burn—the feeling of fullness was almost too much.

"This okay? Too much?" Jami asked, his eyes traveling from my face to my ass.

"So good. Feels amazing. Want your cock."

Jamison smiled and continued to work me open, his slick fingers sliding in and out as he fucked me deeper on each stroke. "Wish you could see how gorgeous this is; you're so good, so open, taking me so deep. Can't wait to see my cock in your ass;

wanna watch as you stretch around me and pull me into this tight little hole."

"Yes," I gasped. "Want that." I could have come with very little persuasion, but I wanted Jamison inside me. "Please, Jami, give me your cock."

He finger fucked me for a moment longer, his long digits brushing my gland and sending electricity coursing through me. "You wanna be on top? Give you a little more control on the depth and angle."

I hesitated. I'd never tried riding the guys who I'd done this with in the past. Maybe that position would give me a better chance at taking Jamison and actually enjoying it.

As if reading my mind, Jamison slowly pulled his fingers from my body. "You start on top. If you want to switch to your knees or on your back later, you just tell me." He moved to lie on his back, his thick cock bobbing against his stomach.

My ass clenched with anticipation and desire. Longing for a cock in my ass was something I'd given up on several years and many bottom mishaps ago, but right then, I wanted nothing more than the burn and stretch of Jamison's dick taking over my ass. I straddled his waist, sitting down so my ass rubbed against his cock. "Never tried it this way," I admitted.

"Love being a first for you." Jamison handed me

the lube. "This is your show. You set the pace, you call the shots."

How Jami could have me in a tangled ball of sex and emotions and yet still make me feel like I was in control was beyond me, but he was exactly everything right that had been missing in my life.

I slicked my ass and stroked lube all over Jamison's thick length before shifting to press his head against my hole. Concentrating only on the extreme pleasure filling Jami's face, I slowly lowered myself onto his shaft. The burning sting was a strange and exquisite pain and I hissed as my body adjusted to his invasion. When my balls nestled against his lower belly, I paused to catch my breath.

"You okay?" Jami asked, his hands stroking my thighs, thumbs caressing my balls, a finger tracing along my flagging dick.

"I'm good. This is already a thousand times better than anything in the past." I lifted myself slowly and sank back down, smiling at Jami's hiss as his hands tightened on my hips. "But I want to move to my back." I continued to rock on his cock, loving the way each down stroke sent pleasure throughout my body.

"You sure?" Jamison frowned.

I nodded and slowly lifted until his cock slipped from me. I moved and settled onto my back, pulling

Jamison between my legs. "Want to spread my legs for you, see you between them, watch as you sink into me." My voice broke with unexpected emotion. "Please."

"Anything," Jami promised as he nestled between my open legs. He took his thick cock in hand and slowly pressed into me with a groan. "Fuuuck, you're so damn tight and hot."

I watched as desire and control warred through Jamison as he entered me. No longer concerned with anything to do with control, I wanted the desire. I wanted the heat and passion; I wanted everything Jamison could give me. "Fuck me," I begged.

Jamison shifted his position, my legs spreading wider to wrap around him, as he leaned in so we were chest-to-chest. "This will never be just fucking," he whispered as he cupped my face and seared my soul with a kiss. "Nothing between us will ever be just fucking. I love you too much." He pulled his hips back before thrusting in hard and deep. "We can do this any and every way you want, but never again think that what we do together is as simple as fucking, you hear me?" He continued to pump his hips, his thick length stretching me as he thrust deeper and deeper.

I nodded, overcome with emotion I never knew

was possible. "I love you so much," I murmured. "Never want to lose this."

"Never." Jami punctuated his promise with a long, slow thrust. He snaked his arms under me and wrapped me in a tight embrace, his face buried in my neck. "Wanna make you come, hear you scream my name as your ass milks my cock."

I moaned and reached between us to stroke my leaking shaft. "Close."

"You want my hot load deep in your ass?" Jami asked as he increased the speed of his thrusts.

My ass clenched around him at the thought of feeling his cum in my ass. "God, yes. Please."

We gave up on words, our bodies doing all of the talking, as Jami pumped his hips over and over and I stroked my cock between us. Sounds of sex filled the air as our sweaty bodies slapped together and our breaths came in ragged gasps and grunts.

"Fuck, Paul, I'm so close," Jamison gritted out between clenched teeth. "Wanna see you come first."

"Close," I grunted. "Talk to me."

"Mmm, love my greedy little bottom. Love how you take my cock. You like to hear me talk dirty?"

I whimpered and gripped my dick harder as I stroked.

"Wish you could see how pretty your hole looks all stretched around my fat cock. Gonna look even prettier when my cum drips out. I'll push it back in with my cock, keep my cum deep in your ass." Jamison's thrusts were hard and fast. "Come for me, Paul. Wanna feel your ass clench around me."

With those words and a final stroke, I erupted, painting long, white ropes between us as I moaned. "Jamison," I groaned, "fuuuuck."

With one more hard thrust, Jami stilled, his cock throbbing in my ass as he shot his load and rode out his release. "Fuck, Paul, fuck," he panted as he trembled above me.

He pulled out slowly and I whimpered in protest. Jami just smiled and licked his lips as he watched my ass.

"Do it," I whispered when I realized what he was about.

"Fuck, so sexy to watch my cum drip from your hole," he murmured as he pressed his cock against my leaking ass and slowly pushed his release back into my body.

I moaned as he entered me again. "Fuck, that was so damn amazing. Never been that good."

"Same," Jamison muttered as he slipped from me and rolled to his side. Pulling me into his arms, he tipped my chin up. "I love you," he said before sealing his words with a warm, sensual, sated kiss. "And there will never be anything as hot as hearing you say my name as you come." He smacked another kiss against my lips. "It was good? No regrets?" A sliver of doubt seemed to be intruding.

I cupped his face. "It was the best ever. I can't say that I'll ever want to give up topping you, but I'm one thousand percent on board with bottoming any and every time you want me to."

"Any and every time, huh?" Jami cocked a brow. "Not gonna fight me?"

I chuckled. "Okay, there may be a bit of a struggle. Can't deny that I love fucking you. Maybe we can play rock, paper, scissors to see who gets to do what."

"Mmm, sounds fun. Next time, I want to fuck you until I come and then have you fuck me until you come, fall asleep with both our asses ruined, and then wake up and rub off together as we finger each other's cum-filled asses." Jami sighed and smiled as he described his fantasy.

"Fuck, that's hot and totally doable. Put it on the calendar for Friday night." My well-spent cock actually attempted to stir at the thought of playing out the scene Jami described.

"I'll pencil it in," Jamison teased. "Until then, we're covered in spunk. Let's shower."

We spent the next hour making out and slowly jerking each other off in the shower before tumbling our damp bodies into bed and sleeping until hunger woke us in the early evening.

"Leftovers?" I asked as I scanned the fridge. "No reason to cook anything since there's still food from lunch."

"Sounds good." Jamison crowded up behind me and pushed the door closed. Leaning in to nuzzle my neck, he whispered, "Today has been amazing. I know this is new, but I need you to know that this isn't just something casual for me. Nothing between us has ever been casual." His arms snaked around my waist and held me tight. "I'm not pushing and we can take things as slow as needed, but I want you to know that this is very real to me. I'm not looking for an end in sight."

I turned in his arms and backed him against the counter. "Good to know," I said with a smile as I devoured his mouth. "Because I love you and have absolutely no intention of this ending. Glad we're on the same page because fighting to get you to agree to making this more of a forever thing would have been a bitch."

Jami chuckled and held me close. "Dinner, news, and then I better head home."

I groaned. "I kinda hate that we can't just stay at each other's places all week."

He shrugged. "I mean, we can. But let's stick to

weekends for now. We'll see where things naturally fall as time goes on. No one needs to talk about selling or a permanent move just yet, but maybe we keep it in the back of our minds."

An excited and anxious thrill went through me at the thought of living with Jami. But he was right, we had plenty of time to think about it and decide what was best for us.

By eleven o'clock that night, the news finally went live from Mayor Smith's concession speech before switching over to newly-elected Mayor Sharp's acceptance speech.

The man finished up his acceptance before switching topics. "And, I'm the lucky guy who gets to announce the referendum for the Valley Hill school district passed by an overwhelming vote today. I'm looking forward to working with the school board in the coming months. We'll get Valley Hill back on track and keep our kids in our district with the best teachers and programs around." Mayor Sharp gave a smile and wave as the crowd clapped.

As the news switched back to talk of other local races, Jamison stood. "I better go. I'll be dragging ass tomorrow."

"Is it bad that I can't even bring myself to watch the national coverage? I guess I'll see what the announcement is in the morning." I yawned.

After several long minutes of hugs and kisses and sweet words, Jamison finally headed out the door and I made my way to my bedroom. The house and my bed—places I'd been alone for several years—suddenly felt cold and empty without Jami by my side.

SIXTEEN

JAMISON

THE FIRST WEEK of December brought a cold snap of early winter weather to Valley Hill. No snow, but we'd been having icy conditions that made the whole town grumbly about what the real winter might bring.

Every aspect of school was going well. Our mid-year testing was under way and showing growth. The grade-level teams and departments were working like well-oiled machines. Our sports and clubs were finding just as much success as our academics.

Mayor Sharp, Betty, and the school board were already in productive talks—unofficially of course as they waited for January and the mayor's term to begin—regarding what the next school year would bring and increasing enrollment as well as bringing more families to Valley Hill. Betty said the plans looked very promising and she was positive Paul and I would co-principal the following year with very good things for the years beyond. It didn't look as if either of us would be demoted.

Before Paul finally gave in and allowed us to be a couple, we'd worked well together as a team. But now that we were together and not hiding our relationship outside of school, Team Powers was a major force to be reckoned with. Betty submitted our names to a regional education publication and we'd been chosen to take part in an interview for an article on successful administration teams and how they led to successful schools.

We truly were running the school even better than before and looking forward to continuing our working relationship. There were no guarantees about our jobs in the future, but I knew we'd both land on our feet. Team Powers would do great things both in and out of school.

A regular Thursday brought warnings of an ice storm coming in overnight. Betty, Paul, and I had watched the radar and consulted with local weather personnel well into Thursday afternoon.

With a sigh, Betty had stood from her chair in Paul's office and said with a firm nod, "We err on the side of caution and make the call. The students can do online learning. Everyone stays home. But we need to announce it now so the teachers have time to get their assignments posted."

Once we'd taken care of all necessary announcements, Paul had caught my eye across the office just as my phone buzzed with a text.

PAUL: Pick up some wine and food then come to my house. We'll spend the ice storm holed-up together.

I'D HAD to bite my lip to hide my smile.

Luckily, the rest of the day had gone by quickly and I no longer had to contain my excitement as I pulled my car into Paul's garage and gathered the wine and food.

As I walked through the door into Paul's house—which was already as comfortable to me as my own home—I called out, "Honey, I'm home," in a sing-songy voice.

"In here," Paul grumbled.

I frowned at the tone of his voice. Putting the wine on the counter and the food in the fridge, I headed toward his bedroom.

"What's wrong?" I asked and then gasped. "Oh my God, what happened?"

Paul winced, a cloth held against his bleeding

head as blood dripped from his face onto his dress shirt. "I'm an idiot. Went out the back to pull the grill in and cover it since more ice is coming. Wasn't paying attention and didn't see the ice on the step. Slipped on it and fell, banged my head on something. I think it was the step, maybe the sidewalk—it all happened pretty fast."

"You need to go to the doctor," I started.

"No, I think it's fine. Head wounds bleed a lot, but it's not a big cut." He removed the cloth and showed me his head.

I didn't like how it continued to bleed, but I agreed that the cut wasn't very large. "I don't know. Maybe just one stitch. Let's just get it covered and see if the bleeding will stop."

An hour later, Paul's head was bandaged and the majority of the bleeding had stopped. But my main concern was symptoms Paul was having. We argued back and forth for another hour, but I wasn't buying Paul's insistence that he was just getting a migraine.

"I vomit with migraines. I get exhausted. I feel confused. Dizziness and sensitivity to light is all part of my migraines." Paul leaned his head back on the couch and closed his eyes. "And I hit my head, of course I have a headache."

I cuddled close to him on the couch. "Look, I've seen you with a migraine. This is different. Some of the symptoms may be the same, but you're weird and I'm worried."

"Gee, thanks," Paul deadpanned. "It's icy out. I don't want to mess with going to the doctor."

"Will you at least call your doctor and see what she recommends?"

He sighed and pinched the bridge of his nose. "Fine. If it will make you lay off, I'll do it. Then I just want to go to bed."

My face twisted. "Do you want me to go home?"

Paul scowled. "What? No. Of course not. I appreciate your concern, I'm just exhausted. Just want to take you to bed and sleep."

"Not a good idea until we know what's going on with your head." I handed him his phone. "Please call."

I got even more worried when Paul struggled to remember his doctor's name. After he finally made the call, he sighed with frustration.

"What did she say?" I asked. I knew he'd been honest about his symptoms, but I hadn't heard the doctor's response.

"She says I should go to the ER just to be safe." He squeezed his eyes shut. "I have no desire to be stuck in the hospital while an ice storm rages. We were supposed to have a weekend together."

I kissed the top of his head. "We'll still be

together. Just a different location and unplanned activities."

Paul groaned.

Two hours later, after a somewhat treacherous drive to the hospital thanks to the already falling ice and a lengthy wait in the ER waiting room, Paul was finally called back to a triage room.

"Do you want your husband to come back with you?" the kind nurse asked Paul as he approached her.

"My..." he started and paused then looked back at me, "yes, my husband should come with me."

The nurse gave a little smile and a nod. "Sir, you can come with us."

Grateful for the little white lie and the kind-hearted nurse allowing me go back with Paul, I followed.

After vitals and several questions, Paul was left to rest while the nurse promised to send the doctor in.

I grabbed the heavy white hospital blanket and draped it over Paul's body with a kiss to his head. "They'll get you all fixed up. We'll go home as soon as possible. Promise."

"Need to let Betty, Leo, and Danika know what's going on. No one is to be at school tomorrow, but they need to know I may not be available," Paul grumbled.

"Once we talk to the doctor, I'll call them." I pulled my chair close to his bedside and took his hand. "Thanks for letting me come back with you."

"Of course. I wasn't following her at first, but then I realized she likely couldn't let you come back with me if we weren't married. Hopefully they won't investigate too closely." He squeezed my hand. "Wanted you here." He closed his eyes and sighed. "Not going to lie, kinda liked the sound of calling you my husband."

My heart fluttered and my eyes stung. "Not going to lie, I kinda like the sound of being called your husband."

The doctor came in a little later. He ordered pain medicine, nausea medicine, stitches, and a CT scan before telling Paul he'd be back in once he read the scan.

"He should be back in this room within an hour if you need to make any calls or grab a drink," the doctor said to me.

I didn't want to leave Paul's side, but he gave me a sleepy smile and assured me he'd be fine.

I took the hour to walk outside. Standing under the canopy of the drop-off spot, I pulled my jacket around me as I called Betty first.

Once I'd explained to Betty, Danika, and Leo what was going on and promised to call them when I knew more, I wandered back into the ER waiting room. A sign with an arrow pointed toward a coffee cart and I gave an inner shrug. I still had quite a wait, so coffee was a good distraction.

After ordering my drink, I held the steaming cup and walked back toward the waiting room. I sipped my coffee, flipped through a worn magazine, and checked the time over and over until I had about ten minutes left before I could head back to Paul's little room.

The sliding doors whooshed open and three figures walked in. I paid them little attention until they approached me.

"How is he?" a voice asked.

I looked up and felt my eyes widen to see Betty, Leo, and Danika. "You guys did not have to come. He's getting stitches and a CT scan. They gave him medicine for the pain and nausea. Doctor will talk to him after he reads the scan." Suddenly, I was overwhelmed with emotions. Colleagues—friends, really—dropped what they were doing to drive in dark, icy conditions to check on Paul. I was touched. But also nervous because what if having them here would cause Paul anxiety about our relationship being found out at school. "I promise I'll give you the info when I get it. I hate that you drove in such bad weather."

"Nonsense. We drove together; Danika is a pro on ice and her vehicle is well-equipped for it." Betty took a seat across from me. "We won't stay long and we know we likely can't see him. Or at least we're hoping that he doesn't get admitted because that's the only way he could get visitors. We just wanted to check on you and make sure you're both good."

Danika and Leo took seats as well.

"So, how did he hit his head?" Leo asked.

I filled them in on the events of the day as I knew them. Of course, I left out the parts of me bringing wine and food to Paul's house with the plan of spending the whole weekend in bed.

"You did the right thing bringing him in. Concussions aren't things to mess around with," Danika said.

"Did the fall knock him out? He's lucky you were there." Leo studied me with interest and a slight smile.

"Oh, um, no. I'd gone to his house to give him a report he needed. He was already inside and trying to stop the bleeding. He doesn't know for sure, but he doesn't think he lost consciousness." Would they believe I just happened to be delivering a report? "So, I guess it's lucky he forgot the report at school and I said I'd drop it by."

Leo smirked. Danika narrowed her eyes. And Betty cocked her head.

I began to sweat.

Shit. I had no problem with people at school knowing about Paul and me.

Paul had indicated he wasn't as worried about it as he used to be.

But I didn't want to be the one who outed us to our colleagues and boss without Paul being part of it.

However, based on the looks I was getting, I didn't think I was going to have much choice.

"Jamison, do you and Paul think I'm an idiot?" Betty asked as she steepled her fingers under her chin and leaned back in her chair.

My eyes snapped to her and I stuttered. "What? No. Of course not."

"Are you really going to sit there and try to make me think you'd simply been delivering a report to Paul's house and found him injured?"

I had no answer, so I simply stared at her as sweat beaded on my brow.

"Have you two seriously been trying to hide what's going on?" Leo's lips twisted into a smile.

"Did you think we wouldn't notice what was between you?" Danika asked with a chuckle and a shake of her head.

Betty huffed. "I didn't realize that you thought

you were keeping it a secret. I just assumed you were keeping it quiet and not doing any grand gestures at work in order to keep things professional." She rolled her eyes. "Anyone with eyes and a brain should have picked up on the change between the two of you. I noticed things were different—not good, but different—after the Indy conference trip. We all recognized the change way back when you both relaxed, started smiling more, increased your production, and the tension between you changed. There's still a tension, but it's not a bad one anymore." She laughed. "I can't believe you thought you could hide it."

Heat crept up my face. "We weren't trying to lie, Paul just didn't want to mess things up for us at work. Then we realized we couldn't fight it, so we decided we'd just keep it quiet at school. We aren't really hiding things outside of school." I shrugged and tried not to worry that Paul was going to be pissed.

"Believe me, I know." Leo chuckled. "I'm dating Todd Christopher's cousin. The kid came home all excited with gossip about seeing you at Paul's house. Not that we all didn't know before that, but the sandwich delivery sealed the deal and took away any doubt."

"Not to mention, there's no way you two can

hide the smiles and glances between you," Danika teased. "It's enough to make a person want to puke, but it's also cute as hell."

"I'll speak to Paul when he's home and feeling better, but please assure him that neither of you needs to worry about your jobs. The school board and I have been beyond pleased with the performance our very own Team Powers has shown these past several months. No matter what happens with the consolidation or reopening the other buildings, you two will always be top choices." Betty stood and glanced at her watch. "Please call us as soon as you know what the CT scan shows. I expect you to get Paul home and keep him company all weekend. Depending on the diagnosis, I don't expect him back at work until at least Wednesday. And I'll need a doctor's note to release him to work. I'd actually feel more comfortable if he took the whole week."

I chuckled and stood, tossing my empty cup in the nearby trashcan. "Yeah, we'll see how that goes."

After expressing my gratitude for the visit and giving hugs, I said goodbye to the crew and headed toward the desk.

"I was told I could join my husband around this time if he was back from his CT scan?"

The young man at the desk smiled. "You can go on back. If he's done, he'll be in the same room."

I found Paul asleep in his little room. His head neatly bandaged and his glasses slightly askew on his face.

"Ah, I see our patient is asleep," the doctor announced quietly as he walked into the room a few moments later. "The pain medication likely made him sleepy. I'll tell you what I told him—he may not remember it; all the information will be on the discharge papers. He has three stitches. They'll dissolve on their own. He can wash his hair tomorrow. He doesn't have to keep the wound covered. The CT scan showed only a very slight concussion—he was lucky; a fall like that can cause broken bones and much worse head wounds. He may have the headache, dizziness, and confusion for the next couple weeks, but he's not in any danger at this time. He may bounce back quickly since the concussion is very mild. He has no real restrictions, just rest and not push himself. If he's dizzy or confused or has a headache, he needs to rest." The doctor made a few notes on the device he held. "I'd say he should feel pretty normal within a couple weeks. I want him to follow-up with his general practitioner in a week. The paperwork will have a list of symptoms to watch for and instructions on what to do if you see them." He glanced up. "You'll be with him constantly for the next few days?"

I hadn't expected the question, but I nodded with no hesitation. "Of course."

"Good, keep an eye on him. He needs to rest all weekend at least."

"What about work?" I studied Paul with a frown. "He's going to want to go back on Monday."

"I'll write it so he can attempt to go back on Wednesday, if he doesn't have dizziness or a headache."

The doctor made a few more additions to his device and then snapped it closed. "I expect he'll make a full recovery. Get some salt and treat the steps; winter is supposed to be brutal. Icy steps and sidewalks are dangerous. He definitely doesn't need another fall."

Three hours later, we finally made it home. Paul had dozed most of the ride and even slept through me picking up his prescriptions at the pharmacy.

The hour was already very late and creeping into the morning and I knew Paul wanted to crash into bed as much as I wanted to. "Hey, let's grab a shower and then we can go to bed. I'll get you a water for your medicines." There was no way he wanted to climb into bed with the hospital funk all over him.

We took a quick shower and Paul gratefully swallowed his pain and nausea pills. As we crawled into bed, he pulled me close and kissed the top of my head. "Thank you for being here today. Thank you for standing by me through it all. Sorry I fought you on it; I appreciate your concern and help."

I cuddled into his chest and sighed. "Nowhere I'd rather be. I'll always stand by your side. Love you."

"Love you, too. And same. You've got me, always."

"WHY DO I have a text from Betty telling me to stay home all week and let my boyfriend pamper me?" Paul groaned as he struggled into a sitting position on the bed the next morning.

I grimaced as I walked into the room with a tray of breakfast.

Paul narrowed his eyes. "What are you not telling me?"

Placing the tray on the bed, I propped my hands on my hips. "Slow down. You were asleep and drugged most of last night. I'm not hiding anything." I helped him move the tray to cover his lap. "And don't overdo it on the phone—the papers from the hospital said screen-time could bring on headaches."

Paul tossed his phone to the side. "What happened? Why is Betty calling you my boyfriend?" He squeezed my hand. "Not that you're not, just wondering how she came to that conclusion."

"After I called her, Danika, and Leo, they all showed up in the ER waiting room. I told them they shouldn't have gotten out on the ice, but Danika is supposedly some sort of bad weather driving guru and has the perfect vehicle for it." I waved my hand. "Anyway, having them there was a nice little distraction while I waited for you to get done with the stitches and CT scan. They were asking about your fall and how I found you. I couldn't very well say I showed up with wine and food so we could hole-up against the storm and spend all weekend in bed."

Paul chuckled.

"So, I said you'd forgotten a report at work and I'd brought it over to you." I ran a hand over my face and groaned. "Which was flimsy at best—they all know we use the shared cloud and anything you needed would have likely been available online—but I kinda panicked. I've never been worried about people knowing we're together—even at school—and I knew you'd kinda indicated you weren't as concerned about it these days, but I didn't want to just out us while sitting right there in the waiting room."

Paul took a sip of orange juice. "Did they push until you spilled?"

I laughed. "Not exactly. Leo kept giving me that knowing look. Betty asked if you and I think she's an idiot."

He snorted. "Oh Lord."

"Basically, long story short, they all three let me know we were ridiculous to think we could hide it and that we've pretty much done a shit job of it. Everyone—well, at least the three of them—feel that we've been better at our jobs since we got together. Hell, Betty says she knew something was up after Indy even though she could tell there was major tension. Danika says our looks and smiles are cute even if it makes her want to puke."

Paul laughed. "Aw, that's nice."

"And I guess Leo is dating Todd Christopher's cousin? So, any thought we had of keeping things quiet went out the window with the sandwich delivery." I winced. "Sorry about that. Totally wasn't thinking."

Paul took a bite of bagel and waved away my concern. "We said we wouldn't hide outside of school. We may not think Betty's an idiot, but I definitely was acting like one when I thought our personal and professional lives wouldn't intersect. There's no way to date and be in love in this town without it following us to our jobs."

"Do you regret it? Want to stop this?" Pain and panic filled my chest.

"What?" Paul's eyes shot to mine. "Hell, no. I'm just saying that we stick with the no PDA and overly couple-y situations at school, but we go with the flow and don't worry about it."

I sighed and leaned in to kiss the uninjured side of his head. "So, at the risk of poking the bear, are you saying that I was right from the very beginning?"

Paul growled. "If I wasn't recovering from a concussion with strict orders not to engage in strenuous activity, I'd totally fuck that smug look off your pretty face." He nuzzled his nose against mine. "But yes, you were right."

"I'm sorry. I had a bit of trouble hearing that. Could you repeat it?" I teased.

"Don't push it," he muttered. "Finally giving in and admitting that it was okay to let go, okay to give up a bit of the power and control, was the best thing that ever happened to me." Paul shook his head. "No, that's not right. You were the best thing that ever happened to me. Being with you showed me it's okay to let go and that I don't have to keep such a tight grip on that control at all times."

I kissed him gently, licking at his lips and smiling as the buttery bagel flavor hit my tongue. "Well, you're going to have plenty of time to practice letting go of some of that power. You're not going back to work until at least Wednesday—doctor's orders. And Betty is requiring written authorization for you to return. She actually wants you to stay out all week."

Paul grumbled as he took another bite of bagel. "Before all of this, I would have likely tried to go into school today. But now? I get to spend at least three days cuddled up with my boyfriend and fake hospital husband, so I'm not too devastated."

"Ohhh, the boyfriend and the fake husband? Threesome time? Kinky," I teased.

"No way, I'm not sharing you with anyone." He swallowed the last of his bagel and washed it down with a final drink of juice. "What are we doing today?"

I snorted. "Well, school is closed, the roads are icy, and my boyfriend has a concussion. I'd say we're being lazy fucks all day. Showers and back to bed. If we're feeling really frisky, maybe we'll move to the couch."

"We should watch cheesy romantic comedies and talk about Christmas plans. Gifts, decorations, meals, that type of thing." Paul wiped his mouth.

I removed the tray and gently helped him to his

feet. When he assured me his head was fine and he had no dizziness, we made our way to the bathroom.

"I have an idea for Christmas gifts. I say we start a Bucket List fund; we each put an amount in as the original gift and then we keep adding to it. When we have enough, we use it to take a Bucket List trip." I turned on the water.

"What's a Bucket List trip?" Paul asked as he gingerly worked his shirt over his head.

"A trip that gives both of us one item from our Bucket List. Dolphins for me and tigers for you. I've been doing a bit of research and I think we can do it in one trip, but it will be a long one. We'll need to save up and plan it for the summer." I helped him remove the bandage from his head.

Paul smiled broadly. "That sounds absolutely perfect." He wrapped me in his arms as the bathroom filled with steam. "I love you. I'm sorry I struggled against this—against us—for so long."

I shrugged and kissed him. "We're worth the struggle, worth the wait, worth it all. I love you. Thank you for the part you've played in my life over the years. You were exactly what I needed each step of the way."

"And now?" Paul asked, his lips feathering over my mouth.

"And now, you're the person I want to spend the rest of my life loving."

"That can totally be arranged." Paul kissed me, long and slow. "Now, get in that shower. I think very non-strenuous blow jobs are on today's to-do list."

EPILOGUE

PAUL

Three Years Later

The heat of Jamison's tight ass engulfed my cock as I moved inside him with long, slow thrusts. "Fuck, Jami, I'm close." I pulled him to his knees, his back to my chest, and stroked his thick shaft as I kissed his neck.

"Me too," Jami gasped. "Oh fuck, so close."

We both groaned as orgasms washed over us.

Completely spent, we collapsed to the bed in a panting heap.

"Three years later, and we've still got it," I teased and kissed him.

"How mad do you think people are going to be?" Jami asked as he cuddled close to my side.

"Because we snuck off to Indianapolis to get married and spend a weekend for our honeymoon?

Or because we're leaving for two weeks to go to Portugal and India without telling anyone until our plane is in the air?"

Jami chuckled. "Both."

"Well, there will be some who are pissy about not being invited to the wedding. But since it was just us and the officiant's wife as the witness, no one can actually be mad. Plus, we're inviting everyone to the party once we're back." I ran my hand up and down his back—my husband's back; that was never going to get old. "And we planned the two-week trip so it doesn't interfere with work. We've got the time. No one can be mad about that either. Leo will likely get shitty he wasn't involved just because he likes to plan travel accommodations and all of that. Danika won't care. Betty will tsk at us, but she won't be bothered that much. As long as they all get to come celebrate with us when we're back home, it will all be fine. We'll bring them souvenirs."

Jami rolled from the bed with a laugh. "We have exactly two hours until we need to leave for the airport. We shouldn't waste time. Let's shower and get packed."

"You don't want another round of married sex?" I teased.

"My ass couldn't take it right now. Yours?" Jami

cocked a brow as if suggesting he could probably go again if I'd bottom.

"Hell, no. You ruined me last night. I'm out of commission for at least a day."

He laughed and wrapped his arms around my waist. "So, we shower and pack. Then we take that pretty AARP card you got and see what kind of breakfast deals it can get us."

I groaned and swatted his ass. I'd been pissed and completely avoiding the AARP membership option since I turned fifty. But when Jami saw another one arrive in the mail the week I turned fifty-two, he made me look into it. Turned out, there were some great travel benefits that saved us a lot on our Bucket List trip. So now, at fifty-three, I was a card-carrying member of the AARP. I hated it, but begrudgingly admitted that the benefits were worth it. Jamison, of course, loved to tease me about it.

"You know, you don't have to be fifty to get a membership. You could get one too." I grabbed a pair of boxers from the suitcase.

"But why would I need to when I have my very own senior citizen sugar daddy who can flash his card and get us ten percent off breakfast?" Jamison cackled and ran toward the bathroom as I growled and gave chase.

Our shower was slow and easy as we tasted and explored before a quick wash and rinse.

"Are you nervous or excited about the trip?" I asked a bit later as we got dressed.

"Both?" Jamison smiled. "I've never taken such a long trip out of the states. But I'm excited to see the dolphins and tigers—plus everything else we might see. This is definitely a trip of a lifetime and I'm so glad I get to take it with you."

We were going first to The Azores of Portugal where we were hoping to see several of the eleven species of dolphins in the area. With pods reaching up to one thousand individuals, we'd been told it was highly likely to see them feeding near the shore without even stepping foot on a boat. But we were also going out on a boat and had heard we might see whales as well.

After Portugal was Madhya Pradesh, India—home to seventy percent of the world's wild tigers. Our research promised a very high likelihood of seeing tigers among several other wild animals.

"This will be a great trip before school gets busy again," I said as I folded clothing to repack the suitcase.

Ever since the referendum had passed and we got a new mayor three years ago, the Valley Hill school district had rebounded from its former money woes.

Through some planned and early retirements, we were able to keep much of our staff. Our class sizes were allowed to stay small—which was a huge part of why we had growing enrollment. Programs that Jami and I had started—along with the district test scores, graduation rates, and college/employment rates—helped to increase the appeal of Valley Hill for families looking for a place to settle and call home.

The biggest change on the horizon was that Betty had announced this coming school year would be her last as superintendent. If plans went well, she would step down from her position at the end of the school year and take the assistant superintendent spot while I was slated to step into the top spot.

I'd never dreamed of wanting to be superintendent of a school district, but I'd also never dreamed I'd be married to a man who used to be my student, madly in love, taking Bucket List trips, and carrying an AARP card. Life had definitely gotten better when I allowed myself to admit that dreams and plans could change and power and control weren't the most important things in life.

Jami and I would complete our co-principal run at the end of this year. Danika had accepted the principal position at the middle school for the next year; Jamison was going to reopen Valley Hill East as principal. Two years from now, Valley Hill West was slated to reopen if enrollment trends continued.

As we zipped up our suitcases and headed toward the door, Jamison turned and pressed me against the wall. "You know, this all started in an Indy hotel room and us kissing against a wall."

I shook my head, teasing my nose against his. "No, this all started a long time before that. I was just too stubborn to admit it."

"I'm glad we took our time. We weren't ready way back then." Jami kissed me.

"Agreed." I deepened the kiss. "No one I'd rather do Bucket List trips with than you. I love you, Jamison Powers."

"And I love you, Paul Powers." Jami took my hand as we walked out the door.

Team Powers headed to the airport to take on the rest of our lives.

Together.

And always.

BROWN COUNTY WINERY Tasting Room
    Salt Creek Winery
    Country Heritage Winery Tasting Room
    Cedar Creek Winery

(this was the first M/M I wrote and you may remember Sawyer and Luke being mentioned in Barrett & Ivan as well as in Ryker & Gavin)

Start Something About Him with a **FREE** short story:

(The Beginning https://instafreebie.com/free/84Cxr)

Then continue with the other stand-alone titles in the series (available to read FREE for Kindle Unlimited subscribers):

Bryan & Jase

Brody & Nick

Barrett & Ivan

Braeton & Drew

Ryker & Gavin

Kade & Cameron

Or grab the boxset HERE.

Plus several other titles:

Devoted (a Something About Him novella)

Saving Us

Stranded Hearts (a short story)

Eli & Gage (a Something About Him short story)

Escape (a 3-book collection of fun stories)

A.D.'s first stories (all male/female except <u>Sawyer</u> which is male/male) are in the Torey Hope and Torey Hope: The Later Years series. Find the 8 book box set HERE or you can find each individual title on Amazon.

For Nicky

Because of Beckett

Christmas in Torey Hope

Loving Josie

Decker

Sawyer

Zach

Kendrick

NOTES

If you'd like to visit Brown County in Nashville, Indiana and go to the wineries mentioned, you can find more information about them below.

Brown County Winery Tasting Room

Salt Creek Winery

Country Heritage Winery Tasting Room

Cedar Creek Winery

ACKNOWLEDGMENTS

It's always so hard to write this part because I'm worried I'll forget someone without meaning to.

Readers- you are the reason I write. As long as you continue reading my stories, I'll continue writing them. Thank you for your support.

Bloggers- your support, reviews, and promotion are very much appreciated. Thank you!

My author buddies- I don't know that I could keep doing this without our brainstorm sessions, laughter, road trips, meals, wine, and friendship as my support.

Thank you to my alpha readers, betas, editors, proofreaders, and ARC readers! Your eyes and input are beyond important to me.

Brett and Gage- as usual, I doubt you even grasp how much your support, input, and friendship mean to me. This author journey has brought many wonderful things into my life, and you both are two of the BEST! I'm blessed to call you friends.

My family and friends- thank you for your love and support, always.

ABOUT THE AUTHOR

A.D. Ellis is an Indiana girl, born and raised. She spends much of her time in central Indiana as an instructional coach/teacher in the inner city of Indianapolis, being a mom to two amazing school-aged children, and wondering how she and her husband of almost two decades have managed to not drive each other insane. A lot of her time is also devoted to phone call avoidance and her hatred of cooking.

She loves chocolate, wine, pizza, and naps along with reading and writing romance. These loves don't leave much time for housework, much to the chagrin of her husband. Who would pick cleaning the house over a nap or a good book? She uses any extra time to increase her fluency in sarcasm.

Find all of Ellis' contemporary romance and male/male romance at www.adellisauthor.com

FREE books-- sign up at bit.ly/ADEllisNews for a FREE male/female romance.

Sign up at http://www.subscribepage.com/

ADEllisNewsMMRomance for a FREE male/male romance book.